Blanket of Many Colors

Rotonger Ronitha
Burns-Walker

Table of Contents

Chapter 1 1

Chapter 2 4

Chapter 3 6

Chapter 4 10

Chapter 5 13

Chapter 6 24

Chapter 7 28

Chapter 8 32

Chapter 9 35

Chapter 10 39

Chapter 11 47

Chapter 12 53

Chapter 13 56

Chapter 14 61

Chapter 15 69

Chapter 16 73

Chapter 17 77

Chapter 18 89

Chapter 19 96

Chapter 20 104

Chapter 21 107

Chapter 22 109

Chapter 23 111

Chapter 24 113

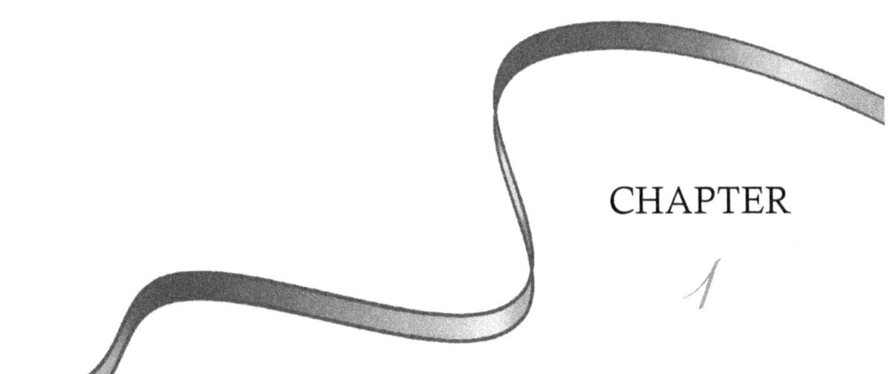

$\mathcal{J}$asmine walked out of her private medical practice and looked up toward the heavens and said to herself, "What a beautiful day to go on a long drive." She got into her car and begin to ride down North Bridge Street toward the beach front. As she was driving, she noticed all the different types of people that were in her town. She thought to herself, I am so happy to be in a place that love diversity and different ages coming to gather for a common purpose., "Having fun and enjoying life."

Jasmine at last made it to the beach. She parked at the nearest parking area by a lively restaurant. Jasmine said, "What a lovely atmosphere to be in. The beach is not so busy today. I don't see a lot of people. This is the best time to enjoy the ambience." Jasmine changed her black dress pants to blue jeans shorts that came up to her thighs. She pulled off her long sleeve white shirt to reveal her turquoise short sleeve T-shirt that she tucked into her blue jean shorts. She replaced her black high heels with turquoise beaded designer shoes.

As she walked along the beach, she took off her shoes. The white sand was so warm under her feet. The sun was very comfortable, it was 80 degrees with a cool breeze. Jasmine felt the warm water run through her toes. It felt so good. Jasmine, signed, and said, "Oh, what a refreshing moment I am having. I work so hard. I really love serving my community with my gift of healing from above, but I never take time out for myself. It is my time to enjoy the good life."

Jasmine looked around, she saw older couples, younger couples, and children running in and out of the water. They were laughing, running, and playing. It was such a change of pace from her busy lifestyle. She looked around and saw people gathering around a man playing a karaoke set. The man that was singing had such a soulful tenor voice. His voice captured the audience of those at the beach. Every last person that was at that beach gathered to hear this man in his latter 20's sings an original song she had never heard before. When he stopped singing his 4th song, the crowd that gathered around him chanted, "More, more. Please give us More."

The man, pulled out his black brief case and shared prerecorded cd's of songs he had wrote and wanted to share his story with the word, but in his own natural singing voice. He did not charge them anything but he did give them his business card that was attached to the cd's. It contained his social media platforms and the ability to download his songs for a small price. Before, the crowd left he blessed them with angelic song that touched the heart of everyone that heard it. They left very happy. His songs were so uplifting. It made them feel so wonderful inside. As, the crowd left, Jasmine was able to see the man that song so beautifully. He was 6'4 with a lean muscular built, with dark almond coloring of his skin with blue sparking eyes. Wow, he was a sight of sheer good looks. Jasmine tried not to stare but she could not help but seeing the most handsome man that she had seen her whole life.

Jasmine was forty years old; she had lived a very enjoyable life going to medical school. She did not do much dating because she did not have time. She was raised by her single father. Her mom did not want children but she became pregnant and wanted to give her up for adoption. Her father respected her choice and he knew the reason why she wanted to do so. Her father was a black man and her mother was Chinese. Her parents were in their Residency of their medical career.

Jasmine, dad, Ramon, would tell her that her mom was a brilliant doctor with a great bedside manner. He talked about her as if she was God's gift to man. He told her that she wanted to keep you in her heart but knew that in starting her new medical career, it would be hard to raise a child and start a career with extremely long hours. Her mom's name was Lorina. Her dad always carried a picture of her in his wallet. She was very beautiful. She had olive skin color with long straight black hair with hazel eyes. She was 5'8 at 150 lbs. She was amazingly beautiful. Her dad was 6'3 with dark brown beautiful skin. He was thin but very toned with dark brown eyes with wavy hair that he kept cut in a fade. Her dad was very handsome even in his 60's.

In a nutshell, Jasmine's mom had parents of Chinese race and cultures. It was hard for her mother's parents to accept Ramon, Jasmine's father because of his race. They believed the cultures and races should stay with their own race. Her parents were not prejudice they just believed in their customs. Jasmine remembers conversations with her mom explaining to her when she was a little girl that although her family felt a certain way of not mixing with other races in relationship matters not all Chinese people believed the same thing. Sometimes it is just the way people are raised. Thankfully, as time went on and Jasmine parents seen her mom's resistance in not giving up her daughter, even if she agreed not to marry the love of her life, Ramon, they did come to want to be introduce to Jasmine. They fell in love with her at first sight and introduction. They became a valuable part of her upbringing as well. Although, Jasmine spent most of her life being around her father, Ramon's parents, and extended family. So, they would not accept a biracial child that was born out of love. It is funny, but as a person, they treated Ramon as if he was their son. They adored him.

Jasmine's dad, Ramon came from a beautiful warm family. They believed that no matter who you are, you should have the chance to fall in love with whomever you will as long as you were compatible. Her grandparents loved her mom, Lorina and thought she would be beautifully matched with their son. Lorina, knowing her parents were true believers of their custom of not mixing with other races, would not accept a bi racial child. At least not initially.

Jasmine's dad, Ramon had asked her mom, Lorina to marry him, but she would not run the risk of losing her parents although she was deeply in love with Ramon. Ramon persuaded Lorina to allow him to raise their child as a single dad but she could come and spend time whenever she liked. Thankfully, Lorina let her dad raise her but she was able to spend a great deal if time with her mom as she grew up. Jasmine's dad, parents were black and had a rich culture of family. They helped her father raise her with his other aunts and uncles. Their culture was, "It takes a Village to Raise a Child." It was so much love in her dad's family. They assisted him while he started his medical practice with her mom, Lorina. Although, they never got married they remained great friends and had a great working relationship. They later met other people and married them and the two couples were thick as thieves. Very good friends.

As, the man turned around he saw an amazingly beautiful woman with long curly hair with hazel greenish brown eyes. She was 5'6 at 145 lbs. She was curvy and very enticing. He looked into Jasmine's eyes and his heart leaped with excitement. Jasmine walked up to the man that was singing so soulfully that captured the audience heart as he sang to them. She held her hand out to shake his hand. He was still captured by her beauty, but he regained his composure, and reached out his hand to shake hers. He introduced himself," Hi my name is Romeo." Jasmine, let go of his hand and introduced herself, "Hello, my name is Jasmine. You are an amazing singer. My heart burned when you sing. How long have you been singing?" Romeo said, "I have been singing all of my life. It makes me feel good." Jasmine said, "I can tell. You melt our hearts as we leaned on every word that you sung. You express them very well."

Romeo said, "Thank you for those kind words. It is always nice when someone tells you how much they enjoyed my gift." I believe if we do not share the gift that God gave us, he will give it to someone else that will use it for the up building of his kingdom." Jasmine reached out her small smooth hands again to shake Romeo's hand. He grasped her hand and held it for a solid minute as if he did not want to let it go. She looked into his eyes in deep admiration and he could tell she felt as if he did, that they were destined to be together. Unfortunately, they both were in two different paths in life. Romeo was pursuing a music career and Jasmine was pursuing a medical degree as a Physician.

Jasmine went home and took a long relaxing bubble bath. She reminisced on her encounter with Romeo. He was so enduring. She wondered to herself what type of relationship they would have with one another. He seemed as if he would make an interesting boyfriend but she wanted more than that, Jasmine was about to fall asleep, so she decided to get out of the tub and put her favorite pajamas on and go to sleep. She had a father and daughter date tomorrow.

Romeo gathered his things and left the beach. He went home and enjoyed a quite evening with his cousin, Damion as they watched the Dallas Cowboys play Green Bay Panthers. Damion flew into town for the weekend to visit his favorite cousin. Dallas won 28-21. Romeo got up the next morning and went to his second job which was Psychiatrist. He had three appointments at his office. Romeo had two careers he wanted to pursue. One was singing and the other one was the human mind.

Chapter

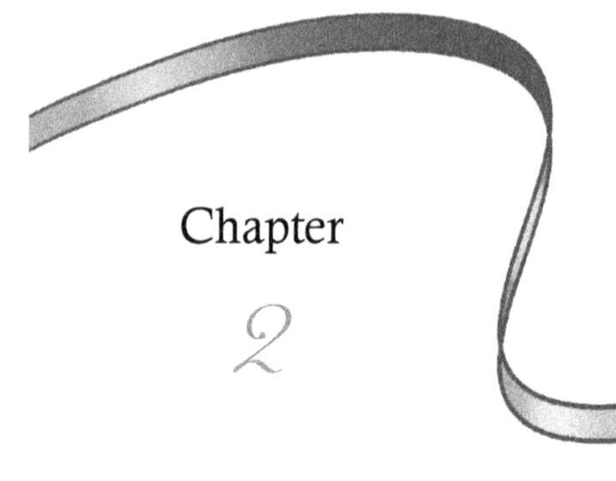

2

Romeo's first client was, Nancy. Nancy was going through a tragic divorce. She nearly went insane staying in an unhealthy marriage to a man that she argued with every day. Nancy was a Christian and was well versed in biblical teaching. She thought that her husband was like-minded but he was not. He was a challenge to Nancy, because everything God taught her regarding the holy scriptures through the holy spirit was so different from what her husband Tom would practice. Tom read the word of God every day at lengths. He even spent most of his time alone with God as he put it. He would often would tell Nancy, it was only he and God as if Nancy his wife never mattered.

Nancy knew the right interpretation of the Word of God that it is not good for man to be alone in Genesis, so God made Adam a help mate and took a rib from Adam and made Eve. God gave Eve to Adam as a companion. Also, the Bible clearly informed man to love his wife as Christ loved the Church. Christ Jesus gave his life so that believers could has a right to eternal life. He became the sacrificial lamb for the believers to be joined to the Father in Heaven as his children to disciple others unto Christ to have life and have it more abundantly as well as have a right to eternal life to be with the Lord.

Nancy life with Tom was very turbulent. They had several physical altercations, whereas, Tom on two different incidents he held her face, neck, and body to the floor and she could not breath and was about to faint. Once he had Nancy in a bear hug and she could no breath and he did not remember not one of those dangerous episodes. Tom would only remember what Nancy, through the strength of God, did to get out of Tom's embrace and break free so she could live. That second episode, Nancy had to get her eldest son Patrick and his wife Lola involved. Patrick told Tom when speaking to him on the phone, "Tom, I know that all marriages have their problems but when it comes to putting your hand on my mother. That should never happen. My mother is my heart and if you ever put your hands on her again. You will have to deal directly with me. Man to Man vs Man to Woman. I am a lot stronger than my mother. Do you understand me." Tom told Patrick, "Yes, I do understand you."

From that point on, Tom, did not directly perform the same deeds, but he still played the same manipulative mind games with Nancy and would pick fight with her so that she would become angry and lash out on him physically or curse him for pessimistically taunting her so much that she could not breath. Tom could never see his part in what angered Nancy, especially since she now suffered PTSD of the past altercations when he physically assaulted her. He would always blame her and tell her, "You have always been a angry violent person and you will always be one." Nancy, would always call him a liar and tell him, "I have never been an angry person or fought back until I made you. I was very calm and could peacefully work through things before I met you. You have done so much to me that I have turned into someone that I don't recognize. You always say it is me because I feed into your plot to make me angry and lash out for the ugly things you say to me so that you can shift the blame on me. I can't live like this. You are too much for me."

Although, Nancy would say this many times when the above altercations and arguments continued every day. Nancy would pray, cry, and try hard to mend the fences between her and Tom. Until God, gave her the strength and courage to file for Divorce. She did file but it was so hard for her to cope with it because she had put so much into saving her marriage that it had drained her so much. She needed counseling to help her to gain her strength back with the help of the Lord. Nancy was making huge progress by working with a Spiritual Psychiatrist. Romeo was young but he was brilliant. He achieved his Master degree in Psychology at age 23 y/o. He did 4 years of Residency at St. John Psychiatric Hospital and Rehab for clients that have gone through multiple mental and physical abuse. He had a wonderful bed side humor and he soothe his patients mind to relax by playing his prerecorded cd's of him singing some of his favorite original songs. Romeo had a 85% healing success rate that helped his client resume normal lives. Romeo knew it was not of his own human strength it was from the Spirit of the Most High God that helped him to help others come out of their darkness into the wonderful light.

Romeo did inform Nancy she has to work through the anger, frustration, and the resentment with the Lord but she will soon be feeling lots better and back to her sweet calmer self in a few months. Romeo informed her that she should leave saving people to the Lord and she is not put on this earth to fix others or their problems. Just continue to be your lovely self and let your heart lead you and you will be fine.

Nancy left and went to her sister, Liza's home. Liza was also fun loving and loved to live very adventurous. Liza was married to Frank and had 16 y/o teenage twins Ralph and Rosanna. They were well mannered children that also had great personalities. Frank was a 6'4 large man that was a teddy bear when it came to his wife Liza. He loved her and his family so much. He was a dentist and Liza was a Registered Nurse. Liza loved working with people. Ralph and Rosanna were not your typical teenagers. They were computer experts and very technical. The two of them completed high school at the age of fifteen and was already a junior in college due to taking a lot of college courses while in high school. They loved both their Aunt Nancy and Uncle Tom. They were wise in their own right because their mom and dad constantly communicated well with them. Teaching them daily in biblical and earthy principles in which how to be successful in living a spirit led life and applying them to live successfully while yet on this earth. Tom and Nancy did not have any children of their own so Ralph and Rosanna became like their very own children. Ralph and Rosanna benefited from having two set of parents. They had their choice of adults to help them with life struggles.

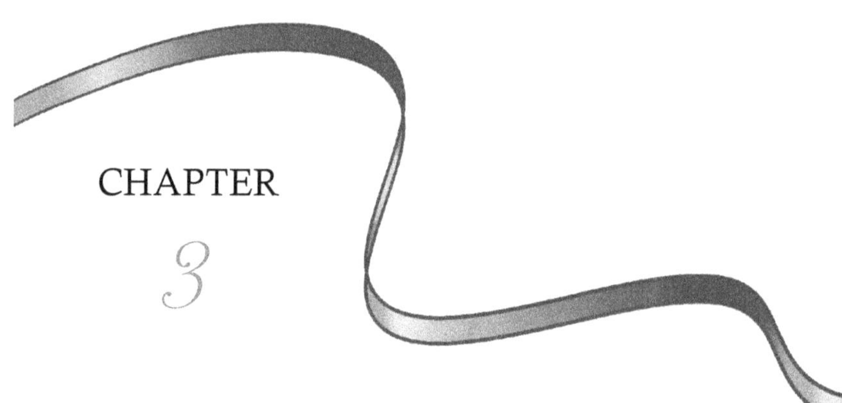

CHAPTER

3

omeo's next client was Tom. Tom did not want Nancy to know he was also seeking counseling. Tom was trying to sort out his mental issues. He internalized everything to the extent it affected his daily life. Tom really did love Nancy and realized because he had a lot of issues, he had not dealt with in his growing up he turned into a self-absorbing person. He thought everyone around him was the person that was wrong if they offended him and would always think that the good deeds, he performed was good for the other person. The problem was he did not consider the other person, he only considered what he thought they would like. Mainly, in his dealings with his ex-wife Nancy. Tom was raised by a single mom and his grandparents. They were very loving toward him but his mother was still in love with his father that left when Tom was 10 y/o. Tom loved his father, but he did not understand why his father would leave them to be with another man.

As Tom grew, his mother put a lot of responsibility on him as the man in her life. Not in the sense as being her partner but yet one that would fix things around the house and console her when she would cry because she would miss his father being with them. Tom was trained in carpentry by his father, grandfather, and neighbors. Tom loved it. As, Tom became older he wanted to become an architect. He Wanted to build quality affordable homes along with great corporate buildings. When he graduated high school, he immediately enrolled in architectural school. His Father and grandparents paid for his tuition and he worked part time with a local house builder and taught him how to build a quality home without having to have all expensive materials. As long as the material was of great quality it did not have to cost an arm and a leg to utilize it. Tom, utilize this training as an internship and he gained great knowledge that catapulted his career into being very successful by the age of 35 y/o he was a mufti-millionaire.

Tom's grandparents passed when he was 40 y/o. They were involved in a tragic auto accident. His mother could not deal with their death very well. She felt into a great Depression. This depression was very debilitating. Tom knew that she would require far more help than he was able to give her. Although, Tom's father, Chance, left his mom, for his now husband, Dan, Chance never left his son. Chance and Dan helped Tom with his mom, Lisa. Lisa depression with the help of a psychiatrist became very manageable. Lisa was so grateful to her ex-husband, Chance and his husband, Dan that they continued to spend a lot of time together. Chance and Dan would have lots of entertaining dinners that they would often invite Lisa to. Lisa met one of Dan's brothers, and they begin to talk not only at the dinners they were invited to by Chance and Dan but they also began to go out on dates. After a 1 ½ years of dating,

Dan's brother, Richard asked Lisa to marry him. Lisa said, "Yes, I will marry you and they had a long happy, healthy marriage together.

Tom wanted that for him and Nancy but he did not know how to love such an independent woman. Tom was always used to looking after his mom and make decisions for their lives, but did not know how to cope with a woman that was good at making her own money and her own choices in life. Nancy was a very loving wife, but it disturbed her when Tom imposed his thoughts and his decisions on her without discussing it with her. Nancy believed that the man was the head of the household but that she was his partner or help mate and not someone he had to oversee. That struggle caused a lot of arguments and friction in their marriage that led to their divorce after six years.

Tom was under counseling with Romeo, whom both he and Nancy had met at one of his father, Chance and Dan's entertaining dinner parties. Romeo was Chance and Dan's special guest to entertain them with his beautiful singing voice while they enjoyed great meals together. Nancy and Tom would often talk to Romeo regarding what other things he did besides being a singer songwriter.

Romeo informed them both, he was a psychologist during daytime hours and pursued his singing career in the evenings at designated special invitations and evens. Romeo had given them both one of his psychologist business cards. Tom and Nancy both were very intrigued. They both thought to themselves that they needed the help of a psychologist or a Marriage Counselor to help them sort out some of the issues they were having in their marriage. Unfortunately, the struggle and the pride of both of them would not let them discuss the possibilities of seeking outside help. They felt they wanted to keep their problems private and let everyone continue to think they had a perfect marriage.

Nancy loved Tom very much. She admired that Tom had the ability to be trusted and that he was very responsible. She knew that he was a key factor in making sure his mom was ok after his dad left their family. She knew that if he loved his mom the way that he did he would be a good husband and father. Tom in the sense became the man of his family even though he was only 10 y/o. He started his long journey of being a strategic business man at the age of 10 being trained in carpentry and building small utility storage sheds by his grandfather and neighbors. He had a plan at a young age to be very successful in something he loved doing and not to just work on a job all of his life. The fact that he did a lot of things for his mom and made the decisions for her was a catalyst of the reason why he and Nancy did not have a successful marriage because Nancy was an independent woman. She knew how to led the man lead in their family structure but she did not like to fact he did not consider her as a partner in their marriage in discussing things first with her when it impacted their family unit. Although she tried to talk to Tom about what she could no longer accept him doing, Tom was determined to persist in his way even though it was causing the both of them to grow further in further apart.

When Tom realized after the 15the year of their marriage that Nancy was done. She could no longer stay in a married that made her miserable, he was too late to try to change his actions. Although, he had a hard time seeing and letting her go because he loved her so much. Pride kept him from going to marriage counseling with her. Both, Nancy and Tom were prideful and would not even bring the subject matter up of going to Counseling. It would most likely have been an asset in both of them coming to terms with what was causing a widening gap in their relationship.

Nancy was overwhelmed in her grief. She wanted Tom to love her enough to alter his ways of having so much control but he would not, and it was so hard for her to forgive him for not doing so. That is why she felt the need to go to counseling to become whole again. She also prayed and started to have counseling sessions with her Pastor to help her spiritual to overcome this physical death emotionally in her life. Nancy and her sister were raised by her parents. They were poor growing up but their mom and dad showered them with lots of love. Although, their parents did not have a lot of money, both of them taught them biblical principles, God first, family, education, and honest hard work was the key to leading a successful life. Nancy parents maintain that status all of their lives and worked hard in their private restaurant business where they sold the classic American Menu with a twist of soul. The business was successful but because her parents fed anyone that came into their restaurant that was hungry but they did not have enough money to feed themselves or their family regularly, her parents with provide them with one meal a day for at least three times a week for an individual or a family.

Nancy and her sister and parents lived in a modest single family brick home with three bedrooms that her mom inherited from her parents when they passed away. They were only obligated to pay the property taxes and upkeep of the home. They had a very Spiritual and happy home. All four of them attended Sunday Morning and Wednesday evening Services. They loved the fellowship and served in the choir and usher board. Their Father was a Deacon at the church and their mom, served on the Deaconess board. Nancy parents taught her and sister the blessing of giving tithes and offering. They would instill in them, Malachi 3: 10: "Bring ye all the tithes into the storehouse, that there may be meat in mine house, and prove me now herewith, saith the Lord of hosts, If I will not open. you the windows of heaven, and pour you out a blessing, that there shall not be room enough to receive. And I will rebuke the devourer for your sake, and he shall not destroy the fruits of your ground; neither shall your vine cast her fruit before the time in in the field, saith the Lord of hosts." Their parents explained to them, you don't give to receive but you give because God blesses a cheerful giver. They kept that biblical teaching from their first job in high school unto the present time.

As, Nancy reminisces on how happy her parents were with each other and the joy of their family unit, she wished that her and Tom would have had the same happiness. She and Tom never had any children because she remained on birth control pills because of the struggles she and Tom was having in their marriage. She did not want to bring children into a turbulent situation. Nancy thought that because she and Tom were an interracial couple that would have caused difficulty in their marriage with society and the different culture and childhood up bringing. Nancy was a black woman raised according to biblical principles that continued the practice of going to church and biblical principles but Tom was a white man that was raised in a non-traditional family that believed in God but did not go to church or teach godly principles. However, being an interracial couple was not the reason why their married failed and led to a divorce, it was because Tom continued to make all of the decisions for their family without consulting her and although she would try to discuss with him how this made her feel, Tom persisted in this way, because that is all he knew. He had to grow up all too fast and be there for his mom in this way when his Father left their family for a man that he fell in love with.

Tom through his counseling sessions with Romeo, was gaining the knowledge that he needed to be able to include the other person in decision making and not be so bossy and unmovable to change. He also worked through anger issues that he felt toward his father for leaving him and his mom, when he knew his mom was not working at the time. He and his mom had to move in with her parents until she was able to grief from her divorce and get herself together in order to get a job to make a living to support her and her son. Tom also had to work through the fact that his mom put him as the man of their household way to soon. He was only 10 y/o and had to learn how to work to earn money to help his mom, but he was making successful strides to becoming a well-balanced person in his emotions and his inclusive nature. Tom gathered his keys and left the counseling session and stopped by the restaurant to eat, before he went home. Tom often worked on architecture building projects for luxury affordable quality family homes at night which was his passion and worked at the office during the weekdays M-F sometimes Saturdays to draw Corporate Office building designs that was unique and classy.

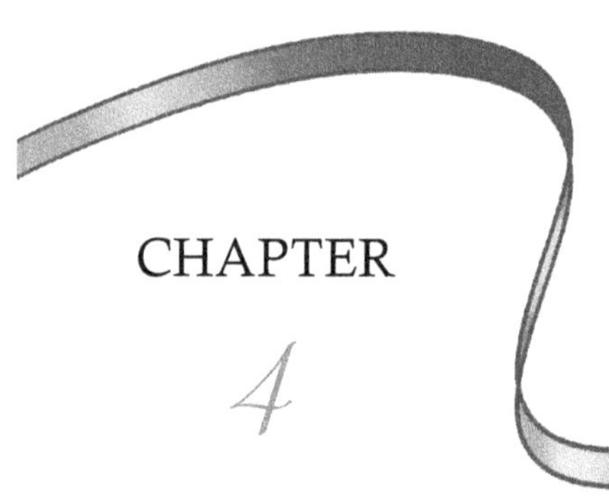

CHAPTER

4

Romeo had his last session for this Saturday, with a middle age woman that was happy but had challenging relations with men that always ended before it could turn into a successful union because her fear to love someone. Her name was Rosette. Rosette was 45 y/o and had never been married. She wanted to find Mr. Right but she could never allow the relationship to grow. She had a chance to do so multiple times because she attracted wonderful faithful men but she was the one that could not commit to growth in their relationship but she could not understand why.

Rosette and her two brothers were raised by loving parents that spent a lot of quality time with them. She and her brothers were athletic scholars that were smart and also great at playing basketball, her brothers playing football and running track. They were a middle -income family that was raised in a good neighborhood. Her dad was mixed with American Indian and white and her mom was mixed with Black and Mexican culture. They were truly blended in American culture. Her brothers always had a lot of their friends over to their home. They were twins and very popular. Their names were Peter and Perry. They were 6 ft 4 and very handsome.

Rosette was tall as well. She was 6 ft and slender. Her parents allowed her to model for Guess jeans when she was a teenager. Peter went on to play College Basketball with Yale University and was drafted into NBA and played with Chicago Bulls for 10 years until he retired. Perry received a scholarship to Division A1 college at LSU and was drafted into the NFL his 4th year of college. He was first round pick as a Wide Receiver with the Dallas Cowboys. He was very successful and loved living in Texas with the blending cultures. He played 11 years in the NFL and retired. Peter also retired and moved to Dallas Texas.

Both of them infested in Real Estate and become brokers of their own Peter & Perry Realty Company. Their business was very successful. Rosette also received a basketball scholarship to play with University of Texas Austin. She completed her 4 years and was drafted into the WNBA with the Houston Comets. She played for 5 years and was asked to become offensive Head Coach for the same team when she had a right knee injury that ended her basketball career but she still had the great moves and she could teach others very well the art of being a great basketball player.

Romeo asked Rosette when did her troubles with not having successful relationship with men start occurring.? He would ask her what did she believe what caused her not to be able to connect with men long term. Rosette shared with Romeo, when all of the young men with come over to their home, because she was beautiful, most of them would ask her out in secret because they did not want her brothers to find out because they were very protective over their little sister who was three years younger than they were. They would always run her away from being around them when they had a lot of guys at their home for that very reason.

In spite of her brother's warnings, she did go out on several dates with a few of her brother's friends. She was only 15 but she looked 17 y/o like her twin brothers because she was tall and very mature for her age. She already had her life planned out what she was going to be in life. So, she thought. Nancy was not planning to become serious with one of the three of her brother's friends but it did occur. She stopped talking to the other two guys and concentrated more so on the young man she was interested in. Although he was only 16 y/o, he was also mature for his age. His name was Ray.

Ray was so handsome. He was about the same height she was. She was just a little taller than he was. He was 5'11 and muscular. He was the star running back on their winning Football team. He also had planned to go to college to play football. Football Scouts were already sending him invitations to play for their D1 colleges. Ray and Rosette kept their relationship a secret because if her brother's found out about it, not only would they end their friendship with Ray, but socially it could limit his success with the guys on his football team. Rosette's brothers were very popular.

Rosette and Ray became intimate at one point in their relationship. Teenage hormones took over. Nancy became pregnant. Unfortunately, once her parents found out about it, they quickly sent Nancy to her mom's Rose, sister's home in Shreveport, LA to live with their family for the duration of her pregnancy which was about 7 more months. Nancy had to transfer to one of those school by her Aunt Rose home. Rosette was very distraught. Her parents did not want her to get an abortion because if she did it may be a chance, she could not have any more children if she so desired later in her life. Rosette did not know this, but her parents had spoken with Ray's parents, to formulate a plan for Ray's parents to adopt Rosette and Ray's child after he or she was born and they would raise the child with family. The only thing that Rosette knew of the plan was that she was to give the child up for adoption even though she personally wanted to keep him or her. Rosette enjoyed staying with her Aunt Rose and her family. Her husband, Adam, was about 3 inches shorter than her aunt Rose. He was 5'9 and Aunt Rose was 6'0 just like Rosette. The women in their family were very tall. Aunt Rose and Uncle Adam had three children two girls 13, 12, and a son 10 y/o. They were very mannerable and curious. Their son had a high functioning autism. He was brilliant but he did not like to be touched much. Although he loved the hugs his mom gave him. He was a little distant at first with Rosette. Although the two families were in frequent contact with each other, Tracy, her Aunt Rose's son was very particular who he let be in his midst. Rosette grew on him and he learned to cherish her presence like all of her other family.

Rosette enjoyed the high school she went to. Because she was tall not many people could tell that she was pregnant because she always wore loose shirts and blouses. Again, she was model like. Rosette even made some close friends both male and female. She was like her brother she had an outgoing personality even though she was sad because she had to give her child up for adoption. Rosette had come to love Ray very much but because of the distance she adapted to not having him in her mindset as she always had. Rosette's family would visit her as often as they could.

Ray continued to do well at school and in spite of him missing Rosette entirely, and him having to keep the secret that his parents were going to adopt their child, he seldom outreached Rosette. He did not want her to think she was in the pregnancy alone. However, it was very difficult to hide the truth from her. He loved her so much. He would have married her if their parents would have allowed it. Nonetheless, their parents thought this would be very admirable of him, but on both sides, they knew that both of them had a bright future ahead of them. Ray during the course of the 7 months visited Rosette numerous times. They remained great friends but the adoption was too much for them to carry because they wanted to raise the child together that the two of them settled to be good friends that would talk on occasions to stay in touch.

The seven months passed. Rosette family became a major support system to her when she had to give her child up for adoption. Rosette began to be very sad because she actually fell in love with her child at first site. She had given birth to a boy. The boy had green piercing eyes that stared at her as if he would remember her face forever. At least that is what Rosette told herself. It was so hard for her to give up her child. Ray was able to be in the birthing room at the hospital along with both set of parents when she gave birth to their son. The nurses took their son to the NICU unit after performing the Apgar scores. Their son had a perfect score 10. All systems checked out well.

From the NICU unit, the child was adopted by Ray's parents. The child grew as Ray's brother and child because Ray's parents Michael and Kathy taught Ray how to take care of his son and trained him to be a responsible and attentive brother/father. As Ray's son began to grow, he did not talk to Rosalyn much because they went into two different paths. He went to college at Duke University in Durham, North Carolina on a football scholarship and later played in the NFL with the Cincinnati Bengals for 10 years and Rosette after given birth to their son returned back home in the summer of that year to get ready to go into her senior year in H.S. She had poured herself during her pregnancy into her school work and was able to skip two years from the 10th grade to the 12th the following year because she could not do much due to her pregnancy.

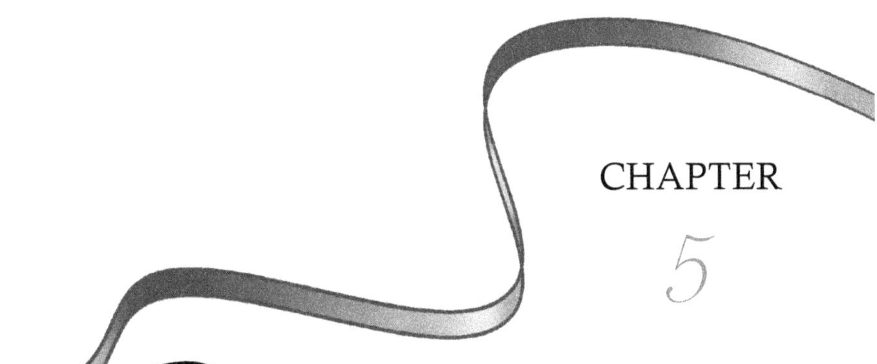

CHAPTER

5

Rosette was always self-motivating and progressive in her goal settings. In her 12th grade she returned back to playing basketball and excelled academically and athletically. This earned her a four-year basketball scholarship at University of Houston to play with the Houston Cougars. Rosette was a star forward. She excelled so much that she received an invitation to play in the WNBA with the Houston Comets. Her life was fast paced to stardom, but in her 5th year, she injured her left knee and was asked by her team, to become head offensive couch because she was always their high point person for the 5 years, she played with them. The upper management of the team would often see her bring some of the community children into their courts to motivate them to be involved in sports to stay out of trouble and learn as much as they can to be able to pursue their dreams and reach their highest potential. Rosette loved children and often thought about her son she had to give up for adoption. She loved her parents but she also resented them for not adopting her child so she could watch him grow up. Rosette would teach the children plays and how to dribble down the court.

Rosette also taught them how to hold the basketball and shoot it in the basket as they were in motion. She was a great teacher. Rosette did not know this but she was often watched by the other coaches who alerted the owner and upper management team that whenever Rosette decides to retire, please ask her to continue her basketball career as their offensive head coach. The owner and upper management team to heed to Rosette coaches' suggestion and after her left injury that was a long-drawn-out recovery period, Rosette decided to tell her coaches instead of coming back to play she would go pursue her life as Physical Therapist in which she graduated with honors in.

Her coaches asked Rosette to meet with the Owner of the team and the CEO before making that decision and they offered her the head offensive coach position at the team she was playing successfully in the WNBA and she accepted it. Rosette couched there for six years and they won the WNBA championships at least three of those years and made it deep into the playoffs the remainder of the three years. With all the success that Rosette was having, she did not have much of a social life. She dated a few guys through those years but she could not bring herself to have lasting relationships with them. Rosette never got married or had any more children. She was beginning to think something was wrong with her. That is how she came to start counseling services with Romeo.

Mary one of her basketball players had talked to her about how she had dated a guy whom she thought was a good man but he had changed into someone she could not recognize. Mary told Rosette how their relationship began. She had just started her basketball career with the Houston Comets and they had dated about 2 years. She had met him at a bar that her and some of the other players had gone just to unwind from playoff series. She told Rosette that she did not drink alcohol but she loved to dance. Mary told Rosette a man named Phil introduced himself to her and asked her could he buy her a drink. She informed him that she did not drink alcohol but her could buy her a soda. She asked him to ask the bartender for a canned drink and not to pour it into a separate glass. Phil did so. Mary said Phil was very polite and had great conversation. She voiced he had the ability to put her at ease even though he was a stranger.

Phil asked Mary for her number and could he take her to her favorite restaurant when they were not so busy with practice and playing back-to-back basketball games. Mary said, "Yes, that would be fine. She gave him her number and did not hear from him in over a month. Phil called and asked her to dinner and that led to them seeing each other as much as they could regardless of her full schedule. He worked as a Realtor so his schedule was more flexible then hers. Mary informed Rosette that, she and Phil dated for about two years. Mary with disbelief, shared with Rosette, how she began to notice how Phil began to change and when she first acknowledged that he was becoming very possessive and jealous over her.

 Mary was beautiful and very attractive. She also had a caring personality that enable her to make friends easily. The guy she was dating, name was Phil. Phil did a 360 on her. He showed his good side the first year and then he started changing because he could not deal with her popularity. On the last night of their relationship, she had invited him to eat dinner with her so that she could break thing off with him. Phil met her at the restaurant. After they had eaten, he had proposed to her. She did not know what to say. Her plans were to end things with him. Mary, thought of an excuse to end their dinner date and maybe tell him later that she wanted to end their relationship because she did not expect him to purpose. Mary informed Phil that it was late and she had to get up early the next morning because her team had a home basketball game. Phil understood and continued to pursue the marriage question to Mary.

Mary told Phil to please allow her to tell him the answer after her game tomorrow. Phil insisted to follow Mary home to make sure she had made it home safely. Mary tried to tell Phil that it would not be necessary but he would not take No for an answer. Mary allowed Phil to follow behind her in his care to make sure she returned home safely. Phil insisted he come in for a night cap. Although, Mary tried to discourage him, he persisted until he came in anyway. Phil asked Mary for a drink. Phil knew Mary did not drink alcohol. Mary said, "You know I don't drink alcohol but I have a six pack of bottle Lipton tea in the refrigerator. I can bring you one of them." Phil said, "Yes, please bring me one and one for yourself."

In Spite of her better judgement, Mary did as Phil requested. She put the two bottle of Lipton tea on round place mats on her living room glass table. Phil asked if she had anything to eat. He was hungry. She said, "Yes. I will fix you a sandwich." Mary went back into the kitchen and fixed Phil a ham and cheese sandwich on wheat bread with mayonnaise like Phil liked it. As Phil ate his sandwich, he asked Mary was she going to drink her tea. Mary said, "Yes, I will take a few sips. I don't like drinking any fluid close to the time I go to bed. It has me getting up to go to the restroom too much." Mary drank a few sips of the tea and begin to get drowsy. Mary told Phil that she did not feel well and she needed to lie down. Phil said, I will walk you to the bedroom. Mary insisted that he just go home and said she could make it to her room buy herself but Phil insisted.

Mary went to the restroom and as soon as she lied on the bed, she fell asleep. The next morning, she had awakened with no clothes on and Phil was lying next to her in the bed naked as well. Mary was very upset. She woke Phil up and asked him why was she naked and why was he lying in her bed naked as well when she had asked him to go home. Phil lied and said, you were complaining that you were feeling nauseated and felt like you had to vomit so I stayed all night to make sure you were okay. Mary asked Phil, "Why are we both naked?" Phil said later on that night you woke up and informed me that you felt better and one thing led to another. We made love and I fell asleep beside you."

Mary was horrified because she did not remember any of it. Mary was somewhat relieved when she saw a rubber package that Phil obviously had used in their encounter, but she could not help but to think he had drugged her with Ecstasy or something. Mary bluntly asked Phil if he had given her something to make her drowsy. Phil became angry with her and lied and said that he did not. They began to argue about it. Mary told Phil that she did not appreciate him staying all night and sleeping with her when she had asked him several times to go home. Phil tried to calm her down, but Mary insisted him to leave her house, now, and told him that she does not ever want to see him again.

Phil left after Mary had threaten him, if he did not leave, she would be forced to call 911 to ask the Police to come escort him out. Phil left reluctantly and she never saw him again. Mary got dressed and rushed to the stadium and despite her morning, she played well as she was one of the Houston Comets best guards. Mary informed Mary she could never really trust men after that and really did not date much after that. Mary said to herself, I am beautiful and outgoing. I want a family someday. I cannot let what this man did to me to stop me from having happiness.

That is when she decided she needed to start going to a spiritual counselor to help her deal with what Phil did to her. She told Rosette she began to ask around and one of her church friends told her about a young man that was very popular at their church because he was a singer song writer and sung at their church occasionally when their Pastor or Pastor's wife would ask him to prepare one of his original spirit-filled songs. The church member's name was John. He had grown up with Mary, and he was one of her faithful friends that kept her encouraged despite the woes of life. Mary and John went out a couple of times but decided their friendship was more important than to pursue a more intimate relationship with each other.

John had told Mary that every time their Pastor introduced Romeo, he would also let the congregation know that Romeo not only song very well but he was also a licensed Therapist. Their Pastor recommended that if anyone needed spiritual counseling, Romeo would be a great person to consult. Romeo did receive quite a bit of clients within their church family. John had requested one of Romeo's business cards at an earlier time because he wanted to work through some of his issues of growing up without a mother. His dad raised him as a single dad. His mom had died of cervical cancer when he was 7 y/o. His dad had re married a lovely wife, but he missed his mom very much. He was very closed to both his parents. They did a lot of things together up until the last year of his mom's life. She became to ill to go out much. John was very distraught from watching his mom waste away from a 5'4 and 145 lbs woman that had a beautiful curvy figure to 5'4 and 80 lbs. The cancer was very debilitating.

Romeo had counseled John for two years and he helped John to work through losing his mom at such an early age. He also shared how his grandparents had adopted him but he found out at about 12 y/o that his grandparents were not actually his parents but the man he thought was a very attentive older brother was actually his father. Romeo shared with John that his grandparent's intent was to help his biological dad to learn the art of being a great father but also pursue his dreams of going to college and hopefully play in the NFL one day. Romeo told John he never met his mom, but his family told him that his father was 16 y/o when he was dating his mom at age 15 y/o and they became romantically involved one evening not thinking about the consequences and she became pregnant. Romeo remembered his dad and his grandparents sharing the above with him and how mortified he was to hear such a story at the tender age of 12 y/o.

They also shared that the young lady that became pregnant by his dad expressed to him that she wanted to keep their baby but instead her parents thought it would be best if she goes and live with her mom's sister and finish out her 10th grade year in Louisiana where aunt family lived and have the baby there. The young lady he dated, Romeo's biological mother did not agree with her parents because she still wanted us to be together and raise our child together even though they were so young. She did not want to give her baby up for adoption, but her parents insisted that she does so to keep her from not pursuing her dreams of going to college and possibly being drafted into the WNBA as she had dreamed of since she was a little girl being trained with her brother by their father how to play basketball. Romeo was informed by his father that he wanted to purpose to his mom and raise their child together with family helping him because they were so young, but again, her parents insisted that his mom give their baby up for adoption. This how, Romeo's grandparents' purpose to his mom's parents that they adopted the child and raise him as their own because they were still in child bearing age and no one would be the wiser that did not know them well. His biological mother's parents agreed to such but never told his biological mom that this was going to occur. She had no idea.

Romeo's father informed him that he and his mother tried to continue their relationship but it was too hard for his mom to bear losing her the son she never wanted to give up so they slowly stopped seeing each other before it became noticeable that his parents had indeed adopted their child. He would make up all type of excuses why she could not come to their home. He was very successful in meeting her at her home or other places besides his home.

John informed Romeo how he appreciated him for sharing his testimony and that did help him move forward in coming to terms of losing his mom at an early age and realized his mom was in a better place and was not suffering anymore. He knew his mom had confessed her belief in the Almighty God and believed in the trinity: God the Father, God the Son (Jesus), and God the Holy Spirit were three but one in the same purpose to redeem men unto God. John remembered how his mom and father taught him biblical principles.

All these things, John share with his dear friend, Mary. Mary shared these things with Rosette as she gave her one of Romeo's business cards. Rosette wanted to have a family. She was only 43 y/o but she could not bring herself to love any other man then the man she had the baby with that she had to give up for adoption against her will because her parents thought it was best for her. At the time, they were not willing to help her to raise her son. Rosette knew the rationale why she could not connect to another man to love him and for it to lead to a lasting marriage but did not know the way to resolve the issue within herself to move forward from it controlling her life.

It was not until she went to a laid-back upscale lounge club that served great food and wine with some of her friends, in which she coached on the Houston Comets, when she heard this strong soulful voice that captured the attention of the participants hearts, mind, and soul with the way he song the lyrics of a very meaningful song. Rosette, asked her friend Stephanie did she know the name of the song the young man was singing? Stephanie asked Sheryl because she did not know. Sheryl told Rosette and Stephanie the name of the song was blinded love. She said the only way, she knew the name was blinded love because she was at an event where the young man was singing to a great crowd of people at one of the local Amphitheater being the main attraction. The young man that was singing had told the audience then the name of the song was, "Blinded Love." It was dedicated to his father from a faithful love of a woman he once knew and what came from that love was him. It was so moving that it brought the audience to tears. Rosette had the same impression. She thought to herself, how coincidental that this young man would sing her testimony. Something, she herself had gone through.

Rosette, listened to the rest of the song, and before she broke down and cried in front of everyone because the lyrics of the song reminded her of the time she loved a man so much, that their love produced a child, but she had to give the child away. She gained her composure just enough to tell her friends that she had to excuse herself because she needed to go over some plays for their next practice. Her friends told her that is all she does, work, work, and work. Live a little. Don't you want to meet someone nice and have a family. We hardly see you with anyone. Rosette thought to herself, yes, they are right but I have to heal first. She could not find the way to heal, she needed some help. She reached into her pocket, and pulled out the card of the Psychologist that her friend Mary had given her. She put it on her Calendar to call him first thing Monday Morning before she went to practice at 10:00 am.

Romeo finished his song, and saw Jasmine, the beautiful lady he had met when he had song some of the original songs, he had written at the beach two months ago. He had called her and invited her to one of the gigs he had singing hoping that she would come. He knew she was busy with her career being a family physician but she did not know that he was still working as a psychologist. He stepped down from the stage in which he was playing the piano and singing. They greeted each other with a hug. Romeo began to talk with excitement to Jasmine. "I am so happy you could make it tonight. I am so sorry it has been so long since I called you. I had actually lost the card you had given me with your contact information on it." It was deep into one of my pants pockets that I had worn a few days after I had met you at the beach. I had another event that I was the main attraction and I had intended to call you that morning to say hello, and possibly invite you to the event but things became so hectic that I did not get a chance to do so. I had placed the pants in my closet in the laundry basket and it had been there all this time. I have so many outfits and do not have to wash very regularly so they were left there this whole time. I usually check my pants pocket before I wash them, and that is when I found your card. I am so sorry."

Jasmine said, "I understand. There is no need for you to apologize. I also have been so busy. We have increased the number of new patients we serve by 30%. I already had a lot of patients but I guess the word is being spread on how I treat my patients and the great bedside manner that I have with them." I also apologize to you because I have wanted to call you as well but putting in so many long hours at work and finally at the end of the day, I was too tired to do anything but fix dinner, take a hot bubble bath with jasmine to whine down, and go to sleep. The next day, I just continued in the same like manner. It became so routine."

Romeo thought to himself, Jasmine is so easy to talk to and she is beautiful. I want to spend more time with her. I will have to be more intentional to ask her out." Jasmine looked into his green eyes and again, became mesmerized with his handsome looks that it was hard for her to concentrate on anything else but being with him in this moment. However long it may last. Romeo and Jasmine talked about more ways they could connect so that they could get to know each other better. They both agreed to not let two weeks go by without taking the time out to call at least to say hello. Even though they both knew they wanted to do more than just talk.

Romeo and Jasmine were seated in a nice quiet but Romantic area in the lounge and ordered dinner and talked the night away. Four hours had passed and it was now 11:00 pm. They both wished they did not have to depart because they began to become very comfortable with other but they knew they had to get up the next morning to do their hustle and bustle all over again with their busy work schedules. Romeo walked Jasmine to her car and asked her to please call her when she made it home so that he would know she made it there safely. Jasmine agreed. She just stayed about five blocks from the lounge where they were. She called him when she made it home. Romeo was relieved. He had another five blocks to go. Out of courtesy, Romeo texted Jasmine to inform her that he also had made it home safely and thanked her for supporting him by coming to his singing engagements. He voiced how she made his night.

The weekend passes as soon as it came in. Monday morning came around to quickly. Rosette got out of bed and went to her restroom in her master bedroom. She brushed her teeth and took a relaxing bath. She got dressed and put the business card of the Psychologist she was to call this morning at 9:00 am that she had left on her night stand on the side she normally gets up on. She grabbed an apple and her car keys and walked to her drive way and got into her black Lexus. She pulled out the Psychologist business card and called him on her way to 10:00 am basketball practice. Romeo's office secretary answered the call and booked an appointment for this Friday at 3:00 pm. Rosette prayed to God that this Psychologist could help her to resolve the pain of losing not only her first and only love but also giving up her son, who she wanted them to keep for adoption. She wanted to move forward in her life, and possibly be able to meet someone she could have a lasting relationship that would lead to love, marriage, and hopefully having children together. The week progressed as usual very eventful and fast. Friday was finally here. Rosette prepared for her first appointment with the Psychologist she had booked an appointment Monday morning.

Rosette parked her Lexus and entered in the office of the Psychologist. It was very classy and beautifully arranged. It was very bright and soothing with bright tropical colors but also had a very appealing fancy leather office furniture to it. Rosette thought to herself, wow, this does not look like a psychologist or a Counselor's office. This is more inviting and soothing. He must have had help from a woman. Maybe his wife or lady friend. Rosette came into the front lounge and was greeted by the office secretary. The secretary was a friendly middle-aged man that had a way with people. He knew just what to say and when to say it. His name was Frank. Franked asked Rosette to have a seat and he would go and get the Psychologist and he would take her back to his office. Frank also gave her the admission paperwork for her to fill out and took her driver's license and her health card and made a copy of it to start her patient file.

By the time, Romeo came out to get her, she had already finished the documents and had handed them to Frank. To, her surprise, as Romeo came toward her to greet her with a hand shake, she noticed he was the same young man that was singing in the lounge last week when she had joined her friends. She almost turned around and left but something in her heart moved her to stay. Romeo reached out his hand to shake her hand as he greeted her with a smile. Of course, she knew right away, how handsome he was. She knew that from when she first saw him at the lounge. Romeo led her to his office and offered her some coffee, water, or tea.

Rosette, politely turned it down. Romeo began to ask her certain knowledge seeking questions to find out a little about her back ground so that he can best know how to help her. The first session was very interesting. She felt like she knew him but never saw him before she laid eyes on him at the lounge last week. It was something familiar about him but she could not pinpoint what it was. It was not so much of the way he looked but more of his mannerism. Romeo was very calm, polite, and choice his words wisely in not to offend because he knew he would have to dig into their past where a lot of pain and sometimes harmful suffering had occurred in order to help them to resolve the past to move forward into the present.

Romeo and Rosette set their goodbyes, and Rosette set her next appointment with Frank to see Romeo for her second session on next Friday at 3:00 pm. This was always a good time for Rosette due to practices with the team were usually over by 12N unless they had a game on that day. Romeo also left the office and on his way home, he called Jasmine. It was after 6:00 pm, so he was hoping she had already left her office and had not eaten anything yet. He was hoping to ask her to meet him at a local restaurant so they could relax and get to know each other. The call was not answered so he left a message asking her to return his call.

Int the next 15 minutes, Jasmine was returning his call. She apologized for not being able to pick up his call before. She informed him she was finishing up with her last client for today. She had approved a late F/U appointment with one of her new patients that she had to give some good news from a diagnostic test two weeks ago to determine if the patient had a debilitating illness. She could not give out any other information due to HIPPA and PHI rules and regulations. Romeo asked Jasmine had she eaten yet. She told him, "No, not yet." Romeo asked her would she join him for a quick dinner tonight or tomorrow night. His weekend was unusually free. Jasmine informed Romeo that she would love to meet him for lunch tomorrow. Tonight, she had to go see her dad to see how he was doing. Romeo and Jasmine made plans to meet at a local Mexican Restaurant in the east end where there was a lot of eateries and entertainment areas.

Jasmine arrived at her dad's home. She noticed that there were three other cars there. She knocked on the door, and her dad, Ramon came to the door to let her in. She saw that his wife, Louise was there, her mom, Lorina and her husband Lou Hong, and her grandparents, Anthony and Rochelle. She wondered what the gathering was about. It was unusual for all of them to be in the same room together or the same place. Jasmine's family greeted her with a hug and a wide smile as if they were up to something.

Jasmine's father, Ramon asked her to have a seat in the living room on the back end of the house. Her dad had two living areas in his home. His parents often spent the night with them. Ramon informed her that they would join her in a little bit. Jasmine's grandparents, Anthony and Rochelle joined her first. Then her father, Ramon and his wife, Louise came in a little later. Jasmine was wondering why her mom, Lorina and her husband, had not joined them yet. Jasmine heard the doorbell rang. She looked at her father, Ramon. Ramon told her your mom will get the door.

Lorina opened the door and let two other people in. They all joined the rest of the family in the 22nd living room area at the back of her dad, Ramon and his wife, Louise house. Jasmine saw a couple that appeared to be in their late seventies, come into the room with her mom and her husband. They appeared to be very healthy looking and quite attractive. Lorina, Jasmine's mom started to talk to Jasmine to introduce the couple that came in with them. They were holding gifts in their hands. Lorina began to speak, "Jasmine, I know this is a bit peculiar and you do not know what is going on. I wanted you to meet this couple that you see now before you. This is my mom, An Ni (Peace, quiet) and Hui (Intelligent, wise) Li. These are my parents and they wanted to meet you. I will introduce them to you and then let them talk to you. They have some things to discuss with you from their hearts." Lorina introduced her parents An Ni and Hui Li to Jasmine her daughter.

Jasmine greeted them with a bow to show honor and respect. Her mom taught her some of their Chinese customs. She had also talked to her long ago when she was a girl about why she could not see or get to know her parents at that time. Jasmine had just accepted that she would only know her Father's parents and his side of the family.

Lorina's mother, An Ni began to speak to Jasmine, "Hello Jasmine. It is our pleasure to meet our granddaughter. I wanted to start out by saying, we always knew of you but because of our upbringing and our customs we did not allow our daughter to marry into another race. We did come to know your dad, Ramon and we admired him greatly. We also adored him but because of the way we were raised it gave us great pause to accept him as our daughter's husband." An Ni paused and allowed her husband, Hui to speak to Jasmine. "Jasmine, I wanted to let you know that it was more of me not accepting the union of your parents then my wife, An Ni. An Ni had come to love your father Ramon because he and our daughter studied all the time over our home. They kept their relationship hidden from us as a couple and told us that they were just great friends. My wife, intuition would always tell her they were more than friends but had a very enduring relationship. She would allude that to me but I would always discourage that idea because I did not agree.

When it came to our full attention that Lorina and Ramon were actually a couple was when they were sharing with us that she was three months pregnant but could not tell us because she knew that we would not approve. She was right. Ramon, was a wonderful man and we both knew how he was going to be a successful Physician but I was stubborn and stuck to our old customs and traditions. Ramon and Lorina wanted to get married but we told her if she did, we would not have anything to do with her or her family. I can tell by the way you are looking at me that you are horrified that we would say such things to the daughter that we loved and her unborn child and the child's father, but we did.

We could not bring ourselves to meet you while you were growing up but that did not keep your mom from telling us how beautiful and intelligent you were. She would show us your pictures as you grew up. She told us how you were following in their footsteps in becoming a Physician as well and would join her and your father's Family Practice once you finished your residency." Hui continued, "I know that we can never turn back the wheel of time and the words and unjust way we treated your parents love for you and each other, but today, this day, we wanted to give our deepest apologies and ask you to please forgive us. We were very mistaken in not watching you grow up to the beautiful accomplished woman that you are. We missed being grandparents like Ramon's parents got to enjoy because of our stubborn ways."

An Ni began to speak to Jasmine and Jasmine's parents, "We apologize to all of you. We lost so much time with you both. We continued to see our daughter because in the since she chose our will instead of her will to marry your father and the two of them raise you together. To our daughter's credit, she was persistent in her way in informing us of her your milestones and the different pictures of your childhood up unto now. We kept every picture and milestone in a photo album that I created. I so wanted to get to know you but I did not want to disrespect my husband. We want to get to know you better, now, if you will allow us. We cannot make up time but we can let time heal all wounds. If you say, no, Jasmine, that is totally fine. I know this is a lot and we have been so unfair."

Jasmine looked at her mom's parents and perceived in her heart, that they were so sorry for the ways they had treated not only her parents but had treated herself as well. Jasmine looked at her other family members in the room. They all were wiping tears from their eyes. Jasmine, went to her mom's parents and gave them both a hug and said, "Yes, we cannot go back in time and change the past, but we can start right now to build hopefully a caring relationship because I would love to get to know you both. I had the pleasure of always having my dad's parents and his family always nearby. I love them all so much for helping my dad to raise me. My mom was always there but she did not raise me. My dad and his family did. Is it okay, if we start right here, at this moment to forgive and let the past rest in the past and build a relationship at this moment."

Lorina's parents, reached out to Jasmine and gave her a big hug and a kiss and thanked her for being such an understanding and forgiving person. Lorina and Ramon also hugged Lorina's parents and said they would like to also build their relationship from here and that they forgive them as well. Wow, that was a happy and a challenging moment in their lives, but they put those things behind them and enjoyed a wonderful dinner with each other. Jasmine and her mom's parent's exchanged phone numbers and they invited everyone that was there tonight over to their home for dinner in two weeks. They all accepted the invitation and was off to a great start. Jasmines' grandparents, An Ni and Hui gave her the presents they had in their hands for her. A Littmann CORE stethoscope and a check for $50,000 dollars. They both said, we are not trying to buy your love, but it is better late than ever to contribute your educational financial needs. It could not have been easy for your parents and Romeo's parents to put you through medical school. We wanted to give you the $50, 000 now and $100,000 later when you decide what account you will put it in.

This gave Jasmine and her parent's great pause. Jasmine, said to them, "No, I cannot accept this. You all are my grandparents. I have already forgiven everything. All is well, now." However, her mom's parents insisted and wanted her to please accept the gift that they should had given her when she was actually going through medical school, but if she accepts, she can use the funds for anything she so desires. Jasmine did accept it and put it into one of her high yield Money Market accounts.

It was an enjoyable rest of the evening and they all left their dad and his wife's home around 11:00 pm. All of them made it home safely that left. Jasmine and her father's parents stayed all night at her dad's home and left the next morning to go to their homes. Jasmine, took a long hot shower and put on her sexy red fitted dress, that flowed just passed her knees with red pumps. She put a red rose in her hair and left to meet Romeo at the Restaurant they had decided upon. Romeo had already made it to the restaurant and got them a table on the left corner in a private area so that they could talk without many distractions. Romeo had a red dress shirt on with a black blazer and black dress pants. He looked very handsome. Again, Jasmine was amazed how well he dressed. Romeo was also taken away by Jasmines curvy figure and how beautiful she looked. Although, by now, they both was bias and had come to the terms that no matter what they wore, they would still be positively alluring. That is just how attractive they were to each other.

Jasmine told Romeo all about last night events with her mom's parents, An Ni and Hui Li and how it was her first time actually meeting them. She also shared the eventful past that her mom and dad had to endure when they shared that her mom was pregnant with her and how her mom's parent could not bring themselves to allow her parents to marry and raise her due to her mom' s parent's Chinese cultures and traditions that they persisted on keeping. Although, they did come to care for her father, Romeo as their daughter's friend, they could not accept him as her husband. Jasmine informed Romeo how they were deeply sorrowful in their actions and asked her and her parents for forgiveness. They also wanted to ask that they allow them to build a bridge of a hopefully getting to know each other now even though so much time had occurred that they will not able be able to get back or retrieve. Jasmine informed Romeo that she and her parents did forgive her mom's parents and wanted to bridge their relationship.

Romeo also shared with Jasmine how his parents had him when they were teenagers. His mom who he has not met and his dad or grand parents have never shared that information, had him when she was 15 y/o and his dad was 16 y/o. Romeo told Jasmine that the only thing he was aware of was his paternal grandparents wanted to adopt him to help his father learn how to raise him. They shared with him how much his mother loved him and wanted to raise him with his dad but her parents wanted her to give him up for adoption because they felt like she was too young to accept such a responsibility or to get married. At the time, they were not willing to help raise me but my father and his parents were.

Romeo shared with Jasmine he did not learn that his father was his actual father until he was about 15 y/o. By that time, his dad had matured, went to college, and playing football in the NFL. He informed Jasmine he always thought his father was a very attentive big brother that share with him a great deal and took him to most of his home college football games and later to NFL football games. He shared that his father was very loving toward him and he was grateful to have such a lovely family to grow up end. Romeo said he started singing in the church choir. His grandmother played piano for the adult choir. She also taught him how to play. He voiced his grandfather was a cool guy. He played the saxophone and people loved it because it made the church music sound like jazz. My grandmother would also practice voice lessons with me to gain more levels of my singing to have multiple ranges of style and pitches. They are so wonderful. I go to their home every Sunday evening for Sunday dinner. My grandmother loves to cook. My grandfather loves to grill. He grills everything even fruit. My dad retired from NFL after playing 10 years. He is getting ready to be drafted in the Hall of Fame as one of the greatest running back of all time. I am so proud of him.

Jasmine asked Romeo, "How do you feel about your mom wanting she and your dad to raise you but her parents wanted her to give you up for adoption? The fact that you do not know her identity. That must be hard?" Romeo answered Jasmine, "Well to be honest, I struggled with not knowing my mom's identity while growing up. I would see other kids being held and kissed by their mom and missed that specific knowledge of my mom's touch after I found out that my grandmother was not my mom. I must tell you that my grandmother, was a wonderful mother to me and I still call her mom and my grandfather, Pop. I call my father by his name because most of my childhood, I knew him as my older brother."

Jasmine said, "I understand. Although, it is not the same exactly, we did have some challenging things we had to endure in our childhood, but as far as the people who actually raised us, our grandparents had a great deal in raising us with our dads." Romeo agreed and was so happy they were off to a great start with things in common. The two of them enjoyed their time together and without telling the others knew that their relationship would be a lasting one. Internally, they both wanted it to be a long-lasting Romantic relationship as a couple. They both had a healthy but filling lunch. Jasmine asked Romeo, "Romeo, I know that you sing but what else do you do?" Romeo informed her, "I am also a psychologist. I work most M-F and if I accept Saturday appointments, then I will try to take off on Mondays so that I can plan out my singing gigs. "Jasmine asked Romeo, "Which do you like best, the singing or the counseling?" Romeo said, "I enjoy them both. I am more of a Spiritual psychologist. I draw from biblical teachings to help people resolve issues in their life. I may never mention the words God, Jesus, or the bible when I am interacting with my clients, but I certainly apply these principles with them. If I know the client is a professing believer than I may mention the quotes by either Jesus, God, or the bible specifically, but most of the time I express them as sound teaching methods that are proven to help any situation to become less traumatic." Jasmine was impressed. She did not go to church often but she was reared with biblical teaching by her father and grandparents. She knew that her father and grandfather were very Spiritual good men and she had hope to marry someone similar when she took that great leap of faith.

Jasmine and Romeo had another lovely night together and they embraced each other in a big hug as they finished their lunch and Romeo walked Jasmine to her care. Romeo asked Jasmine would it be ok for him to call her one evening next week? Jasmine voiced, "Anytime. You can call me anytime. If I am not able to answer please leave a message and I will call you as soon as I can." Romeo leaned over to her face and kissed her fore head and said, "Great. Until next time. Hopefully soon." Jasmine almost melted with sheer excitement when his soft perfect lips touch her skin even if it was her fore head. She actually wanted to be her lips. Jasmine said," Yes, until next time hopefully, we will see or talk to each other again next week.

You have great conversation and I feel at ease with you" Romeo said, "I feel the connection with you as well. It is definitely special and I want to get to know you even more." Jasmine smiled as she got into her car, but before she did so, she hugged him very tightly as if she did not want to let him go." Romeo, had to ease out of her embrace because he could feel his temperature rising and not just his body temperature. Romeo walked to his car and went to the grocery store to pick up some items. He wanted to have Jasmine over for dinner next week instead of going out. He wanted a more intimate and private setting.

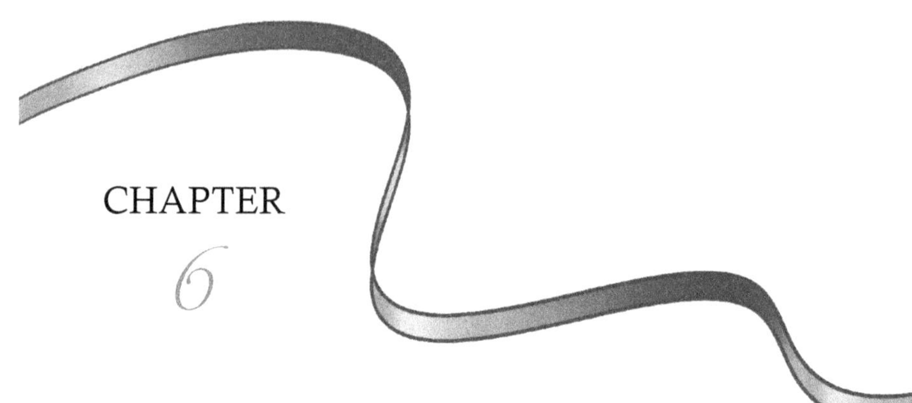

CHAPTER

6

*T*he weekend came and went very fast as usual, Monday came along and he had an appointment with Nancy. Wednesday of the same week, he was scheduled to counsel Tom. Nancy arrived at her appointment with Romeo a little earlier. She went into the office and set in the lobby until Frank called her to notify Dr. Romeo Mitchell his appointment was here. Romeo came out to meet Nancy. He outreached his hand to shake hers as they walked together to his office. He was just finishing with another person.

The man was a very handsome rugged man that was about 45 y/o and had a pleasant disposition. As the man was about to pass them, Romeo reached out and touched the man on his shoulder and called out his name as he spoke to him. Romeo voiced, "Ray, I want you to meet Nancy." The man stopped and was greeted by Nancy with a very beautiful smile. Ray, thought to himself that she was a very attractive woman. He did not stare to much because he was dating someone, he had met when he first retired from the NFL. It was not as serious to get married but he has been dating her for a few years. Romeo informed Nancy that Ray is my father. Nancy, looked in amazement because Ray did not look much older than Romeo. Nancy, looked into Ray's bluish green eyes and said, "It is very nice to meet you. I can see where Romeo gets his good looks." Ray blushed and said, "Watch out now, you are going to get me in trouble." They both laughed as they said to each other, "It was a pleasure to meet you." Romeo and Nancy continued to walk to Romeo's office as Nancy laid on the couch. Romeo gave his clients a choice to sit in a comfortable plush leather chair or lay down on plush leather couch.

Romeo started asking Nancy his therapy questions to get more to the core problem of what is presenting her from moving forward and healing from her frustration with Tom. She had already let Tom know that the core things about Tom, she loved because he was very responsible and knew how to provide financially for his family. Meaning he and her because they did not have any children. He had started working early in his childhood after he learned the trade of carpentry and how to build things. He was gifted in that so naturally he would be a great fit to choose architecture designs and building homes and corporate offices as a lucrative career. The thing that caused great distance from him was he was never inclusive when he made major decisions for their marriage and life. She was independent and waiting a long time before she decided to marry. She viewed marriage more so as a partnership rather than a dictatorship as she described Tom. Tom had one way of doing things. IT WAS ONLY HIS WAY OR THE HIGHWAY. At least that is how it seemed to her.

24

Romeo asked Nancy how was her childhood. Was there a male figure that was very Authoritative that Tom reminds you of and that is why you detest that characteristic in Tom? Nancy said, "There was my mom's husband of 10 years. He was my step dad and not my biological father. My mom never married my dad. My dad and my mom were high school sweethearts and my dad was planning on marrying my mom because he loved her so. My mom also loved him. My dad had accepted a job in New York after they had finished college as a computer design advertising specialist. He went to New York to get settled and he was going to come back home to Atlanta Georgia to Marry my mom, but after a month he was involved in a severe airline crash when the plane was landing."

Nancy continued, "One of the wheels came off of the plane and it caused a lot of un balance and they crashed into the west wing of the airport. Her dad was one of the 20 people that died on impact of the crash. The Airline notified my mom, because her dad did have her listed as an emergency contact in his wallet. The sad thing was, her dad did not know my mom was pregnant with me his child. She was planning to tell him when e made it home. Unfortunately, she was never able to do so. It took my mom a long time to recover from the death of the man she loved dearly. My mom had me seven months later and she cherished me greatly because I not only looked like my dad but I also had a lot of his characteristics. My mom met my step dad Ralph when I was five years old. They dated and took things slow. One day, Ralph asked my mom and myself out to dinner and he purpose to my mom. My mom said yes. I was 8 y/o. "

"Ralph was a good man. He treated me as if he was my biological dad. I really did come to love him as my father. Again, he and my mom were married for 10 years but cumulatively they were together for 13 years. So, we got to know him very well. He was a loving husband and dad. He was a great provider. My mom worked as a RN full time as an OB and Women Surgery Nurse, so she was financially fit as well. Like Tom, Ralph struggled with my mom's independence. She did not really need Ralph to provide for them. She just wanted his love, inclusion in important matters of their marriage and life together especially when it came to decisions about me."

"My mom was very beautiful. She could grow her hair very long but she loved having a nice short hair glamorous style. She had naturally curly hair so when she washed it, she could wear it naturally and she could manage it well with the long shifts in nursing at the hospital. She had was about 5 ft 4 and curvy but about 135 lbs. She was a sight to see. She walked so proudly and held her on even though she was a petite woman. She would always capture men hearts when she walked past them even when her husband, Ralph was with her. I don't believe he handled that very well. He started to be very controlling with my mom in various ways and mom struggled with him regarding that. They would get into some serious arguments that eventually led to Ralph and my mom separating. They eventually, got a Divorce when marriage counseling was not being very effective in their case. There divorce really affected me greatly. I loved Ralph as my father. He was a caring father to me. I hated to lose him and I missed seeing him every day. Fortunately, for me, my mom allowed Ralph to continue his role as my father even though they divorced, she did not want me to be estranged from the only father I have ever known just because they were no longer together. Ralph is still in constant contact with me. He is a person that I trust and respect and he did change. He remarried and his wife is enjoying the fruits of his now, more inclusive nature. He is still a great provider but now he is more of a partner than a sole provider in his mind set like he was with my mother.

Nancy was happy that Romeo asked her pointed questions. She had never taken a moment to analyze why Tom had made her so angry when in her mind set, he was the perfect man she had always wanted. Loving, handsome, strong, and took care of others. She realized the main thing she was attracted to him about was the main thing that made her crazy. Romeo asked Nancy, "How does that make you feel?" Nancy paused because she did not tell Romeo what she was thinking about. Nancy said, "Excuse me. I don't know what you mean." Romeo said, "I can tell the way that you were sitting in such a stoic way that you were thinking about something very heavily. So, what was it? "Nancy said, "You have a gift. Are you sure you did not study behavioral science?" Tome said, "As a matter of fact. I did study Behavioral Science and body motion psychology in tune with the mind."

Nancy confessed, "I was just thinking ask you ask certain pointed questions why I believe I upset me the most about Tom and led me to realize he was not the man for me and that I could no longer be married to him. Consequently, did Tom remind me of someone that acted like Tom in my childhood because often times what we experience in our childhood it is revisited in our adulthood. Nancy said, "Yes, Tom reminded me of my Stepfather, Ralph. Ralph had a lot of characteristics as Tom but the one thing I did not like of Tom was the exclusive way he did things. Rather than talked to me about important issues that would affect our marriage or our Livelihood, he would make the decision exclusively and would tell me about after the effect. It continued to happen even though; I had tried to inform him many times how much I did not like him doing so. It drove me crazy just like Ralph drove my mom crazy. It led to their divorce. The sad thing is, the very thing my mom divorced Ralph about was corrected by him but another woman benefited from the change and not my mom. That was hard for me to forgive him for because he was and is the only father I have ever known. I did not deal with their divorce well.

So, I guess when Tom refused to deal with that issue, I still had unresolved issues of unforgiveness that I was harboring in regard to Ralph leaving my mom and I. I see it so clearly now, but during my marriage with Tom, I could not see it at all. I only seen him not dealing with the issue because he felt he was not doing anything wrong. Tom had a complex. He could see my faults very clearly according to his thoughts but he would not acknowledge his own faults. As a matter of fact, Tom did not think he had any faults. So, naturally, I was always blamed for everything that went wrong within our marriage."

Romeo said, "Exactly, the mere fact that Tom was everything you have always thought you wanted in a husband and partner he was not because of the latter. He did not include you as a partner in your relationship because he made all of the important crucial decisions regarding your marriage and livelihood as you pointed out earlier." "Those same issues led you to divorce because he did not want to change those things about him that you had some unresolved issues and unforgiveness in regard to your Stepfather, Ralph. The point that Ralph corrected his but it was too late for his mom to enjoy the benefit thereof, he, meaning Ralph, gave the reward or prize to another woman that was not in the trenches of the muddy water or the struggle like your mom had with Ralph. You felt like Tom was not going to change for you, but like Ralph, another woman would reap all the rewards of your struggle with him by Tom deciding to change for the other woman that came after you. Or, so you felt it was inevitable going to having the same way, it had occurred with your mom and Ralph."

Nancy felt ashamed of her unresolved issues with her stepfather, Ralph and his mom. She concluded and admitted it did play a lot of the struggles she could not accept about Tom. She felt like if she could have just forgiven her step dad, Ralph for leaving her and her mom then she could have still been married to Tom or at least know why she could not deal with the exclusive ways he was treating her. She could not stand the fact he only saw what he wanted even when he thought he was truly doing things for their benefit. Romeo ended their session for today and asked her to make her next appointment with

Frank. Frank made an appointment with Nancy for the next Wednesday evening in two weeks. She wanted to go see her mom and see her and the new man she was dating for the last three years. Nancy had promised she would have dinner with her and Michael. She had met Michael several times before. He was a Caucasian man that was very culture. He knew how to treat a woman. The only thing she disagreed with regarding her mom dating Michael was that he was 10 years younger than her mom. Looking at the two of them no one would be the wiser, because her mom always looked far younger than she truly was. That was why, Ralph became so jealous and controlling over his mom. Ralph could never see that in himself, but as a child she saw it so clearly. Although, Nancy looked just like her dad, who was very good looking in his own right, her mom did pass that youthful gene along to her. She also looked very young well younger than she actually was.

Nancy said goodbye to Frank and said, "I will see you next time." Frank said, "I will look forward to it." Frank was a nice-looking man too. He was very rich and did not have to work but he loved working and being a part of other people lives. His family was from England and he never went home to visit much. He had a few cousins that moved to the U.S. but they stayed in too far from him for them to fellowship very often. Every now and then, he would date a woman and spoil her but he could not meet Ms. Right yet. He would often be teased by Romeo and her that is was no such thing as a Mr. or Ms. Right. Frank had met Romeo in College. They became close friends with each other because they shared a lot of the same classes. Although Frank was gifted as a therapist as well, he did not want to start his own practice of yet. He was struggling in remaining in the U.S. or going home, back to England so that he could be with his parents and siblings. Frank did not want to get a lot of clients only to leave them. He did not want to carry that burden because he knew once he started, he could help them because he had a sixth sense regarding psychological issues.

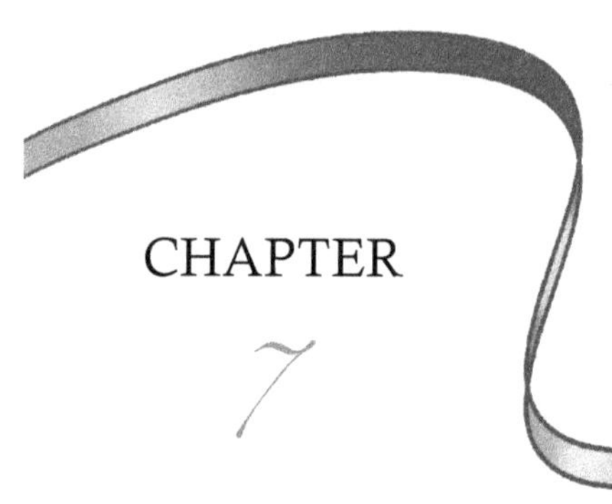

CHAPTER

7

When Romeo became overwhelm with clients, he would ask Frank to step in to do a few therapy sessions especially with dealing with clients that were suffering from PTSD from being abused. Schizophrenia and Bi Polar behavioral health conditions ran in his family. They were high functioning but when they would go a while without their medications some of their struggles would appear as light in darkness. His mother personally had B.H. needs and her father had to be more than a husband to her. He also was her personal Therapist. For the most part, he kept his mom medications titrated very well because he studied her behaviors. She was able to live a normal life and was a great loving wife and mom to him and his two older sisters.

Nancy knew that Frank had a crush on her. He would often flirt with her in a professional manner if there was such a thing. He would laugh and try to present himself so professionally but it was obvious. Nancy thought to herself, if she did not have all of these unresolved issues about Tom, she would probably have started to date Frank, but in her heart, she still loved Tim very much.

Nancy stopped by the grocery store near her home and picked up a few food items to re stock her pantry and a few snacks so she could have her sister kids over sometime so she would not feel so lonely and miss being with Tom.

Tom visited his mom. She was so happy to see him. He husband was a good man. They lived comfortably in a new residential community not too far from where he was living. After he and Nancy divorced, he moved into a small loft community that was near his job so he could continue to work late and burn the midnight candle and crash in his bed when his eyes became too heavy to continue to design corporate buildings and build unique affordable residential homes. He thought of how he never though he was wrong in he and Nancy relationship but he never knew why he could not ever think that he had any faults. He could recall the many times that Nancy would try to talk to him about what she was struggling with him about but he would never accept it. He would just tell her, "That is not me!"

Tom was restless as he drove home from work which was only two blocks from where he lived. He made him a ham and cheese sandwich and got a back of plain lays out of the cabinet with a bottle of citrus fruit Lipton tea as he sat down before his 50-inch screen TV and watched Netflix and Tubi channel until it put him to sleep. This had become his routine during the week and on the weekend, he would travel with some of his golfing buddies and they would enjoy the night life afterwards.

Tom was never a man that went out regularly. He just did not enjoy that. He only did it now, because he was still in love with his ex-wife, Nancy. He wanted her back but he could not bring himself to admit he was wrong in making most of the decisions in their marriage because he felt that he was looking out for their best interest and she should just be appreciative and not nag him about. At least, at the time, he felt she was nagging him. That is why he could never resolve anything with her. He felt like he was never wrong about anything. Tom fell asleep on the couch and got up the next morning and took a shower only to work long hours and crash at night at his apartments alone. Tom was growing tired of this life. He knew he was good marriage material but he needed help to accept some responsibility in seeing his own faults. That is one of the main reasons he was seeing a therapist. Too figure out why he could not see any faults in himself but he clearly blamed others and not himself in every issue.

One day at work Tom, had a business lunch with one of his prospective clients that wanted him to design an entire Residential single-family home in an up-and-coming small town on the east side of town. This town was very sought after because it had several lakes which were surrounded with concrete pavement for walking and bicycling. It was very naturally beautiful because they were surrounded by big green trees. He believes they were Evergreen trees because they would stay green in all of the seasons.

Tamara was her name. She was about 35 y/o slim and tall. She was highly intelligent and she went after the things that she wanted. She was not born rich but she developed wise business savvy that earned her a lot of money. She also diversified some of those earning in stocks and bonds. She became well off and wanted to give back to her community by developing affordable luxurious homes and increase her fortune in residential properties. Not so much for her wealth but to create scholarships for local talented children that could not afford to go to college but they were smart enough to make something out of themselves. She was recently divorced from her college sweetheart. They actually started dating in high school and went to the same law school.

Tamara worked in the corporate world for 10 years as a brilliant lawyer. She even made partner at the firm she was working but because so many white-collar criminals that were stealing money from their clients won their cases when they were sued and taken to court, she became burnt out and wanted to give back to the people as a result. She actually won her cases, but too many of the lawyers at her firm struggled with the idea that their white-collar clients benefited from their services and would never be prosecuted for their civil crimes.

Tamara had showed interest in dating again, as she had shared with Tom on several occasions. Tom was tempted to ask her out but did not want to mix business with pleasure. He also did not want to confuse his attraction toward Tamara with the fact he was missing his ex-wife, Nancy and the life they shared. For the most part, Tom knew he had lost a good woman due to his Pride, but he would never admit that.

Tom shared with Tamara that he had been working some late hours in completing this project. He told her that in 2-3 weeks he will finalize the drawings and be able to show her the blue prints. He did share that he does not want to show her the results as of yet, because he is still tossing around a few unique plans for recreation in the residential neighborhood that will draw a mix range of clients both young and older. He informed her it would be muti purposeful and it would be a great place to retire and start a family. Tamara loved that idea and continued to be patient. Tom had great work reviews and she knew he was well worth the wait even if they should get more involved romantically. She had a intuitive feeling that he was a great man in so many matters.

Tom and Tamara finished their meeting and said their goodbyes. Tom thought to himself how lovely Tamara was and how easy she was to be around. Tom stopped by his mother's home before he went home and had given her some flowers that he had picked up florist shop that was near his home.

She and her husband greeting him at the door and invited him in to have dinner with them. He gave his mom the flowers and she was so happy to see him. She begged him to stay but he. Had to politely decline. He said, "Mom, I am so sorry, I have a Residential drawing that I have to complete. I am at the brink of creating it to be a hub for Retirees and Families."

Tom's mom, was so happy that he was doing well at work. She felt like he was working too much. She knew how much he loved his ex-wife, Nancy. She felt in her heart that she was a great choice for her son. She was all that she wanted to be, strong, independent, beautiful, and sure of herself. Tom's mom, was beautiful but she was gaining her confidence back in being sure of herself. She was still recuperating from her first husband leaving her for a man. She did not know when she married him, he was struggling with his identity rather he was attracted to women or men in a romantic manner. He still loved her. That was obvious but he did not want to continue to live a lie. She forgave him and now her ex-husband and his partner are her best friends. They both raised Tom in two separate homes.

Tom left his mom's home and walked in his apartment. It was a cozy environment and he learned how to make a home colorful and inviting. He taught interior decorating on the side and staging for Real Estate Agents. His friends loved to come to his apartments for the big basketball and football games. They all missed Nancy because she cooked so well and made all of them eat all the food before they left because she did not want to waste any food. Tom did not eat much leftovers and she definitely, was not going to add any extra pounds. She loved her thin size. Her dad was tall and thin and she was his female version as her mom use to tell her all the time when she was growing up. Tom added some more recreation areas like pools, walking parks, and playground equipment for parents to take their children. He also drew basketball goals, stabilized metal bikes in the cemented into ground so that no one would take them away. He wanted the walking park to have a wide pavement big enough for bikers and walkers surrounded by a large body of water.

Tom also drew beautiful trees and tropical flowers that would bloom in their season so that year-round it would be so appealing. It would be like a ministering sanctuary of land. He thought about Nancy, he voiced how he discouraged her from wanting to start a family because he wanted to make sure his business got off the ground firsts so that they both can spend a lot of time with their children. He loved children but he did not want to be an absent father. Tom made himself a cup of beef soup and a grilled cheese sandwich on buttered Texas toast. That was his specialty. Nancy loved that he helped her cook meals and did housing chores. He does not know why they broke up. He still could not come to term with why he thought he was always right and others were so wrong. He could see himself always accusing her of being a nagging wife when she just wanted her to include her in the decision making regarding their family.

Tom ate his dinner and took a long relaxing bath. He lit some beautiful Jasmine candles that could be smelled all over his apartments that relaxed him. At the same time, it reminded him of his mom and Nancy. They both did the same thing on a daily basis because it relaxed them. They had that in common. Tom was very manly but he shed some tears because he felt his mom and his ex-wife Nancy was the women, he loved the most in the world. He afterward smiled as he also thought about how they both loved to sing their favorite hymn. In particularly these two verses, "Lord, I want to be a Christian in my heart. Lord, I want to love everybody in my heart."

Tom, lifted himself out of the tub and dried himself off. He put on his pajamas and he put some of his favorite music on that relaxed him. He put one of Romeo's original song CD collections inside his CD disk player and went to sleep. His music was so heart stirring but relaxing. He had the perfect tenor voice with a wide variety of pitch to make the words of the song so impactful. Tom, did not understand why Romeo was not a Pop Star yet, he definitely had the talent for it. Tom looked at his pocket calender and noted that he had an appointment to see Romeo on Wednesday at 4:00 pm until 5:00 pm.

Tom woke up and got dressed and went into the office. He had a few meetings and went to the park to his favorite area, where the white ducks would gather for the people to feed them. They had become very domestic. They even allowed some of the children to stand close to them while their parents took them pictures. Tom imagined that if he and Nancy was still together, maybe they would be some of the parents, that were taking lots of pictures of their children. He remembered his mom doing that with him quite a bit as he was growing up.

Tom met one of his friends that was woman for dinner. She was married and was known by her and Nancy. She became a great friend to both he and Nancy. She was a childhood friend of Tom. He has been knowing her for over 25 years. They were 40 now, and she had three children. She has always been more like Tom's sister than a romantic love interests because both of their moms were best friends and helped look after the others child as they went back into the work force after they both got a divorce from their husbands. Tom's friend name was Priscilla. He nicked name her Prissy. He would pick on her when they were little as if she was his sister.

Priscilla was very athlete back them. The ratio of girl to boys in their neighborhood growing up was 5 to 1 in favor of boys. She loved to play basketball and catch football with him growing up. He was amazed how she grew up to be a beautiful mature woman. She was his confidant. She knew him very well. As a matter of fact, Priscilla was the one who introduced her new friend, Nancy to him. Priscilla told Tom in her corny way, "Tom, you are a good guy, and since you are more like a brother to me, I would want you to have a good woman like me, and not the millions of girls that are lusting after you since you are growing to be such a hunk. Tom was growing very tall and he had that cold black wavy hair. He had olive skin with hazel eyes. He looked like a Greek god. He was absolutely gorgeous and she was tired of getting in fights with the girls at school because they were jealous of their relationship. Tom went to work on Tuesday morning and ate dinner at his favorite restaurant and went home and took a shower and watched Dallas Cowboys play their Rival Atlanta Falcons. He did not have a favorite. He liked both teams and was rooting for them to be one of the teams to make it to the Superbowl. He went to bed and went to work Wednesday Morning as his routine except he went an hour earlier at 8;00 am instead of at 9:00 am as usual because he had a counseling appointment with Romeo at 4:00 pm.

Tom finished his day at the office at 3:00 pm and finalized some of the key recreational methods at the affordable Luxurious Residential neighborhood he was working on for Tamara his business client.

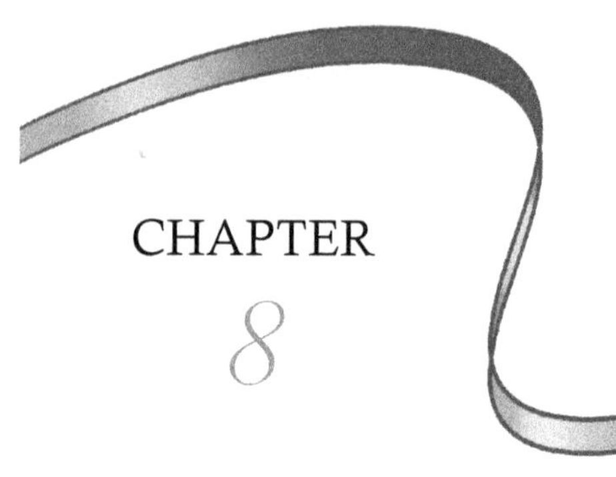

CHAPTER

8

The drive to Romeo's office was about 35 minutes with normal traffic usually, so he gave himself at least 15 minutes to make up time in case the traffic is heavier than usual. Tom made it to Romeo's office. He was greeted by Romeo who was standing while he was talking to Frank.

Romeo had asked Frank to see one of his clients that was having the development of two personalities as a result of the multiple raping by his father who had also been abused in the same manner when he was young at the age of 10 y/o. The young man was now, 21 years old and struggling with wanting to commit suicide because he could not fight off the memory of his father sexually abusing him from age 5-7 y/o. If it was not for his mother walking in on his dad committing such acts when he was 7 y/o. It would be a good chance he may have continued to be sexually abused and not living because he would have committed suicide by now. Thankfully, his mother left her dad and started the process of divorce him instantly. His mother also called the police and his father was charged for child endangerment, child abuse, rape and physical assault. His dad was sentenced to 30 years with Psychological Rehabilitation. His dad was abused the same manner by a distant older cousin. His dad torn between liking women and committing the same tragedy on someone else as he was done. An unfortunate learned trait.

The only difference between the young man and is his father, is the fact, he knew he was unequivocally attracted to women and he was determined not to abuse any children. That is why, he was in college studying to be a psychiatrist. The young man's name was Phillip Reins. Phillip was still taking had completed his medical basics and was starting his Psychiatric courses. He was about to have a mental breakdown because during class a case study was read: It was about his dad and himself but of course, the case study could not reveal the names of the individuals. Phillip though he was fine and had resolved the tragic memories because at the time his mother divorced his dad and press charges on him, she had immediately enrolled him in a series of counseling sessions. She wanted her son to survive this tragedy. She felt so bad she could not protect him even though her own therapist told her respectively that she was not the one at fault but her ex-husband was solely responsible for the grievous acts he performed on their son. His mother had enrolled herself and with Phillip In group counseling session to help herself and her son to cope with this tragedy. Phillip intentions were to get stronger so he would not have continued relapses that would cause him to want to escape such as via suicide.

Phillip was yet strong enough to not commit suicide but he did not want those thoughts to enter into his though processes. He wanted to overcome the negative attributes that came through being abused. He also wanted to learn from Romeo and Frank on ways to combat these thoughts so that he can also pass that knowledge to his clients whenever he passes his license for Psychology when he completes the program. Romeo had already had 4 sessions with Phillip.

Phillip was making great progress because Romeo incorporated biblical principles with Phillip consent in order to help him to be an over comer. Romeo knew that Phillip had not only had to have physical, emotional, and mental breakthroughs but he also needed to have breakthrough in the Spiritual realm of things as well. Romeo was aware that Phillip was utilizing him as a Mentor as he followed his Psychiatry curriculum. Romeo had asked Phillip to consent to at least 5 sessions with one of his skillful colleagues in such manners. Romeo informed Phillip, that he already knew his colleague. Romeo informed Phillip, "Frank helps me with the administration of my office duties and he also consults with a few of my clients. Frank is between setting up an office, here, in the U.S. or moving back home to England to set up his office. Phillip voiced understanding and consented to see Frank for at least 5 sessions. Franks had an impressive background in Psychiatry with clients that have been abused in a variety manner. He will bring forth a wealth of experience to assist in finding breakthrough mythologies to help deliver individuals from such trauma in a positive manner.

Romeo finished his conversation with Frank regarding Therapy sessions with Philip and asked Tom to walk with him backed to his office. Tom laid down on the plush leather couch instead of sitting in the leather chair because he was a little tired from the long nights, he had put in in developing the Residential project for Tamara. Romeo began with a recap of his last sessions and started the current session with a question, "Tom, are there any developments to why you feel that you are always right and you can't ever accept that you are wrong in any issue as I had asked you to think on from the last session until the time we meet again." Tom voiced, "Well, I don't know why or how it began, but I did think a lot about what Nancy would discuss with me her feelings about me making all of the decisions about our marriage without ever consulting her. Back then, I told her to stop nagging me because it is not like I am doing anything wrong. I have doing it for the benefit of our marriage." Romeo asked, "Please give me an example."

Tom said, "Well when she would bring up having children and starting a family. I told her no, not yet. I am just getting in the grove of building a successful client base. Give me more time." Back then, I was not thinking about a women biological clock of having children before 35 y/o to lessen her chance of have a child with down's syndrome chromosome. I later learned that by talking to a few of my colleagues and female friend that was my confident after Nancy and I were divorced. I was too ashamed and prideful to bring the subject up before we divorced and when Nancy, receptively, brought the subject up of having children."

Romeo asked Tom, "What do you feel was the reason why you were so nonzealot toward Nancy pleas that you all start a family?' Tom said, "I thought I was helping bring more stable money unto our household and building our bank accounts to become financially stable and successful and ignoring her pleas to have children before it was too late for her. I believe she had even mentioned the urgency of her biological clock running out passed the age of 35 y/o. His mother had hi in her 30's so I felt like we had time. Looking back, I was just being selfish. It was not that I did not want to have children but it was more of me getting to a point that we can afford to have children." I can remember vividly, how I had to start working at about 10 y/o to help his mom financially, when my father left my mom to marry his male lover. He had hidden from my mom that he was bisexual. I guess, I was traumatized regarding he and his mother's experience, and was now, developing PTSD symptoms regarding it."

Romeo, agreed with Tom and said, "Yes, you may be going through some latent s/s of PTSD from what you and your mom experience in regard to your dad leaving your family and left your mom in a state of depression that became very debilitating. So much so, you and her had to move in with her parents so that they could help raise you and provide emotional support to your mom so that she could get through this ordeal."

Romeo asked Tom," Did your mom seek any counseling? She went through some extensive counseling from my grandparent's pastor at their church. She had grown up under his leadership but had stopped going church as often when she married my dad who never went to church. My grandparents took me to church when I would spend the weekends with them on occasions. My grandmother taught Sunday school and My grandfather was on the financial committee. They both practiced biblical principles in their daily lives. I respected my grandparents a great deal. It helped their marriage to stay solid as they too went through life's challenges. Nancy and I use to go to church regularly together for most of our marriage but as my clientele grew, I had started to accept Sunday appointments and Wednesdays, I worked late night." Romeo asked Tom, "Why did you feel the need to stop going to church with your wife? Did you stop believing the reason why you grandparents stayed together was because they applied biblical principles regarding marriage into their relationship?"

Tom said, "No, I did not stop believing the reason my grandparent's marriage stayed strong was because they studied the word of God together, went through spiritual marriage counseling when times became really complicated in their marriage. Wow, I can remember my grandparents dropping me off to the children church on Wednesday as they went through Marriage Core class on Wednesday night to strengthen their relationship when I was 12 y/o. Wow, I never thought about these things when Nancy and I was going through our marriage struggles. I remember my grandmother asking my granddad can she talk to him in the other room. He did not want to discuss things in front of him that would have possibly led to a fight between she and my granddad. Lord Have Mercy, I was so wrong treating Nancy like that. I was selfish and prideful. I see that clearly now."

Romeo said, "Tom, it looks like you are developing some breakthroughs. Let us stop here and I want you to continue to think on things that possible could have helped you and Nancy have a totally different outcome than divorcement. Please stop by Frank's desk and set an appointment within 2 weeks. I will be out of the office next week. I have some projects I have to take care of. Will Wednesdays continue to be a good time for us to meet.? Tom said, "Yes. Wednesdays are good for me." Tom walked Tom to Franks desk and went into his break room to get a package of apple juice out of the refrigerator. He also fixed him some lunch and set down to take a break.

Romeo finished his break and talked with Frank a bit about his upcoming schedule for Friday. He made sure that Frank had it on his schedule that he was going to be out next week and to make sure Frank had it on his schedule for his first of five appointments with Phillip. Frank informed Romeo that he did have Romeo already blocked off for next week to not have any appointments and that he had already added Phillip to his client schedule for next Thursday. Frank informed Romeo that he was scheduled for an appointment with Rosette on this upcoming Friday at 3:00 pm.

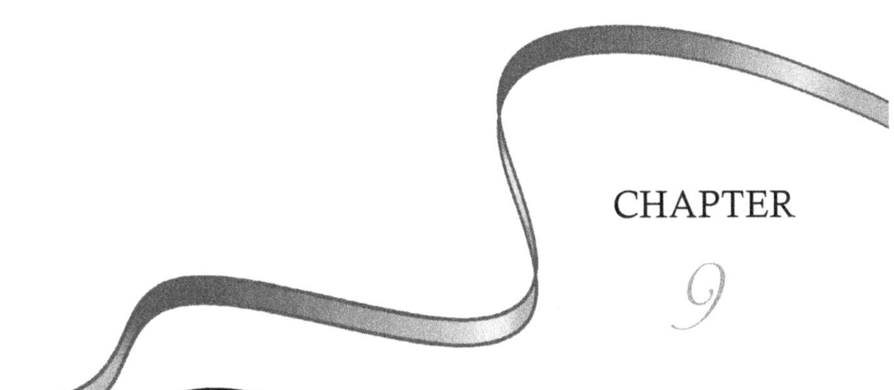

CHAPTER

9

Thursday came and went and Friday came storming in. It rained all day. Rosette finished coaching drills at her basketball team practice with the Houston Comets. They had comprehensive drills and perfected their offensive and defensive plays. They were looking very good to give a strategic playoff run this year. Rosette safely travelled to her appointment with Romeo. She was looking forward to her counseling sessions. She felt like it was something familiar with him that was comforting to her. She could not pan it out but she felt like he was going to help her to have amazing breakthrough so that she could love again. She so desperately wanted to do so.

Rosette parked her car close to the office entrance and ran into the office. It was raining heavily. Romeo was taking a short break in the break room and heard Frank laughing with a person that had a female voice. He had determined it sounded like Rosette. Rosette was a happy go lucky type of person. She was definitely a people person from what he noticed in the few interactions he had with her. Rosette and Frank were teasing each other. They had developed a corrode type relationship that seemed to be developing into a friendship. Frank was teasing her because she had become soak and wet in the rain and her wavy sandy hair was all over her face. He had asked her, "Rosette, I am glad you can see through the all of that hair because I couldn't." They both burst out laughing out loud. Rosette said, "If I couldn't you would be the first to laugh because I would be stumbling all over everything." Frank said, "No, I want laugh. I will be running to catch you." Rosette said, "Yea right, Frank. You are just trying to make things better while you are sitting in dry areas while I have to run through heavy rain." They both laughed out loud again.

Romeo walking into the front office, greeted Rosette with a smile and said, "How are you, Rosette? Rosette said, "I am doing well besides being wet. "Romeo looking at her grabbing some dry sweats asked her if she wanted if she needed to change her clothing. Please feel free. The lady's lounge is very spacious and comfortable. I will wait in my office." Rosette said, "Thank you for letting me change. I did not want to be distracted from our counseling session by being wet and uncomfortable. "Romeo said, "No problem. I will see you in a little bit." Rosette said, "I will see you soon."

Rosette changed into sweat pants and shirt. She also put on dry socks and tennis shoes. No matter what she put on rather it was dressed down or dressed up she was always beautiful and drew attention to herself no matter where she went. That is why Frank was so drawn to her but he kept it on a professional fun level in which she enjoyed. Rosette hurriedly, rushed into Romeo's office to start her counseling session. Romeo said, "How do you feel, now? Are you comfortable?" Rosette said, "Yes, I am good, now. It is a good thing I watched the news last night and seen the forecast that it was going to rain all day today. I packed me an extra set of clothes just in case. Romeo said, "Good. Let's get into some deep conversations."

Rosette, we discussed a few preliminary things at our last sessions. It is customary for me to do that during my first one or two sessions. I will get a little deeper in trying to ask pointed questions so that you can elaborate on what do you believe is preventing you from moving forward with someone ad having a family. I know you shared last session you do want have a deep desire to do so. You said now, is the right time to do so but you can't let yourself get close to anyone to start that process."

Rosette said, "Yes, I do feel like it is the best time to fall in love and possibly get married and have a family. My heart is there already but my mind is not letting me move forward." Romeo asks Rosette, "Why do thing that is occurring in that order? Why isn't it the reverse? Meaning, why isn't your mind saying I can do this? I am ready and your heart being the one that is holding you back? "Rosette honestly said, "I don't have any idea. I don't know what all of this mean."

Romeo said, "It is reassuring to know that your heart would like to move forward because the heart is the window to your soul. The mind is a battle ground that is at constant war with decisions but because I can already see your strength, this is a war you are going to win. You will have positive outcomes." Rosette was re assured when Romeo said these things. Romeo asked Rosette, Tell me about your love life. Have you ever been in love? Rosette said, "Yes. I was really young. I was in high school and was not intending to fall in love but it just happened. The young man that I fell in love with and I started out as friends. That friendship started to develop quite quickly."

"I have always been athletic and loved to play basketball and football with my brothers and their friends. It is funny because my brothers did not want me to be around their friends because all of them would always tell them how beautiful I was. My brothers did not trust anyone. They kind of knew that one of their younger friends that was only one year older than me, were getting along quite well. They brushed it off by saying, Rosette is just a happy and friendly person. She can get along with anyone. Little did my brothers know, I had already start dating about three of their friends off and on. Well not seriously dating. They would have me to meet up at study sessions with them to help them with either Math of History. Those were my favorite subjects. My brother's friends did that to disguise us being together to learn more about each other to doing so because they were about to be kicked off the basketball or football team because they were failing a class. Unfortunately, the younger guy that I secretly met up with could not use that disguise because he was brilliant. He was already two grades ahead. My brothers again just brushed it off because we were close in age and quite naturally, we were going to bond more than their other friends when were three years older than I was."

Romeo said, "Good, we have a starting point. We were end now. I just wanted to get the flood gates open so that over the next two weeks you can think about how you want to inform what happened with that love affair that has caused you not to let yourself moved forward with someone else.' Rosette paused, She could not help but to hold her head down. She was about to shed tears but she gained her composure. Romeo noticed her reaction and wanted to give her a re assuring hug because he knew it had to be very tragic for her to have such a reaction. He felt that she had suppressed those feelings for such a long time to at least move forward with her life even if she could not move forward in love.

Romeo walked Rosette to the front lobby to have Frank to write down her next appointment two weeks from this Friday, again at 3:00 pm. This was her best time. Frank seen her countenance and knew that the session must have been quite complicating and deep. He looked at her and said something corny to make her laugh. She liked that about Frank. Frank said, "Rosette it is good thing it stopped raining because I don't know what I will do if I had to see you looking like a little wet lamb. So sweet are you my dear." Rosette and Frank burst out laughing yet again. Rosette said, "Frank, I have just the woman for you. You both will get along so well. I believe you met her before. I will introduce her to you." Frank said, sheepishly, "Why can't it be you? It would be fitting, don't you think?" Then he said, "I am just planning. I have to keep thing professional."

Rosette shook her head and said, "Frank you are so Special as she teased him. Special like a yellow short bus." They laughed again. Romeo heard them laughing together and felt good that Frank had found him a friend. Obviously, Rosette was letting her guard down with Frank. Maybe that was a good opening to find love again even if it might not be with his dear friend, Frank. He was not worried about Frank because he knew that Frank knew how to guard his heart. Rosette thought within her mind, that Mary would be perfect for Frank. She deserves a good man. All of the patients had earned that Frank was a brilliant Psychiatrist that was very wealthy. They knew the only reason he did not have his own set of clientele or office was because he was still between not knowing rather, he would remain in the U.S. or go back home to England to be around his family. His parents were now in their mid 70's but still very healthy.

Romeo and Frank gathered their things and they both walked out to the office together. Frank asked Romeo did he want to grab a little dinner before he headed home? Romeo said, "Yes. It has been a long time since we talked outside of work. What type of food do you have in mind? Frank said, "What about seafood? Romeo said, "That sounds like a plan.' They headed to a seafood restaurant not too far from the office. It was still raining as they drove separately to the restaurant. Frank had called ahead to see what the wait time was like. It was Friday night and it is usually very busy on the weekends. The host at Poppin Hot Seafood told him they had a 30-minute wait time due to the rain. It is usually 45 minutes to 1 hour. Frank informed Romeo of the wait time should be about 10 minutes when they get there because it was about 20-minute drive from the office.

Romeo and Frank made it to the restaurant and walk in together. Frank gave their names to the host and she assured them they only had about 10-minute wait time and if they would like to they could order them some drinks from the bar while they waited. Romeo and Frank walked over to the bar. Frank only drank on rare occasions and Romeo did not drink at all. They both ordered a Sierra in light ice with a cherry so that they can appear to be cool. 10-minutes passed and the host led them to their table. Romeo and Frank did not talk about their clients or politics because they wanted to keep things light, fun, and relaxing.

So, Frank came out with it. "Man, what is going on with you and that beautiful woman Jasmine that I saw you talking with at your last gig? She seems like a keeper. At least you guys look great together." Romeo said, "Frank, actually we are trying to get to know each other better. She is a sweet woman. She is a little older than me but she looks very comparable to my age. She is a doctor and is very busy like us but she makes time to see me. She and I have similar past regarding who raised us and we have an easy-going relationship. She is easy to talk to." Frank said, "Man, that sounds great. It is about time you started to settle down. If you are not seeing your clients, you are singing at your events. It is a wonder if you find time to eat, sleep, visit your family, or just have some fun time for yourself."

Romeo said, "I know. I know. It has been a long time since I enjoyed a woman's company other than a few dates here and there. Yes. I really like Jasmine and would love to develop a romantic lasting relationship. I can already tell that she would be a great person to do so with. She seems very honest and committed in all of her endeavors." Frank said, with a fist bump with Romeo, "I hear you. Man, I hear you. I am happy for you. Do you believe she feels the same way?" Romeo said, "Honestly, Man. I believe she does. She at least is sending me positive vocal and body language feedback.' Romeo asked Frank, how about you? Have you met any women or women that you have connected with. He said as a matter of fact, I would like to get to know Rosette a little more. I know she is older woman but, Da___, she looks amazing and we just click. Before you say anything, I know about what our pack is, No dating our clientele. However, for her, I would move mountains to get to know her better."

Romeo said, "Yes. I hear you guys talking and laughing a lot. I have joy seeing you both found a friend in each other. I know it can't be easy on either side, especially with you not knowing if you will stay here in the U.S. or go back home to England to set up your office." Frank said, "Yes, I am still not sure what I will do at this time but I will figure it out. I know that I will keep the line of communication open and honest with the woman that I choose to get to know better so it will not be any surprises." Frank said, I hear that. That is the way to approach the matter. Honest and informative." They both ordered and enjoyed catching up with each other. It had been a long time since they shared details about their lives with each other. It was nice. After an hour they finished eating, laughing, and talking and vowed to each other to do this once every one to two months. They both walked to their cars and drove home.

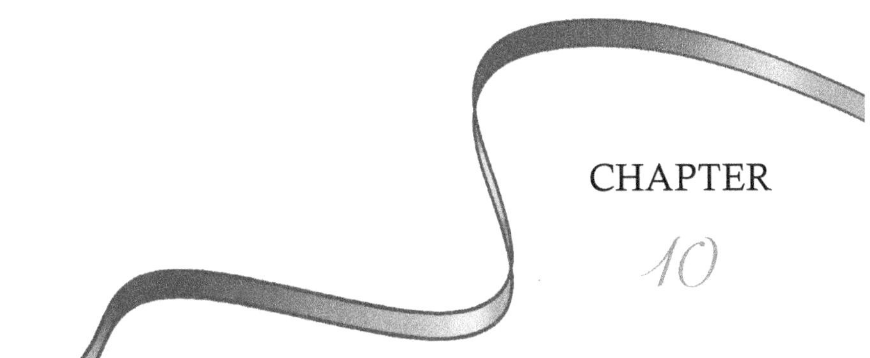

CHAPTER

10

On the way home, Romeo called Jasmine to see if she was still prepared to come over to his home for dinner Saturday evening. Jasmine answered the call, 'Hello. How are you, Romeo. It is nice to hear your voice." Romeo said, "Hello Jasmine. I am well. How are you?' Nancy said, I am doing well Romeo, What do you have going?" Romeo said, "I was calling to see if you are still planning to come over to my house for dinner on Saturday around 6:00 pm?" Jasmine said, "I would not miss it. Will you please text me your address?" Rome said, "Sure. I will text it to you when I make it home. Frank, the guy, I introduced you to at my last singing event, and I went out to get a bite to eat after work tonight. We just left the restaurant. By the way, he was impressed with you and thought you and I would make a great fit for each other. He said we looked great together." Jasmine was reassured. She could not tell much, how Frank's first impression of her was." Nancy said, 'That is wonderful. I really did not know he had such a great first impression of me. That is re assuring." Romeo said, Yes. He had very positive comments about you and I." The rain was still coming down heavily. They got of the phone with each other so that they both could make it home safely.

Romeo text Jasmine his address when he got home and became settled. She text him a quick response stating, "Wow, who knew we were only few blocks from each other. That's good. I am surprised we never ran into each other." Romeo asked if she would text her address as well. She said yes, and did so. Romeo text her back and said, "Yes, we do live near to each other. That is something. Here, I thought I was on one end of town and you on the other. Well, we have no excuse to see each other now do we?" Jasmine text back and said, "So true. So true. Well, have a good evening. Get some rest. I know I need some." Romeo text her back and said, "You do the same."

The next morning Jasmine got out of bed and took a brisk walk. She loved doing this. It helped her clear her mind and relax. Jasmine called her mom. "Hello mom. How are you doing this morning?" Lorina said, "Hello sweetheart. You are up early." Jasmine said, "Yes mom. I am up early. It is a beautiful day. I wanted to go on a walk to clear my head. I work so hard and I usually don't have any down time. How did you and dad cope with your busy schedules in helping people at your practice?" Lorina said, "Well, we had to figure that out. It was a little hard at first. We saw a lot of patients in the beginning then we built it up to the number of clients we wanted to have a full-time practice and then we started opening it up for other doctors to join. Now, we are up to six doctors of all physical specialists except for a Psychiatrists and Psychologist. We of course had to get a larger office space but it is a great thing.

Now, your father and I are able to spend time with the families we chose since we did not get together ourselves."

Jasmine wanted to ask her mom, "But, why didn't you and dad get together? You loved each other so much. Why didn't you choose him?" Jasmine knew the reason why. She knew that she could not bear losing her parents and the man she loved so entirely. She had to make a hard choice to keep them both in her life. She made the choice to succumb to her parents' wishes not to marriage a man outside of her race no matter how much she loved him and the baby she was giving birth to. She felt like to have them both she would stay great friends with Ramon especially since he would be raising their child. He was set against the child they had as a result of their amazing love for each other. Lorina asked Ramon to work with her to build a practice together with all types of Specialists to treat all conditions both mind, body, and soul.

Lorina told Ramon she could not bear to lose him. She wanted him desperately but she could not make the choice her parents wanted to the fullest. Ramon could not bear losing Lorina either, so after a long while of thinking about it, he decided to do so. Ramon did not know how he could stop loving Lorina especially since they were going to be spending a great deal of time together but he made the choice to do so, since he wanted to keep Lorina in his life. Jasmine knew this because they told her this when she was 8 y/o when they believed she could process such a decision. They told her that they both wanted to raise her together but the above was the reason why they could not. They did say although we are not together, we can still have a great part in you knowing the both of us as your parents and we would still do things together and individually with you. Later as Jasmine grew up and started college, they both told her how hard it was to stop wanting to be together and to ease the pain of not being together they both agreed to start seeing other people. That is how we ended up marrying the spouse we have now.

Jasmine said, "Mom, I met someone. I believe he is the one but I do not know how to stop working so hard in order to see if my assumptions are correct. How do I break away?" Lorina told her daughter," Well, baby, you just have to break away. You have to appoint another physician to see your patients and invite this man to a long trip to get to know him if he is available." Jasmine said, "How do I do that? I do not want to come across as being forward." Lorina started laughing, "Daughter, you are full grown and the times are that women are in control of their lives. You can ask anyone anything you want."

Jasmine new her mom was wise and telling her the truth. After all she knew her daughter well enough to know that before her daughter said anything she thought and analyze it multiple times to see if it was worth her time or effort. Jasmine thanked her mom and ended the call with her. She jogged the rest of the way home. She was over zealous of being with Romeo tonight. She started tingling all over and her heart start palpitating very quickly as she thought about the rush of being in an intimate setting with the man she was falling in love with. She looked into her closet and found a beautiful turquoise dress with yellow flowers embroiled in black. It was beginning to be Spring season in mid-April. She laid it out on her bed and pulled out a pair of comfortable black pumps with a turquoise flower on the front of it. It was very sexy if she did say so herself. She knew when she saw it at one of the boutique shops, she visited near her office, last weekend, would be perfect to wear on one of the dates she had Romeo. Jasmine felt tonight was the perfect night to wear it. She knew in her heart that she wanted to go the next level with Romeo.

Before Jasmine took her bath, she left her home to go see her dad and his dad's wife Selena. They both met her at the door and gave her a big hug. They invited her to eat breakfast with them on the patio by the pool. They had a beautiful patio in their back yard. The patio furniture was black with red trimming. It had tropical plants on each four corners in beautiful dark reddish stone platers. The Gazebo had a long couch, love seat, and two comfortable large end chairs with a dark brownish stone fireplace grill. Selena was was Caribbean women. She was absolutely beautiful. She was 5 feet tall and medium built. She was curvy and spoke with an accent. She was strong minded woman due to her high intellect because she thought things out extensively before she spoke.

Selena was good for her dad. She was so sweet to him. She loved hard but at the same time she gave him the freedom to do what he does best, heal. Her father was a brilliant Endocrinologist. He has had many successes and awards in diabetic breakthroughs in helping people eat a more balanced diet and exercise. He worked with an esteemed Nutritionist that helped him to find a more holistic way of treating Diabetic without Pharmaceutical medications like oral diabetic medications and insulin. It was a challenging scientific study but after 5-year trials. They finally felt comfortable in going to the FDA (Food and Drug Administration). After long deliberation, their nutritional plan mixed with exercise treatment plan was finally approved. Shalena was a Optometrist. They met at a medical conference. They were surprised they lived in the same town and become friends that then led to romance.

It took a longtime before her dad let go and allowed himself to fall in love with another woman. His love for Lorina ran deep. Selena was aware of his long history with Lorina because he shared it with her. After all, they were friends first. He had to have someone to confide in, because he struggled working with a woman, he was still in love with, but knew that she would never choose to marry him because she knew if she did, she would also lose her parents. In his heart he understood her dilemma but it still hurt nonetheless. Selena was patient and kind. She was there for my father and that led to the development of a beautiful romance,

Shalena said to Jasmine, It is so good to see you. Come in. We are in the back yard. it is a beautiful morning. I guess after all of the rain, God saw fit for us to see a little Rainbow in the sky. We are having bacon, eggs, buttered grits, cinnamon French toast with butter syrup, pineapple, seedless green grapes, and strawberry fruit platter." Jasmine said, "Wow. Do you all eat like this all the time? Selena said, "No, but today is our 5th Marriage Anniversary so we decided to go all out. We will be going to Hawaii on Monday. We will be staying 2 weeks.

There is a Medical Conference we are to attend the first week in June. I am gathering, you did not see the email that was sent out inviting other Medical Professional to attend? Jasmine said, "No, I am so sorry. I have been working long hours and had not had a chance to review all of my emails. I knew that I still had a few of the earlier week's email that I have not reviewed yet, and had planned to do so Monday." Selena said, "Well, you actually have up to tomorrow which is this Sunday by 8:00 pm to register. The Medical Committee that is sponsoring the Medical Conference in Honolulu Hawaii knew that Physicians and other Medical Professionals tend to work very long hours and sometimes do not have time to look at their emails and let alone plan an event. "Jasmine said, "I will certainly look into it. I can ask my assistant to have one of the other Physicians in our group to see my patients. I will give that person a briefing of my patients before I go over the phone if I decide to go. Do they have airline tickets that I can purchase even up to the last minute that want be so expensive that it put a large dent in my savings account." Jasmine said, "Yes, they do. They made sure they made it easy for those that could not plan their event at an earlier date." Jasmine said, "Perfect. What better time to take a little break and learn at the same time. Hawaii. Yes, this would be a treat."

Jasmine's father, Ramon said, "What brings you by my dear?" Jasmine teased him, "You mean you are not happy to see your only daughter?" Ramon said, "Now Jasmine you know I am always happy to see you. We work in the same building but I hardly ever run into you. I have to purposefully step into your office to tell you to pull away and take a break. You are as driven as your mom and I." Jasmine said, "Yes, the blood runs deep. The reason why, I came is because I wanted to ask for you all advice. I have been seeing a man for about six months now. It has really been six months 3 weeks and 24 hours but who's counting?"

Ramon and Shalena laughed and said, "Yes, who is counting? As they stared at her. They all moved to the table with their plate of food and sat down in the Gazebo as Jasmine went on, "Well, to be honest, I have already talked to mom about the man that I have been seeing. I believe he is the one but I don't know how to move to the next level with him. You all know how I have never really had a serious relationship. I have only casually dated from time to time due to my work schedule." Ramon and Shalena said, "Yes, we know and we have always encouraged you to stop working so hard and think about having a family. We want grandchildren." Jasmine laughed, "Yes. You both along with mom and her husband has shared this with me multiple times." I am sorry. I do work too hard. Anyway, the real reason, I bought this up is because the guy that I am seeing is at least 9 or 10 years younger than I am" Ramon and Shalena looked at each other and then faced Jasmine and said, "And? Is that a problem?" Jasmine caught their sarcasm and said, "I guess not. Thank you for pointed that out so humbly.

They all laughed and finished their breakfast. Ramon and Selena walked Jasmine to the front door and hugged her goodbye. Ramon kissed her on the forehead and whispered in her ear, "Baby, we trust your judgement. If you believe in your heart that this young man is for you, then we trust that it is true. We know that you think on things a long time before you act on them. Especially, with matters of the heart. If things do move forward bring him over to meet us. I will notify your mom and her husband and we will all get to meet him together." Jasmine said, "That sounds like a plan. I will definitely let you know. In the meantime. Let me rush home. I have decided to register for the conference. My assistant had bugged me to look at a certain email. She told me to call her this weekend if I decided to go but she did not tell me what it was. I asked her when I hired her to not be afraid to look at her emails to notify me of important events because I knew I worked to hard to review them.

Jasmine made it home and quickly went to her computer. She had access to her office emails on her home computer. She found the Medical Conference and called her Assistant Rochelle to please book her trip and flight. Her assistant informed her she had taken the liberty to notify one of the other Physician in her group to see her patients over the next few weeks. Dr. Riley Walker had already agreed to do so and informed Michelle to please call him over the weekend. He was on call anyway and would be near to his phone. Rochelle did call Dr. Walker and of course he agreed because Jasmine had filled in for him on numerous occasions when emergencies had arrived with one of his children or his wife felt neglected and he needed to spend some one-on-one time with her on a romantic weekend starting on Friday Morning ending on Monday afternoon. Dr. Walker was determined to keep his marriage so he worked hard to have a work life balance. Jasmine finally ran a hot bath and relaxed a little by listening to her favorite singer," Brian McKnight' classic hits. A mixture of the old and new. She had a busy morning and almost fell asleep in the tub which was deeply troubling. She thought to herself. "My body is giving me tell, tell signs that I need to rest more and stop working so hard."

She got out of the tub and took a short nap and woke up a few hours before she was to meet Romeo at his house for dinner. She was a little anxious and excited. This is the first time they would be alone in an intimate setting. Meanwhile, Romeo was planning his dinner menu. He was a great cook. He had taken a few cooking classes and mastered Italian and Korean cuisine. He often cooked several dishes exploring both cultures. He loved them both. He also learned to cook southern food from his grandparents. Both of them cooked very well. They were taught by their parents and family. His grandfather grilled everything and was good at it. His grandmother taught him how to cook biscuits, pies, and cakes from scratch. He loved cooking just about as much as singing and counseling. It was a means in which he relaxed and had down time.

Romeo walked to his refrigerator and pulled out a couple of T-Bone steaks, a head of lettuce, two tomatoes, one cucumber, one small purple onion, croutons, and shredded cheddar cheese. He also pulled out Olive Garden Italian salad dressing he got at Sam's Club and ranch dressing out of his refrigerator. He walked over to his cupboard and pulled out two large potatoes to back them. He sliced and diced the lettuce, tomatoes, cucumbers, and small onions to make a salad and place it n the refrigerator after putting it in a covered salad container. Romeo placed the croutons, cheddar cheese in a separate closed container. He placed the steaks in his special marinade that his grandfather taught him to make the meat very flavorable and tender. He covered them and placed them in the refrigerator to marinade for about 4 hours before he cooked them indoors on the grill of his range.

Romeo washed the two potatoes while they were still in their skins so that he could put them in the oven about 4:30 pm giving them plenty of time to bake before Jasmine arrived at 6:00 pm. He also put white and red sparkling grape juice in the refrigerator for them to drink in his favorite wine glasses that his grandmother had passed down to him. It was their tradition to pass them down to the eldest child from generation to generation. Romeo's father did not have any other children. He really never seriously dated after he and Romeo's mom broke up. Romeo could not believe all of these years they never revealed his mother's identity. They at the time thought it was best because his mom felt in a depression when she was forced to give him up for adoption because she wanted to raise her child with his father together. They thought by knowing the child and the child knowing her would be too hard so her parents talked it over with his father and his father's parents to do just that. Romeo was told all of these things as he grew older and his reasoning skill and understanding had evolved enough for him to understand such serious matters.

Romeo got 3 ¼ cups white sugar, ¾ pound unsalted butter, at room temperature, 6 extra-large eggs, at room temperature, 2 teaspoons pure vanilla extract, 3 cups all-purpose flour, ½ teaspoon baking powder, ½ teaspoon salt, ¼ teaspoon ground nutmeg, and 1 cup 1% milk to make homemade pound cake out of the cupboard and mixed them in a bowl. He poured the batter in a Bundt cake pan and baked it for about an hour and so that they could eat it with ice cream and strawberries for dessert.

Romeo cut a loaf of fresh Italian bread into six pieces that he had baked last night because he was so anxious of he and Jasmine finally being able to spend some alone intimate time together that could not sleep. After Romeo felt all was well with his prep work for their dinner he was making for their big night, he went into the bathroom and took a nice hot shower. He dried himself with his large fluffy beach towel and sprayed a small amount of Gucci for men cologne on. He took out his closet a turquoise dressy button-down shirt, a turquoise and black beautifully designed neck tie, black dress paints, and his black Stacy Adam shoes and laid them neatly on the table he had in his walk-in closet. He made his master bedroom walk in closed out of a small dress lounge.

Romeo loved to dress well. He was taught that by his grandparents. In the meantime, Romeo put on his dressy lounge jacket with silk black pajamas with no shirt with black leather house shoes to lounge in while he prepared dinner. He wanted his clothes not to smell like the dinner he was preparing for them. He watched Houston Rockets play Cleveland Cavaliers. He was a Lebron James fan. He appreciated his approach not only to basketball but also his devotion to his family. He too wanted a wife and children one day. He felt like he was finally ready for the whole package, now that he had built his Counseling Practice. He also was at the point that his singing events were becoming more stable that it did not take up all of his time. He did a lot of single events at adult lounges and opened up for big concert acts that came into to town. His name was becoming very popular and he was approached by several labels. Romeo had a different plan for his music. He wanted his own creativity and not have to follow any other person views or plan with his music he produced. Romeo fell asleep on his sofa while watching the game.

Jasmine had awakened from her nap and made her a hot lavender bubble bath and lit a few candles. She was a little anxious about the first time she and Romeo are going to be an intimate setting. She wanted to move to the next level in their relationship to become closer but she did not want to move to fast. She wanted them to really learn more about each other before they engage into a more physical relationship. However, she made a decision to let the night flow as it is meant to be and not put too many pre conceived notions or limitation on it. It was now about 3:00 pm. Since she knew that Romeo's house was only a few blocks away from where she lived, she could wait a little before she got dressed.

She put on the beautiful the turquoise dress with white flowers embroiled in black with her black pumps with the turquoise rose on the top of the shoes. She uses the flat iron to straighten her hair after she shampooed and conditioned it so that it will be long and sleek. She wanted to be very attractive and desirable to Romeo. She was not trying to tease him but she did want him to desire her.

Romeo woke up when the crowd went into a loud frenzy cheer when LeBron James drove to the basket and slam dunked on one of the Houston Rockets forwards. LeBron had also drawn a fowl as he went to dunk the basketball. He made the free throw. Romeo took the marinated steaks out and laid them on the grill. He also wrapped the potatoes in foil and put them in the preheated 350-degree oven. He placed a beautiful white table cloth on his dining room table and placed the bowl of salad, the salad fixings, the both bottles of sparkling red grape and white grape juice in a linear silver bucket filled with ice and set the table with his fine cook wear, and place the pound cake in the oven to cook 1hr and 45 minutes. Romeo turned the steaks over and brushed melted garlic butter he had prepared unto the pieces of Italian bread slices he had previously cooked on the griddle part of his range. Romeo placed the steaks on a beautiful oven wear white platter and covered it and placed it in the oven to keep warm. He placed the grill bread unto a small white basket container and covered it and placed it on the table. Romeo smelled the aroma of the food and his stomach started to growl because the food smelled so good. After Romeo had everything in the oven or prepared. He went to wash up and get dressed.

He looked into the mirror in his bedroom and rubbed his chin, and said to himself, "I look good if I do say so myself." After a while, he looked up and saw that the food in the oven had cooked between 1 ½- 2 hours, so he took out the potatoes, place the care on the rack to cool before he transferred it from the Bundt cake pan unto a beautiful glass cake saver. He looked at his watch and it showed 5: 45 pm. Romeo finished placing the food items on the table and awaited Jasmine to make her appearance. He had pre envisioned that she was going to look absolutely beautiful. At 6:00 pm sharp. Romeo heard a light tap at his front door. Romeo perceived It was Jasmine. Romeo answered the door and invited he into his home. Romeo took Jasmine's purse and light sweater and placed it unto a nearby wall in the hall way that was near to the dining room.

Romeo said to Jasmine, "Hello my dear. How are you this evening?" Jasmine said, "I am well Romeo. I am happy to see you. My day just got better." Romeo said," OK now, you don't have to work hard to get me to blush." Romeo started smiling. He reached out to hug Jasmine and kissed her on the forehead. Jasmine hugged him back while trying to hold back her excitement. Romeo asked Jasmine, "Are you hungry or would you like to sit in the living room to talk before we eat?" Jasmine said, "No, I am ready to eat. I ate a little at my dad's house this morning. They were celebrating their anniversary and they cooked a beautiful Caribbean breakfast. My dad's wife is Caribbean. It was so good but I could eat much of it because I knew I was coming here tonight."

Romeo said, "Well, I cooked a special dinner tonight for us. I hope you like the traditional steak, potatoes, and salad" I did not want to cook my Italian or Korean specialty dishes yet. They are so..... good. I wanted to see if you deserve my expertise in those dishes first." Romeo laughed out loud. He was only teasing Jasmine. Jasmine said, "Ok, I shall see. I hope I can live afterwards to tell you if I like it or not." Romeo said, "Ok, you got jokes. I see you." They both laughed out loud as they moved to the dining table. Romeo said, "I have already placed the salad, salad fixings, garlic toast, and sparking red or white grape juice on the table. I do have some champagne if you wanted something a little stronger. I will bring the steak and bake potatoes over as well. Do you need any sour cream. I have a little container on the table filled with butter and another with shredded cheddar cheese. Already." Jasmine said, "Yes, I would like some sour cream as well." She sat at the table. He joined her as he put the two T-bone steaks and baked potatoes on the table. He sat across from her so there would not be too much room between them.

Romeo did not take his first bite until he watched her take her first bite. She sensed that was what was going on. Jasmine cut a small amount of the steak and pit it into her mouth. She said, "Wow, this is so good and tender. What is your secret?" Romeo said, "I am glad you like it." She said, "I love it. It is really good." She ate a little of the bake potato with butter, sour cream, and cheddar cheese on to it. It was great. Romeo did not have to asked her how it tasted. Her face told it all. She thought it was also good. Romeo also began to eat. She was right it is good. They ate, talked, laughed, and enjoyed being with each other. After they had eaten, Romeo put a CD of his greatest POP and R&B hits. He clicked #8 and played the song, "You" by Jessie Powell, https://www.youtube.com. Jasmine heard the lyrics of the song, and easily moved into another place of ease because that was her favorite song. He laid out his hand in front of hers and asked her to dance with him. Jasmine placed her hand in his and he led her to the living room floor. They began to slow dance. Mary thought to herself, "Wow, he moves so seductively." She was beginning to get weak with desire for him. Romeo pulled her closer, they moved in one movement as if they were in perfect sync. Romeo was also getting aroused with her being so near to him. He eased from being so close to her so that she could not feel him physically that he was definitely feeling her with great passion. Jasmine leaned more into him and he moved closer to her as well. He leaned to kiss her. It was a deep passionate kiss. It lasted for three minutes. He loved being with her and his body showed her so.

Jasmine also loved being close to him she was melting. He pulled her closer to him and she followed him over to the couch. He led her to the couch, he pulled her down to him as he laid on it. She was on top of him initially, and then he shifted her so that he could be on top of her. He moved his hands under her dress, then over her breast. She began to moan with pleasure. They began to passionately kiss again. They both were becoming very loss in the moment. Then suddenly, Romeo said, "Jasmine as much as I want to make love to you right now, I don't want to create a path for us that will not be right. With you, I want to wait until we are sure that the path we are going to take is forever. Will you wait with me until, we are sure." Jasmine could not believe it. Most men would have taken advantage of the moment and made love to her. She was definitely willing

Romeo stood up and pulled her up to him and kissed her again. He said, "Jasmine, please understand. My desire for you is great and just not physically. I long to be with you because you stimulate my body, mind, and soul." Jasmine, was more turned on with what he just said then not being satisfied with the hot pleasure she was feeling with the moment they were experiencing. Jasmine said, "Although, you know as well as I do tonight, we could have gone all the way, but I am happy to hear you respect me enough to wait until, we are sure. With that, "I will be leaving. Romeo, this night was all I had imagined. I wanted us truthfully, to take our relationship to higher level. I feel that we are closer, don't you think?"

Romeo said, "Jasmine, I L____," but before he could get the words out, she placed her finger to his lips and said, "Romeo, please. I believe I know what you are going to say but please, If it is really the way you feel. I know that you will say it when it is not such a heat of the moment.' Romeo, said, "Jasmine it is still what I feel no matter the moment, but out of respect, I want say it until you are ready to hear it.' Romeo kissed Jasmine passionately on the lips. Romeo asked Jasmine if she would like him to see her home? She said, "No, I will be okay. I will call you when I make it home." Jasmine left. Within 15 minutes she made it home. She called Romeo to tell him so, and she undressed and went straight to bed. She dreamed about her and Romeo being romantically involved all night long. Romeo did the same. They were more in sync then they realized. Romeo and Jasmine forgot to tell each other that they were going to be out of town in the next two weeks starting Monday, but both thought within themselves that they would let the other know. Monday came and went and both of them were so swamped in flying out to Hawaii and getting settled in with their Conference itinerary that they had unfortunately forgot to do so.

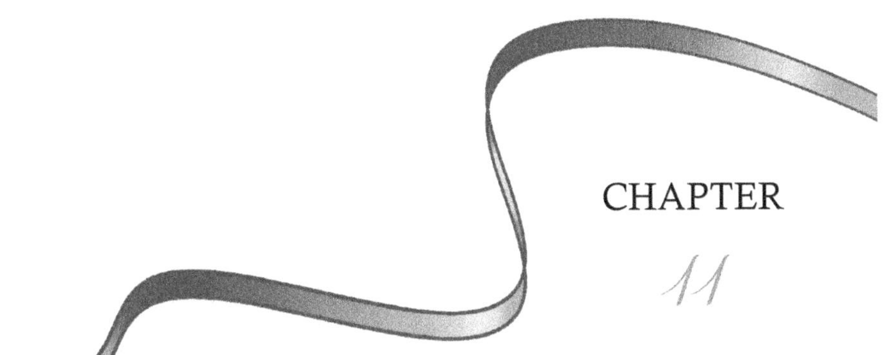

CHAPTER

11

rank continued to go the office to make sure the calls were answered and to set follow up appointments with Romeo's clientele. Monday and Tuesday passed slowly, and then Wednesday came. Romeo's severely abused client was scheduled to come meet with Frank. Psychiatry was Franks specialty. The young man entered the office on time. He appeared to have it all together. He was neatly dressed in business attire and he was very articulate. He shook Frank's hand and informed him his name was Sylvester. Sylvester thanked Frank for being able to meet with him to talk about some of the things he went through as a child.

Frank invited Sylvester to follow him in his office that was down the hall from Romeo's office. This is where he seen the few clients that he had on his roster that he could easily manage before he decided rather, he would stay in the U.S. or go back home to England to start his full Practice in Psychiatry. Frank informed Sylvester that Romeo had discussed his background and that we both would serve as your mentor as you go through Psychiatric/Therapy school. Will you please share with me in your own words what brought you hear today?

Sylvester bean to share with Frank, saying, "I am here today to discuss with you some tragic events that occurred with me when I was very young and because some of the nightmares were returning, and I did not want to go into deep depression again. i had recovered and was doing well and then one day in one of my Psychiatric classes, my instructor was going over a case study. The case study was about me and my father. It disturbed me in a negative manner and it was bringing up some horrific memories that I had worked so hard to manage and get passed. My father sexually abused me from around 4 y/o up until I was about 10 y/o. What makes matters worse, my father was also sexually abused as a child and he was repeating the cycle.

To give a synapse of what happened and how it came to an end, my mother walked in on my father molesting me one evening coming home from work. She worked the night shift as a nurse and was not feeling well. So, she got off a little earlier. Apparently, my father did not hear her when she came into our home. She walked into my room as she always does to kiss me good night on my forehead and make sure all was well. However, my mom walked in on my father molesting me. She was devastated in what she saw. She blamed herself for not noticing any signs in me. She quickly told my dad to get out and never come back. Of course, he left saying, "I am sorry. I am so sorry to both of us as he was crying gathering his things. After my father left, she called the police to have him arrested. The Police department asked her to bring me in for questioning. Her mom said she was not comfortable with bringing her son in at such a tender age of 10 y/o to be questioned by the Police but she would come in and give a statement of what she had just witnessed. She and I went to Police station and reported the incident but she would not let them question me directly. She was the mediator between them and me.

She also had placed a restraining order out on him preventing him from contacting her or me. My mother scheduled us several Psychiatric counseling and therapy sessions that same week because she wanted us to be able to get through this terrible ordeal. We had sessions together and some individualized. Both of us improved but it was a long hard road. That is why I wanted to become a psychiatrist myself, so that I could help others that have went through similar abuse that I have. I also want to specialize in dis association personalities."

As Sylvester shared with Frank. Frank was taking a few notes in his note pad. He asked Sylvester had he heard from his dad since he became an adult. Sylvester told him, "No, not directly but my father did see one of my mom's close relatives that was known to accept people as they are. My father apparently had asked could he stop by his house to talk with him. Our Uncle Lance had given him consent to do so. He and my father apparently had talked quite a bit. My uncle was also a school counselor. So, he knew how to relate to people that had been abused. He also helped my mom and I along with our regular Psychiatrist to make sure we had someone to talk to that was also family. He wanted to make sure we would become healthy mentally and physically.

My father asked our uncle Lance to please inform my mother that he also had sought out extensive Psychiatric treatments because he did not want to continue to repeat the cycle of abuse to anyone else. He told our Uncle Lance that I was his the only one that this too and he feels terrible that he did this to me and my mom. He loved us both very much and he feels that he was just sick, and although he tried all of those years to suppress the memory of his abuse. He never wanted to act on those memories but he, unfortunately, succumbed to the ugliness of it. He wanted my Uncle Lance to tell my mom he did not want to repeat such a horrific thing. He did not consider himself to be homosexual or bisexual. He felt like he was just repeating the horrific cycle of abuse that was also afflicted upon him by a family friend. He never told anyone about it and, therefore, he never received any help for it. My father did tell my Uncle Lance he wrestled with those memories and repeating the cycle daily as if it was a demonic force in his life that he was having trouble controlling. That is why he practiced going to church on a regular basis to fight those demons but in a moment of weakness he felt into the same trap and it was difficult for him to stop once he had started even though he knew it was greatly wrong. It was like it was no longer him but the demonic force that continued to use him to abuse me sexually.

Frank asked Sylvester, "How did you come to know all of this. He said my mom told me when I was a sophomore in high school. She wanted me to know that my father loved me but he just did not know how not to repeat the cycle of sexual abuse that was also afflicted upon him when he was a child. She also informed me that she had forgiven my father but she did not want to ever see him again. She encouraged me to forgive him to so that they could heal once and for all from this great tragedy. She said, although I do not want to see your father again, I will leave that up to you if you want to start seeing him again."

Frank said, "Have you heard or seen your dad since you were 10 y/o?" Sylvester said, "No. I have forgiven him but I have not invited him back into my life again. I am still not stronger enough to do so. I feel that if I do see him now, I would want to fight him. When I was little, he had control over me but now that I am adult, I feel like I can defend myself."

Frank said, "Have you had any suicidal thoughts?" Sylvester said, "No, not now, but when I was younger, I did not know how to process what had happened to me and I fell into a deep depression. If it wasn't for my mom enrolling us in Therapy sessions, I really don't believe I would have made it. I probably would have committed suicide. Well, let me take a step back. Not actually, but I would sometimes entertain the thought of it. Therapy sessions helped me to process the abuse and I was able to turn those negative thoughts into something that I could use to propel me to help someone else that went through similar abuse." Frank said, "Great. Thank you for being honest. Please when I ask these hard questions, it is not that I am trying to make you re live the past but I want to know the details so that I can best help you to move forward."

Sylvester said, "I understand." Frank asked him another question before he ended their session for today? In what you have undergone with the sexual abuse and from a significant trusting family member have it altered your course of sexuality and have it affected you mentally?" Sylvester said, "Well, I do not have desires to be with a man, I do not think much about my sexual orientation or having sex. However, I am attracted to women. As for as mentally, yes it has affected me. I feel as if I am more cautious in getting to know others and letting them get to know me. I am ashamed of what happened to me and much more it was my dad who did it to me. So, even now, I don't make friends easily." Frank said, "Thank you. Now, I have something to help you grow into letting down your guard and letting people know who you are. You do not have to tell them exactly what you have been through but you can use this tragic event to understand when other goes through the same flight in life and helped them to become an overcomer just like you obviously have. Naturally, the field of Psychiatry that you have chosen is a great fit for you. You have firsthand experience in it and can talk to your clients on a personal understanding to help them get through the pitfalls of such memories and tragic events to move to a healthier place in both mind, body, and soul.

Frank ended their session and set up a continuation appointment once a month for four more sessions. In the meantime, he invited him to come by the office at least twice a week to see how he and Romeo ran their Psychiatric/Counseling practice. Sylvester accepted and was pleased the way his initial session went with Frank. It was not easy, but he did feel like Frank could help him to get to a healthier place. Sylvester left the office. Frank stayed behind and he went back into his office to look over his notes. Although he was never molested, physical, or sexually molested he did grow up with a mother that was Bi Polar. His dad spent most of his Psychiatric career being both husband and Psychiatrist to his wife.

Frank's dad had tried all type of counseling and medication therapy until he found the right combination of therapeutic medications that he had to occasionally adjust to enable for his wife to lead a normal happy life enjoying her entire family. Through the study of Franks dad with his mom, Frank also desired to go into the field of Psychiatry. He studied under his Father and became almost as brilliant in the field. The only difference between the two is that Frank depended more of the faith he had in God to intervene then his skillful education that he learned. Truthfully, that is why his clients improved so well. He never enforced his clients to adopt his faith, but he did witness to them that he drew his wisdom from the most high God to best help his clients. Frank began to pray to God, that he, help him to help Sylvester to heal so that he could lead a productive and healthy life. Even to have a family himself and to be a great husband and father to them. Frank prayed for hours. He really wanted to help this young man. Sylvester's thirst for Psychiatry reminded him of himself.

Frank prayed from 8:00 pm to 1:00 am. God did not speak to him until he went home and fell asleep. God visited him in his dreams around 4:00 am. He gave him the tools and therapeutic techniques that did not involve medications. He would teach him the butterfly effect which is a simple dependence on initial conditions in which a small change in one state of a deterministic nonlinear system and result in large differences in a later state with tender concern, guidance, and renewing counseling therapies. Frank wanted to be an example to Sylvester although he and Romeo were not fathers as of yet, they are men that knows how to properly love and be an example of how to teach and guide their children to be able to live successfully and independently in this world.

Frank immediately was awakened with the revelation and was very happy that God informed him how to help Sylvester in the best way possible over time but yet successfully. Frank slept in. It was Saturday and instead of getting dressed and calling one of his friends in his black book to hang out with. He gathered his strength. Over the next two weeks, he knew he would prepare himself to best help Sylvester to get to the point of success that he could also teach others as he goes deeper in the field of Psychiatry. Frank wrote each step down that God had revealed to him. He felt relief that this was going to be an educational journey.

Later, Frank got up and took a shower. He put on dressy clothes and went to one of his favorite restaurants. To Frank's surprise, he ran into Rosette. He was intrigued by her. Not only was she tall and beautiful, she aged very well. Rosette was in her mid-forties and she looked as if she was in her mid-twenties. She also carried herself as a strong confidence especially around men. She related very well around men. Possibly because she grew up with brothers and played sports with them and their friends. She was very natural and she had an uncanny wit about her that made him feel amazingly comfortable around her. He noticed that she was with a female friend. He did not want to interrupt their conversation so he asked to be sat a far off from them. The host did so. Rosette turned as she was talking with her friend and noticed Frank. She smiled because she liked laughing and talking with him. Besides, she wanted to introduce him to one of her friends. She thought about keeping him for herself, but she knew that she was not healed from the traumatic thing of being torn from the man she deeply was in love with and the child that she gave birth t out of their love through her parents insisting she do so. Rosette parents meant well but it was not well received by her. It really prevented her from loving another man and moving forward with any man in order to marry and have other children. Here it is, she was almost forty-six. Well passed common child bearing days but she was still determined to get well enough emotionally and physically in order to do so. Rosette did not want to put Frank through any psychological or physical distress because of what she had gone through. She felt that he deserves better. He deserved a woman that is ready to love him with the passion he deserves.

Rosette kept looking over to Frank until they made eye contact. She waved at him. He waved back at her in a way to invite her over to his table. She accepted and she and her friend walked over to him. Rosette introduced the female friend she was with. Rosette said, "Hello Frank. How wonderful to see you." Frank said, "HI my dear. You know it is always a pleasure to be in front of good company.' Rosette chuckled with a satisfying laugh and said, "Only you will make such a Korney thing sound enticing." Frank said, "In your case I truly mean it. I do have a certain charm that woes the ladies." Rosette shook her head and said, "Frank, you are something else." Rosette said, "By the way, this is my friend Mary, I think you may remember her. Years ago, Romeo counseled her and helped her to become healthy." Mary held her hand out to shake his hand as he extended it to her.

Mary said, "Hello." Frank said," Hello Mary. How are you? It is a pleasure to meet you." Frank thought to himself but said it out loud, "Is all of Rosette friends as lovely as you?" Mary smiled and said, "Do you say these types of lines to every woman you meet or just the ones you find beautiful? Frank was taken back a little from her words. He felt that she was very witty. Just like her friend Rosette. He invited them to sit and talk with him. He offered to buy them anything they wanted to eat or drink but they declined because they had already had their share of what they wanted before they had noticed he was there. They both shook their heads sideways ad said, "No thank you we have already eaten and we had strawberry Kiwi teas which is the best drink here." Frank said, wonderful, then, I will also order that drink on you guys' word." Frank did so and it was proven they were correct. It was very good. Frank, Rosette, and Mary had a great time laughing, telling jokes, and sharing how Rosette came to their office and how Mary had greatly been helped by Romeo because of the sexual assaults that she had gone through.

Rosette, also shared with him of the challenges she still has in putting things in the past of having to give up the man and the baby they had together up for adoption insisted by her parents. Mary was already aware of Rosette's struggles. They had been friends and each others confidant for at least 10 years. They went to college together and played on the same team before Rosette became one of her coaches. Frank was so sad for his friend, Rosette and now his new friend Mary for what they both had gone through, especially for being so beautiful and having a strong will about them to live life in spite of what they had been through. Frank offer to help them anyway he could both as a faithful friend if they needed to talk to anyone and as a Psychiatric Professional. They knew that Frank meant well and accepted his offer by saying, "We will contact you if we need any extra counseling."

Frank gave them both his card which contained his personal cell number and informed them that it is only a professional gesture. Please do not misunderstand." Rosette and Mary both re assured Frank that they knew he was being professional. They stayed an hour more and Mary and Rosette left the restaurant together and hugged Frank as Frank stayed a little longer. Frank thought to himself, how rare it is to find two people not related as Rosette and Mary that had very similar traits; in character, physique, beauty, intelligence, and wit. He believes he had hit the jack pot in making two friends like them. Rosette did inform Frank when they hugged each other goodbye that Mary was the friend she was saying would make a good match for him as she whispered in his ear. Frank would have loved Rosette to feel she was the perfect fit for him but he respected what she had told him. She was not ready for a lasting relationship right now. She still had to work through somethings so that she can give a deserving person such as himself all she had to give and not just her body. Frank knew that this is why she started therapy sessions with Romeo.

Frank finished eating and thought a little more rather he would stay and make his practice there with Romeo or move back home to England and be with his family more since they were aging. His siblings were also still in England. When he thought of Rosette and Mary and the fun time, they just share he thought to himself, how lovely that would be to do this again. He paid for the meal and drinks they had and he left and stopped by the grocery store to pick up few items. He made it home before dark. He made him a turkey sandwich, chips, and glass of milk with a couple of chocolate chip cookies and sat before his 70-inch TV and watched his favorite show. Then he went to sleep in his comfortable bed and got up and prepared to go to the local church in his neighborhood. He had been there several times before but had not joined yet. He decided to join this Sunday. When the Pastor of the church gave the invitation to open the doors of the church to join, he went up to do so. He was already a confessed Christian and believed the Lord Jesus was the true Son of God., and the Holy Ghost was a part of the Trinity of God all three are one for the same purpose for the Salvation of all Mankind. The rest of the day was very nice. He went by a local park with a big body of water and walked around it several times for exercise. Before he went home, he visited one of his friends and they watched one of the pro basketball games.

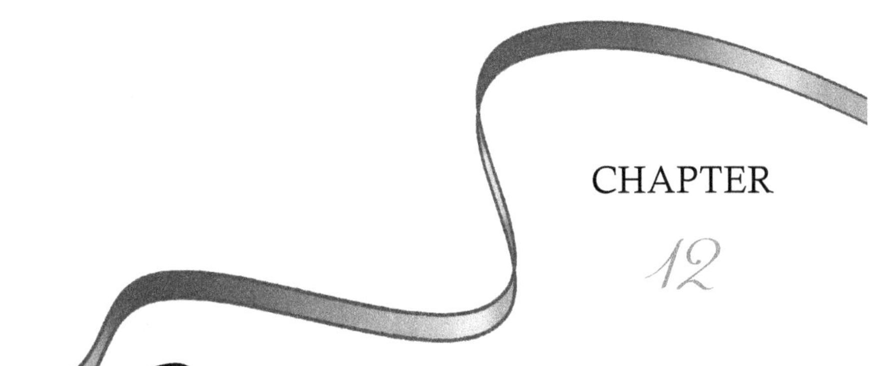

CHAPTER

12

$\mathcal{M}$onday came and he showered and went to the office. It was no patients scheduled for the next two weeks but he went to take calls so he could set appointments for Romeo to have when he returned. He loved working with his college friend. They were like minded in their approach to life and their profession. Romeo came close to getting married to a young lady he was dating in college but after his junior year they broke off their engagement. She was a bit wild and liked to party a lot more than what he wanted to accept in the woman he wanted to be married to for the rest of his life and raise his children. Although, he did not experience having his biological mother's love while growing up, he did have his grandmother and extended aunts who was very loving to him that showed motherly love. That helped shape him into a very loving and caring man. His grandfather and his biological dad who he thought was his big brother were also great examples of a loving father and great provider. Romeo and Frank were able to experience the was a man and a woman having a mutual loving successful marriage that helped shape them on what type of husband and father they wanted to be.

What a week, it has started to be on the first day, Jasmine thought to herself as she walked to her parent's and spouses' room to go the first day of the Medical Conference. They greeted each other and walked to the conference together. It was beautiful in Hawaii. The days are sunny and warm and the evenings are very romantic and magical. Jasmine only regret was not having anyone to spend time with in such a magical place like her parents. Jasmine reached into her purse and grabbed her phone. She text Romeo to inform him that over the next two weeks, she would be out of town on business and she missed him greatly. Romeo text Jasmine back thanking her for letting him know. He also informed her that he was out of town on business for the next two weeks. Neither dared to asked where. They did not seem to be presumptuous. They text each other again on Wednesday to tell each other they miss each other.

The first day of the conference was good, there is four days left. Jasmine and her parents enjoyed the first day of the Medical Conference. They met a number of contacts to start a good network of Professionals all over the U.S. They gathered together and met up with each other for a buffet dinner at the beach. It was a warm beautiful evening with a cool breeze coming from the water of the beach. There were beautiful women performing their Hawaiian dance. It was a beautiful thing to see. Jasmine and her parents with their spouses went out to dance with the ladies as they bid them to come. They danced for at least 30 minutes trying to learn the Hawaiian Laua dance. Surprisingly, Jasmine dad and her mom were the ones chosen to come and learn the dance more in debt so that they can present it to the people on the great Laua that is to occur on Thursday evening before the last day of the Medical Conference. They all ate well of the Hawaiian delicacies and fruit. Afterwards, they went to their rooms, bathed themselves, and went to sleep. They were so tired because they ad danced and ate very much.

Tuesday and Wednesday they met again at the Medical Conference and strengthened their network and learned. In the evening they went out to eat and tasted the great Hawaiian cuisine that was very rich and flavorable. Jasmine's mom and dad met with the Hawaiian women to learn and perfect the Hawaiian Laua dance to present it in the Laua on Thursday night. It was Traditional at that Resort that they choose two guests visiting the resort to participate in the Hawaiian Laua dance which help aide in more customer satisfaction on their reviews. Jasmines parents rekindled their love for one another but remained committed to their spouses whom they had grown to love and never wanted to depart from them. The good thing was that their spouses new of their love for one another and was not intimidated for it because they knew that they had gained their love and trust. They all ate well and went to their rooms again and was fast asleep.

Thursday, came and the Medical Conference was wonderful but everyone lay in wait for the Laua on tonight. That great night came and it was full of great Hawaiian cuisine, tropical drinks, pineapple and fresh fruits, and an award winning Laua dance and party. Jasmine's parents nailed it. They had perfected the Hawaiian Laua dance and their spouses observed with great pride. Everyone enjoyed themselves immensely. It was a definite wonderful night to remember. They took so many pictures enough for several picture albums between each of them. The night was precious, then the host arose and stood before them and informed them that they had a special guest to serenade them with song. The host did not announce the person's name. Then they heard a mesmerizing male voice but did not see the individual that was singing. The person clearly had a mic because all heard him.

The words of the songs were so enduring. It was about a man's solemn love of a woman that he loves but the woman does not want to give into our enduring love affair. Our love surpasses all joys upon this earth, and it is better than riches and gold. The taste of her precious lips is as the honeycomb and sweet as milk chocolate. Her breath smells like the lilac of the wild flowers in the fields. Her skin is as soft as the cotton pillows. Her breast as the bountiful melons. She is as the sun, moon, and the stars in the heavens. She is special, my love is special to me. Jasmine melted, for she knew the man was Romeo. She had learned his voice and his captivating power in the lyric of his songs. Romeo appeared unto the people and showed himself unto them all. Romeo did not know that Jasmine was present nor her family. He had not seen her at all at any of the days of the Medical Conference. He did not go out to the different parties or buffets. He ate inside his room. He was in love with Jasmine and he could not do much else. He was enjoying the Medical Conference but he was missing her entirely. Romeo sang so beautifully that the people got unto their feet and clapped mightily. The shouted, "More, please give us More." Romeo sang few more original love songs and when he song the last song, he looked up and saw Jasmine. His smile was so wide. He ran to her and pulled her to him and song the most beautiful love song that moved everyone to tears. There was not a dry eye at the Laua party. Even the employees shed tears.

Jasmine and Romeo spent the remaining night together discussing their surprise that both of them was at the Medical Conference but did not know that the other would be present. They stayed up unto 2:00 am laughing, talking, and loving each other. They did not make love yet because Romeo wanted to give Jasmine time to know that he was truly hers and would be for the rest of their lives together.

He did not want her to think that he just wanted her body then he would leave her. He wanted her to know his love was everlasting.

They fell asleep in each others arms fully clothed in Jasmine's room. Romeo got up at 7:00 am and kissed Jasmine on the forehead. He told her he had to go to his room to shower and get dressed for the last day of the conference. He informed her that he would call her when his class was over. He did as he had informed her. When the Medical Conference was over. Romeo called Jasmine. Jasmine had him to meet at one of the Restaurants close to the Medical Conference. Jasmine told Romeo that her parents and their spouses was also at the Medical Conference and she would love for them to meet him. He agreed and met them and they all was very pleased of her choice. Her parents and their spouses informed Jasmine that they had made preparation to go to the Airport and fly home. They hugged each other and shook Romeo's hand and they departed for the Airport. Jasmine had informed Romeo that she was there another week to relax and take a long-awaited vacation. Romeo, coincidentally informed Jasmine that he had planned the same thing. They both was delighted and excited to be together in such a romantic place.

Romeo and Jasmine had such a great time laughing, talking, and getting to know each other better. They did not argue but they learned to disagree in peace. They were starting to know each others triggers but it was good to learn the others passions or faults so you could know will this person be the one to have a long-lasting relationship. Both agreed that the other was worth having a long relationship with but they did not share it with each other because it was a mutual thing that need not to be spoke, it was just felt. They slept at their own hotel rooms every night but spent the majority of their last week together in Hawaii. They had great romantic excursions and nights. Although they came close to the notion of giving in to their romantic desires, they decided not to make love, yet, until they both was ready. Romeo, in his heart, did not feel that Jasmine was ready yet even though he knew that he wanted her for more than a person to have sexual encounters with. He did not want to start anything before it was time. He wanted to make sure they have a chance of success. Sex, although it can be very pleasurable especially when it is with a person whom you want to be a part of each other's life for long-term for the rest of your lives.

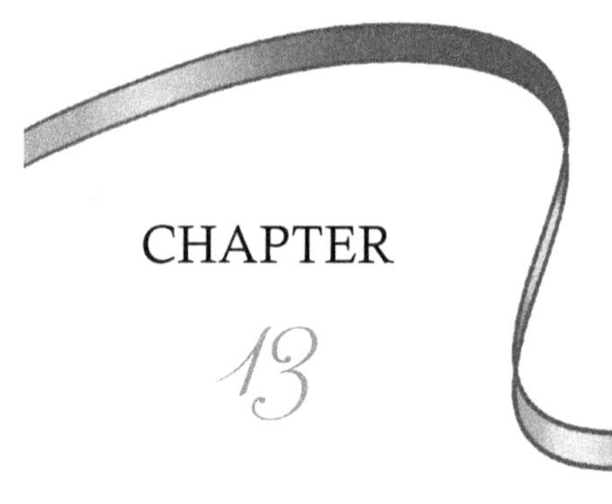

CHAPTER

13

heir week in Hawaii together after the Medical Conference, thankfully, went slowly in Paradise. They were able to enjoy the warm breeze, Luas, beaches, snorkeling, and island food and shopping. They took a lot of pictures to remind each other of their first romantic experience of truly getting to know each other. The two of them arranged travel together to the airport via taxi. They also flew home together on the same plane and at the same time. It seemed so coincidental because they did not know that the other was coming to the Medical Conference in Hawaii, but it was not, it was fate. When certain things happen, it is not always chance, but the way it is designed by God himself according to his perfect plan. He gives us the choice to follow it or not but he loves us through his Grace if we choose not, and gives us chance after chance to accept his love and salvation or deny it.

They fortunately, landed safely, and because they lived within blocks of each other, they both traveled together in the same taxi. Just as they were, turning the corner along their neighborhood, they were involved in a serious motor vehicle accident. A couple that was walking on their evening stroll, Stephanie and Samuel, witnessed the accident called 9-11. They knew both Jasmine and Romeo not as a couple but individually. They went to Romeo concert's many times. They loved his soulful voice and the lyrics of the songs were heart stirring. They knew Jasmine as a doctor in one of the most prestigious Medical Offices in their town. She was not their personal Physician but her reputation of an amazing doctor as her parents went before her wide and far. Stephanie knew that Romeo was also a psychiatrist. Some of her friends were his patients. She knew this because they would discuss how he is so patient and gives wise counseling. He truly was able to assist them in coming to term with their difficulties of life. Stephanie called her friend, William to get Romeo's office number so that she could call to alert them of the accident and that the ambulance is taking them to Primrose Rehabilitation Hospital. It was an excellent and safe Hospital. While Stephanie called William, Samuel called one of his friends named Rochelle that knew Jasmine's parents, Ramon and Lorina.

Stephanie was given Romeo's Psychiatry office number and she called there. The answering service was able to call the doctor on call. The doctor on call was, Frank. Frank called Stephanie back after receiving the message. Stephanie was able to inform him of the car accident and he and the young lady, Jasmine. Frank was very sorrowful to hear the news and immediately called Romeo's father, Ray to inform him. Romeo's father called his parents on the way to the hospital and they told him that they would meet him there. Samuel was able to reach his friend, Rochelle, and she gave him both their numbers, and he introduced himself to them separately over the phone, and informed them he regrets to inform them that their daughter was involved in a serious care accident and was transported to Primrose Rehabilitating Hospital via ambulance, both parents and their spouses rushed to the hospitals as quick as they could. The traffic was heavy but not to its normal chaos, they were able to make it to the hospital within 45 minutes.

Ramon and Lorina with their spouses were nearer to the hospital for they all had went out to dinner with each other and it was near the Primrose Rehabilitation Hospital. They were very familiar with the hospital. It has a great reputation of safety and skillful employees. Some of their patients has informed them of the reputation of the hospital. They arrived there within 20 minutes and quickly went to the hospital registration to inquire about their daughter and Romeo. Stephanie had informed them that Romeo and Jasmine were together in the same taxi going home that was involved in the accident. The attendant was able to give them the information about Jasmine, but because they were not any kin to Romeo, they could not give his information. They were informed that she was in surgery now, and should be in recovery within 30 minutes. Her right ankle was broken but was easily repaired by one of the best orthopedic surgeons in their region. The attendant notified the surgery department and one of the recovery nurses came out to inform them of Jasmine's progress and she will be out of surgery soon and would need to be in recovery for 1-2 hours and transferred to her private hospital room as she requested. The nurse had informed them that the couple arrived at the hospital unconscious. They both had head concussions from the car accident.

Ray and his parents saw each other pull up into the hospital parking lot and hurriedly walked into the hospital together. They asked about Romeo and if they had any news of how he is doing. The attendant asked the relationship to Romeo and was informed that Ray was Romeo's dad and his parents was Romeo's grandparents. She quickly informed them that Romeo's arms were broken and he was out of surgery. He is in the recovery room and he will remain there for two hours before being transferred to his private hospital room. The attendant notified the recovery room nurse, and she came out to talk to them. She informed them that Romeo came through the surgery well. His forearms were put in casts to immobilized them while the bones healed.

They were able to go into the Romeo's recovery room one at a time. Ray went in to see Romeo firs. He hugged his son and ask him why he did not call to notify them that he was in a car wreck. Romeo informed his father that he was apparently unconscious and did not even know how he and Jasmine actually got there. Ray said, 'Jasmine", Is she a friend of your?" Ray said, "Dad she is more than a friend but a woman he is in love with and would like to get to know better. We without knowing the other would be attending the same Medical Conference in Hawaii, thankfully, was able to spend a great deal of time together and it served a great purpose." Ray said, "Romeo, I am happy to hear of your happiness and I am especially happy that you, my son, is still with me. I feel sometimes that my parents and I not telling you initially that I was your father would have damaged out relationship, but you my son, are not like most. You are full of wisdom and knowledge beyond your age." Romeo said, "Thank you father but I know where my help comes from, it is a gift from God, that I do not take lightly. That is why I went into the field of Psychiatry." Ray said, "Yes, your Profession of Choice fits you perfectly. Ray and Romeo finished their talk and then Romeo went back out to his parents, to allow them to come to talk to their grandson.

Ray informed them of the conversation Romeo and he had on how he was unconscious when they made it to the hospital and did not know how or when they arrived. They hugged him was happy to see his handsome face. It had a small scratch on his forehead when his head hit the back of the hard front seat and they were knocked out unconscious as a result of the impact of the car wreck. Romeo's grandparents talked with him a little longer and they left saying, "We will be in the recovery waiting area to be informed what floor and room you will be transferred." Romeo kissed his grandmother's forehead as she hugged hm and he shook his grandfather's hand. His grandparent joined Romeo's father, Ray, in the Recovery waiting room.

Jasmine was now in the recovery room after surgery and her parents and their spouses were able to go see her two at a time. On the way to the hospital each of Jasmine's parents had notified their parents that Jasmine had been involved in a serious auto accident and she is at the Primrose Rehabilitation Hospital. Both set of parents informed each of them that they were familiar with the location and would meet them up there. Both sets of Jasmine grandparents had met their children at the hospital just as Jasmine was transferred to Post surgery recovery room. They were able to go in to see their lovely grand-daughter after each of her parents and their spouses saw her. They were relieved to see her and that she was looking as well as she did. She had suffered a broken right ankle and it was now in a cast from orthopedic surgery. Her parents and her spouses tried to find out as much information as they could without imposing on her because she was undoubtedly still under Anesthesia from the surgery, before their parents came in to see her so that they could pass the information along to them.

They were already aware that she and Romeo stayed an extra week in Hawaii together and they flew home together. They also caught a cab to take them home together because they lived within blocks of each other, and unfortunately, was involved in an auto accident near their neighborhood. They had already informed their parents of that so they were there in support of Jasmine and wanted her t know they were aware of what happened so that could be the least of her worries. Both set of her parents had saw her, and then the grandparents saw her as well. The rest of the evening even after she was transferred to her private room. Romeo was also transferred to his private room and his family followed them up to the room. Romeo and Jasmine's family waited in the waiting room and became very familiar with Romeo's dad and family. They found out that their families had a lot in common.

Jasmine and Romeo both were able to talk with their surgeons and attending hospitalist doctor and nurses later that evening. Jasmine and Romeo's grandparents stated 3-4 hours more for support and said they would be back tomorrow to see them. Their parents stayed 2-3 hours until visiting hours were over and promised they would be back in the morning before they went to work to check on them. They also said they would bring them some extra clothing, house coat, and personal items to have during their hospital stay. When Jasmine and Romeo were more comprehensive from the being under Anesthesia, they wondered were the other one was. Their family had tried to inform them both that their private rooms were on the same floor, but they were on opposite sides of the area.

Jasmine and Romeo slept okay in the hospital bed. They were as comfortable as their beds at home. Jasmine and Romeo's parents had come to see bot of their children respectively and asked how the other was doing and left for work detailing for them to call them if they needed them for anything before, they had a chance to come back this evening after work. They both said emphatically, they would do so, but they are sure they will be fine with the hospital staff having such a warm response to them and their safe good reputation proceeded them.

When Romeo's father and grandparents left, he immediately went to ask the from desk of the orthopedic unit they were on, what room was Jasmine Peters in? It was in each of their hospital records the two of them were both involved in the same auto accident and arrived at the hospital together in the same ambulance. Romeo was informed by Jamine's nurse where her room was. Romeo walked down the hallway and went to the other side of the unit and there she was, as beautiful as ever, sitting in one of the lounge recliners with her right ankle that was in a below the knee cast to immobilize her ankle was prop up on several pillows for comfort. When Romeo entered her room, Jasmine grinned from ear to ear. She spoke. "Oh Romeo, are you alright? Bless your heart. It appears both of your arms were broken in the auto accident we were in." Romeo said, "Yes, my dear it is so. When, I saw that other car getting ready to run into us head on, I tried to lean over to place my body somewhat in front of yours as much as I could when I loosen the restraints a little from my seat belt so that your body would be somewhat protected from the impact of the crash."

Jasmine said, "Thank you Romeo, it must have worked because I only ended up with a broken right ankle, as you can see, it is in a cast now. I am so happy to see you up and walking. God was truly with us. Wow, you never know what danger lies ahead. I am happy we were with each other else we probably would not have known the other had been in an accident until sometime later." Romeo said, "Yes, you are definitely right. Some of the people that knew us saw the accident and called 911. When the Paramedics came and pulled us out of the taxi, they recognized us and called someone they knew that was aware how to get a hold of our parents. One of them called Frank, and the other knew someone that knew you and your parents from your doctor's facility. Look at God. He always works thing out." Jasmine said, "Yes, thank God. Have you heard from Frank? Yes, my parents informed me that he came to see me on last night but I was still under the influence of the Anesthesia from surgery, I pretty much slept through the night after the surgery. He called me this morning to check on me and said he would take care of everything at the office with my clients this week and also if needed over the next two weeks thereafter. He told me he would come to see me this evening.

Jasmine said, "Yes, indeed. My parents had informed me that they would get someone from the office to see my scheduled patients too. They told me not to worry. They will alternate seeing them if needed. They wanted me to relax, gather myself, and to think only of recovering. Spoken like true doctors, huh?" They both laughed shaking their heads in agreement. Jasmine said, "Romeo, have a seat. It is no need for you to stand. I will tell you the same thing my parents told me, concentrate on relaxing, gathering yourself, and getting better." Romeo said, "Well said, I will do just that." Jasmine said, "I can tell you what will make me feel better if you are up to it." Romeo said, "What's that?" Jasmine said, "Sing me a song, unless your vocals got injured during the auto accident." Romeo said, "No, I believe God spared them from injury. Ok, let's see. I think I know you a lot better now in regard to the genre of songs you like. I will sing, "Back at One" by Brian McKnight." As Jasmine heard Romeo sing to her, basically serenading her once again, she started to melt in his presence. She felt weak and dazzled by his loving demeanor and how he chose to carefully look into her eyes as he sung directly to her.

Of course, his serenade of "Back at One" was highly noticed by the staff and visitors. They gathered outside of Jasmine's room to hear that great voice that was widely heard on that side of the unit. They had heard great voices before but not in the context of the way Romeo sung. He emphasized the words from the song so intently that it was very striking straight to the heart. When Romeo finished the song, they all clapped saying, "Wow, do you sing professionally. If so, when and where is your next concert?" Romeo informed them what room he was in and asked if they would stop by and leave him a card or their contact information and he would certainly inform them where his next event would be. They all agreed saying, "You can count on me being there. I have not heard good singing like that in a long time." Jasmine of course, was in tears, as she said, "Romeo, you have a true gift from God. You really need to pursue your singing career more." Romeo said, "Thank you so much, but right now,

I am pursuing both of my callings. One of them being singing and the other in Psychiatry. There is a great need for both especially in the season we are living now." Jasmine said, "You are so right. I cannot argue with that." Romeo talked with her a little a longer, and kissed her on her lips stating, "I will see you a little later. Please rest." Jasmine said, "I Promise." as she put the medical book down that she was reading before Romeo came to see her.

Romeo went back to his room. Some of the male and female nurses had already given him their cards as they saw him walk by the nursing station. They said, "Please don't forget to call us when you are better and start having singing events again." Romeo said. "Will do. Enjoy the rest of your day." By the time, Romeo turned the corner to go in the area of where his room was located, he saw Frank walking toward his unit. He called out to him, "Frank. Wha's up buddy?" Frank said, laughing and shaking his head, "She looks too good for you to leave her alone while you take a day to recuperate. Man, you got it bad, don't you?" What happen with you two over in Paradise? It was that good, huh?" Romeo said, "I don't kiss and tell but it was magical. We really connected." Frank said, "I am happy for you Romeo. It has been long and coming for a good woman to come into your life that deserves the kind of sincerely caring man you are. I know, I have been your friend for over 10 years. Finally, you found a good one that did not want to take you for everything you had counting on your good-natured heart." Romeo said, "Yes, you may be right. I can count on one hand how many relationships I have been in. 2 out of three of those relationships was not noteworthy. There was one that I thought I was going to marry but after college, she was offered a job overseas, and I did not want her to miss such a great opportunity. With that being said, even that relationship does not compare to the way I feel about Jasmine. Man, I believe she is the one for me." Frank said, "Man, Sincerely, I have to agree. I have seen you two together. There is some powerful chemistry and vibes going on between you two. Strong vibes, my Man."

Frank sat down and talked with Frank for an hour and left and said he will check on him tomorrow. Romeo fell asleep, and slept well this time because he had saw Jasmine and knew she would be alright. Later that evening, his father and wife with his grandparents came to see him. Jasmine parents, their spouses, and both sets of grandparents came to see her. Jasmine stayed in the hospital for two weeks. She was discharged to Rehab where she stayed another two weeks. She had Physical Therapy sessions twice a week her last week in Rehab and was discharged for a 30-day Episode of Home Health Physical Therapy for two time a week during the first two-week and decreasing to once a week the final two weeks. Jasmine was getting a little stir crazy and her doctor released her to go back to work with a cane for safety when walking for at least two weeks more.

Romeo stayed in the hospital also for two weeks more and was transferred to Rehab to get Occupational Therapy during the two weeks of his stay after the casts were removed from his arms. As Promised, Frank honored his word. He saw Romeo's patients during that period. Jasmine's parents had a new doctor that started his practice soon after she was hospitalized to see her patient's as he builds his clientele while she was out.

CHAPTER

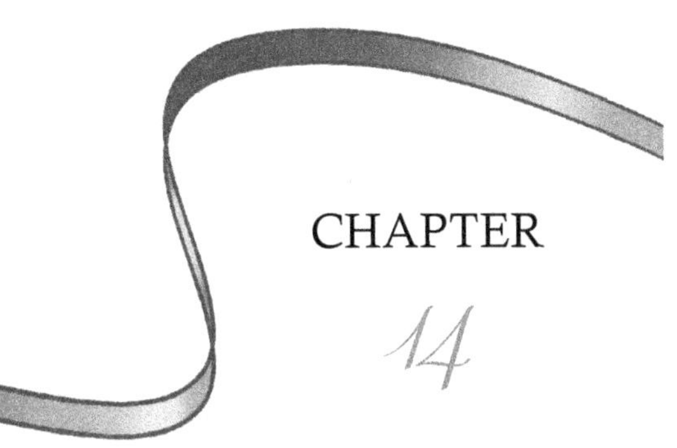

14

$\mathcal{F}$rank counseled Romeo's clients starting with Nancy. Nancy had great report with Frank as well. She felt comfortable in talking to him about her relationship with Tom. Frank has always been quite funny and professional with her. She knows of his reputation of being a brilliant Psychiatrist with a great bedside manner just like Romeo. What set the two of them apart from most of their colleagues in their area is their dependence on God, Almighty through the Holy Spirit to give them the Spiritual guidance in knowing just how to help each client individually. As expected, Nancy had some breakthrough strides in forgiveness regarding Tom. She realized that it was not necessarily Tom that she was upset with but yet her father whom she never knew dying and her step father whom she loved leaving her and her mom when she felt like she needed him most growing into a beautiful young woman. She needed her step father to be her rock. Tom reminded her of her step father so much that she did not realize it. As she began to look back over their life together, she could now see what a wonderful, strong, loving provider and husband. She felt ashamed that she has judged Tom wrongly and she was not mature enough to see him for the good man that was perfect for her that he truly was.

When they were done, Frank walked Nancy to the door because it had already become dark outside and he wanted to make sure she got to her car safely. Frank had already set her next appointment in the counseling room in two weeks giving Romeo more time to heal and possibly being back in the office to see his clients. On the way home, Nancy thought long and hard how she can make recompense of her sins in misjudging Tom, her ex-husband, by holding on past grudges she had with the men of her own family misgivings and weaknesses.

Two days following Nancy counseling session, Frank was now counseling with Tom. Tom was a strong character but yet gentle in his approach to people he cared about. Frank talked with Tom about his upbringing. He apologized for having him to repeat the subject manner again with him. Frank already knew he had previously talked with Romeo about his relationship with his mom and dad. Frank informed Tom that he believes that he had to grow up to be the man of his mom's household because of the tragic way his father left his mom for a man and what stain it left on their family legacy. He knew that this misfortune left his mom in a deep depression and that therefore affected you because you no longer had the nurturing care from the mother you loved, and how his mother's parents had to step in and be the actual ones raising him for at least the next four years. Frank informed Tom that none of these things were his fault. You loved your mom so much you started learning a trade in carpentry at the tender age of 10 y/o that most men take up when they are fully grown, to help support you and your mom financially. Although your grandparents were highly capable and had the means to take care of both you and your mom financially, physically, and spiritually, you still took this upon yourself to somewhat ease the pain you and your mom were going through when your father left.

Tom being a proud man. Knew that Frank was indeed telling him the truth. He realized that the carried that same need to take care of his family with such precision and passion into his adulthood, even unto his marriage with Nancy. The woman he was still greatly in love with. He wishes so much, that Nancy understood that very fact, he loved her and he wanted to make sure she felt loved and well taken care of. Tom also realized that same precision and passion he had to take care of the people he loved, he also was a bit controlling not allowing them to contribute to the decision making or be individualists. Make up their own minds. Frank and Romeo gave him the insight that it stimmed from his mom being a deep depression of losing the husband she was still greatly in love with to another man and he living his family to be with another.

She felt that she and her son was not good enough to keep her husband with them. He accepted his controlling nature. He now realized he still was thinking about his mom being deeply depressed, not fulfilling her duties to take care of him and nurture him as she should have had she not been so deeply depressed and lost all of her desires to function in this present world. He now realized the strength of Nancy being so very independent that drew him to her initially, was what truly he destroyed in her when he did not give her the opportunity to have any say so in their marital affairs. He made all the decisions alone and he never considered her in any of the plans. He knows this was a great disservice to Nancy and this very thing was what led to the demise of their marriage, and possibly not having any children within the 10 years of their marriage because he felt he had to build his clientele first to be able to afford bringing children into the word. He now sees, how wrong he was. Tom was determined to apologize to Nancy even if he could never restore their marriage.

Frank gave Tom a strong hand shake and commented how far he has become. Frank encouraged Tom to keep humbling himself and if need be, ask the Lord for strength to change the things he can and accept the thing he cannot by depending on God's guidance in doing those things he can't do on his own. Frank set Tom's appointment within the next two weeks, hoping that Tom will be well enough to come back to the office to counsel with his clients. Frank walked Tom to the door and locked the office door. Tom left encouraged knowing he had to seek his ex-wife, Nancy to at least apologize to her for his controlling manner that drove her away from him because he did not allow her to be the strong independent woman he fell in love with within their marriage.

Friday came, Frank knew that Rosette's appointment was this afternoon at 3:00 pm. Frank had prayed for God's insight to help Rosette with breakthroughs of her current situation that has inhibited her from having a meaningful lasting relationship with a man. He felt like because he already cares deeply for Rosette that it may somehow interfere with his ability to be open enough to share hard truths with her. Rosette was a little early for her appointment as usual, but this time was different. This time she would be counseling with him and not Romeo. She did not know how she felt about that because the two of them had become close friends that enjoy each others company. Frank discussed this very thing with Rosette before they started their counseling session. He wanted her to know if she felt uncomfortable revealing her deepest wounds because of their friendship he would understand.

Rosette told Frank, "Don't be silly. Because you have already broke down walls for me to confide already confidential information to you at the lunch my friend, Mary and I saw you, you need not worry if I feel some kind of way other than relaxed and confident in your abilities to help me. For, I know your professional experience in Psychiatry and you have already expressed your care for my well being. So, don't worry. I feel just as comfortable with you as I do with Romeo. Both of you are quite spiritual depending on God for guidance even over your Psychiatric skill level of experience."

Frank led Rosette to his counseling office and asked her to make herself comfortable to her choice of the plush leather couch or the plush comfortable reclining chair. Rosette choice the plush leather couch. It secluded her from looking directly into Franks beautiful blue eyes and his chiseled strong check bones and jaw line and his raving rusty blonde hair. Yes, Frank was truly a very handsome man, indeed. He had already broken the walls of her ever thinking she could be close to a man again, although right now, she wanted to focus on her emotional healing that led to her physical manifestations of not wanting to love or be close to another man other than her first love with Ray. Of course, at this time, Frank did not know who it was that Rosette had this great love with and the experience with him that occurred that prohibited her from becoming close to another man since then.

Frank asked Rosette some very pointed open-end questions that revealed the identity of the man that had broken her heart and the dreadful tragedy that led her to give up their baby that she wanted them to raise together as man and wife. Rosette knew that she and the man she loves so entirely were too young to marry much more to raise a tender boy child that came out of the great love they shared. She held great resentment toward her parents for not taking up the responsibly to help her and Ray to raise their child and give them consent to marry. She was 16 y/o and Ray was 17 y/o but the two of them were greatly mature for their ages.

Rosette wanted her parents to do as Ray's parents did in taking on roles of parents until their son became comfortable enough within himself to be a father to the son who he obviously loved. The resentment she felt such disdain of her parents was hiding behind the love she had for them. She understood, the mere fact that her parent's intentions were good, but they did not know how devastated it made her feel to give up the man and the child she wanted to keep, to obey their feelings of her to give her son up for adoption and stop having any contact with the man she loved because it would confuse their child when she could so obviously not be able to reveal her identity to him because her parents felt it would hinder her from becoming all that she can be in life. Little did they know how truly it would have propelled her to be even greater than what she had become because she would have had a purpose for being great. She would become an example of strength and achieving one's goal to her son because he and his father were the true love of her life. Unfortunately, she did not really know that Ray's parents would raise their son.

Rosette only knew that Ray distanced himself from her but she did not know why. It did not add up, because he definitely made her feel his eternal love for her in everything he said and did prior to her giving birth to their son. Rosette tried to forgive her parents and Ray, the love of her live and she thought she had moved on. However, this what not so. Rosette began to realize that now that she was going through therapy in which her Psychologist, Romeo, and her now friend and Psychiatrist, Frank has helped her see and work through. Rosette was just as open to Frank as she was with Ramon, possibly even more so because she felt Frank's love and friendship toward her although he never spoke those words to her. Even still, Rosette although she was developing romantic feelings for Frank, she had determined within herself that she was not well enough relationship wise to give Frank the love he so deserved. She felt that her friend, Mary was more suited for Frank at this time then she was. Although she was becoming more healthier in regard to wanting a more lasting relationship with men and not dwell in the past of wanting only Ray, she still was not there, quite yet.

Frank at the end, asked Rosette, do she feel comfortable in informing him of the man she has held on to all these years and why she cannot forgive him and her parents for what she feels, as the worst thing they could do to her, by being instrumental in not helping her to keep the man and the baby she so desperately wants to keep and raise. She was devastated in her mind, body, and her emotions. It left a lasting doom on her heart. She had attachment issues with men and also with trusting others. Her brothers on the other hand were very sympathetic in what had happened to her. They loved and supported their sister in everything. They shared all through her pregnancy that they would help her to raise her baby even if her parents or the father would not. After they had heard that their parents had made her give the baby up for adoption and soon found out that Ray and his parents was raising their child. It hurt their heart that they too had to keep that knowledge from their sister.

Although through the years, Rosette brothers, Peter and Perry, tried to comfort their sister that they are sure her son is being raised by people that love and support him. They tried to encourage her she can meet someone else when she is ready and have other children one day, but now focus finishing high school and going on to college. You are so brilliant, her brothers would always tell her, to not be the person you are meant to be to be instrumental in helping so many people. You are very loving and caring. You are the most beautiful woman that we know. We will continue to be your support system and encourage you because we love you and we do want you to be able to live lift to the fullest and become such a independent thinker again, strong, and willful. A force to be wrecking with. It is true because of faith and her brother's continuing to be her greatest cheer leaders, she did finish high school with honors and went on to be #1 basketball scholar in both men and women sports at her college, go on to be top 10 basketball player in the nation in WNBA and NBA, and end her career coaching the same WNBA team she was so successful in playing for. Rosette did admit that in her lowest moments, God was still there for her. As, she looked back over her life, she realized that Jesus had carried her through those rough moments just like the great poem stated in the "Footprints in the Sand."

Rosette told Frank that right now the only thing she felt comfortable in revealing was that she sees now how her never really forgiving the love of her life and her parents for not staying the course and helping her raise the son she so desperately wanted to keep, as far as the man who she still loved after all these years, she did not feel comfortable enough to reveal his name because she had heard from her brothers that he had retired from NFL after a lustrous career and up for a nomination into Hall of Fame, had moved back home. They also shared that because he was not there for her after she had delivered their son and seemed to have cut her from his life, they did not continue their friendship with him, after they had heard he was indeed the father of her baby. It was years afterwards but they could not maintain their friendship with him because they did not want their sister too feel even more uncomfortable than she already was. Rosette did share how the man she had loved all of these years that had fathered their child to a tee. As Rosette, began to describe the man, Frank almost gasped and drop the pen he was writing notes on his note pad with. He could not believe his ears, as Rosette was describing someone that both Romeo and he knew quite well. Romeo's father, Ray. Frank never mentioned his thoughts of this because he was more interested in Romeo continuing his sessions with Rosette.

Frank imagined in his heart that Romeo himself will come to know the identity of the man very soon. Frank knew that Romeo would learn of the truth very soon, because he had the ability to help his clients reveal their oppressors rather in people, thoughts, actions, or circumstances. Franks said, "Very well Rosette. I feel that you have made great strides to know where you are and where you need to go to move forward in your live and even have a more fulfilling life with a man, I feel now, you will let into your life and trust him knowing that you have the ability to trust better. It is going to continue to be a work in progress, but as you forgive people that have hurt you, you will be able to be healed, mentally, physically, and emotionally. Frank walked Rosette to door after he made her next appointment in two weeks. He informed her that maybe Romeo will be back from his Rehab from his car accident by then, if not, he promised that he will still be present for her as her Counselor. She was happy on both fronts as she got into her car and drove home. Rosette decided to stop by her eldest brother's home first. He had three children with his lovely wife of 10 years. She adored her two nieces and her nephew who was the oldest. She had imagined in her heart that her son would have been much like him.

Rosette made it to her eldest brother, Perry's home. Her nieces and nephew met her at the door and hugged her waist so tightly, that it was hard for her to breath. Perry's wife, Sarah said, "Guys let her breath." They finally let up her and she was able to breathe again." Rosette said, "I love you all as well." By that time, her brother, Perry, walked to the door and hugged his sister just as tight as their children just did. That is most likely where the children got it from but Rosette knew it was out of love. Perry said, "What's up little sister? You are as gorgeous as ever. As always it is so good to see you." Rosette, hello big brother any my sister, as she waves to Perry's wife, Stephanie, how are you all? As always it is so wonderful to see you all as well. I just missed talking with you guys. Peter is out of town on business. It is hard catching up with our other sibling isn't it, Perry?"

Perry said, "Yes, definitely. Since he does the traveling portion of our business, he stays on the move. He is like you in many ways. Me, myself, after retirement, from the NFL, I was done with all the traveling. I just wanted to do a 9-5 in the career I went to college for, and that is to be a computer analyst, but of course, because of my fame, they bumped me up to an administrative managing role because they knew I had a lot of back ground in it since I did a lot of interns in the summers while going to college and even during my NFL career." Rosette said, "Yes, Perry, we know that you loved playing football but did not like the traveling so much. You have always been a home body. It is a good thing it did not interfere with your game. You were one of the #1 Running backs in the NFL and all times. I also hear that You and Peter are going to be inducted into the Hall of Fame this year. You guys already told me about Ray is up for nomination to the Hall of Fame."

Perry said, "Yes mam. Peter and I was blessed to have all yes on our vote to be inducted in the Hall of Fame last year. Peter in the NBA Hall of Fame and myself in the NFL Hall of Fame. We are honored to join our heroes in the game. Yes, we heard by some of our old colleagues that Ray will also have a unanimous yes vote to be inducted into the Hall of Fame. We may have cut ties with him after the traumatic history you two had together but we respected his game, He was something to behold. He was tall but 6 ft 4 with lean muscle but as fast as lightning. He was one of the best Receivers that I ever seen in the game." "Rosette said, "I have to agree. Although we went through what went through, I checked in on him from time to time just to make sure he is okay. Perry it is funny, I would always see this young man with his parents cheering for him in the stands. He looked a lot like Ray. Oh well, maybe it was one of his nephews."

Perry said, "Maybe, that would be a good question for Ray. Maybe, you ought to call him and you too reconnect. Maybe, after all of this time. The air will be a little clearer, and you guys can get some closure so that you can possibly heal. I know how traumatic it was for you to not only give your son up for adoption but also to lose Ray at the same time. I am sure Ray had his reasons, but I unfortunately, cannot speak for him. Sister, just know that Mom and Dad regret not helping you raise your child during that time. They just though it may have hindered your pathway to great things. They did not take heed to Ronnie and I when we told them that we will also help in raising your son. They thought we were too young as well and knew we were in our last year of high school and had already accepted full scholarships to out of town colleges to play Division A1 football and Peter to play Division A1 basketball. They did not see how it was going to work out when they were also super busy in their careers. They did not believe in abortion so they thought adoption was the best way to see that the child gets with a great loving family if you or them could not raise your son at the time. Please forgive them sister. I have seen mom and dad go from happy go lucky to just getting through the day sort of thing. They simply adore my three children and Peter's twin girls with his wife, but they regret that they did not help or at least raise your son so that they could also be a part of his life. They also knew that even now; it has put a strain on you and their relationship. Yes, you call to check up on them to see how they are, but they miss seeing you as often as they believe they would have if only they would have supported you during the time you needed them most."

Rosette said, "I know Perry bear, as she often called him even when they were growing up, I am working on forgiving mom and dad completely as well as Ray, even Ray's parents for not stepping up to help him raise our son, but there is still things that I am trying to work through because to me both our parents should have assisted us in raising our son. That is what I can't seem to get passed. I am not a shame to let you know now, I am going through therapy to help me to resolve this issue in my life that has prevented me from loving another man or even having a lasting relationship with a man because I keep seeing Ray, the man, I truly have not stop loving." Perry shook his head, "Wow, Sister, that is something else to have on your mind all of these years. I am so sorry you had to endure this terrible situation. I know when you see my oldest son, Donnie, it hurts your because you believe your son would have possibly been a lot like him being his first cousin." Rosette said, "Yes, how did you know?"

Perry said, "Because I know you my dear. I know my sister. You, Peter, and I were very close growing up. Although, you did a lot of girly things with your female friends, you were still a tomb boy and could play basketball better than any of us. Girl, you were darn good even in Middle School. I guess it pays when you just had brothers with no sisters to play with when we were growing up." Rosette said, laughing, "Thank you Perry Bear for saying darn good because I know you wanted to say something else. Yes, I know you love to say four letter words, but you respect your wife, children, and me so you are a lot more cordial especially now that you have matured. Perry, your mouth was very foul growing up away from mom and dad. Peter and I use to get on you all the time. We do not know where you got that foul mouth from. You use to say a curse all the time."

Perry said, "Yes, I know. They also put up with me in college and the NFL. No one could believe how a nice guy as they looked at me had such a foul mouth. I believe it was Stephanie who helped me tone down my cursing because she witnesses how well my vocabulary was and encouraged me all the time to use the vast words that I knew and not to substitute them with curse words. She would always say, people will respect you more so by being intelligent then having a foul language, especially if you want to be known for more than just a football player after your NFL career ends. Man, she really got me to thinking about life after football." Rosette said, "I agree. You and Peter got the best of the best women to marry. Professional, intelligent, and beautiful." Perry said, "Yes, just like our little sister and our mother. We could have it no other way. With mom and you having the bar set up so.... high. We definitely got dad's taste in women"

Rosette said, "I don't know about all of that but I can say you and Peter did a great job in your choosing the cream of the crop." Perry said, "Sister we all want you to be happy like we are with the person you choose to spend the rest of your life with. Forgiveness is definitely a key to moving on, but sometimes you need help from God to do so. I know mom and dad did not take us to church a lot while growing up, but I believe they now, wished they did. Sister, they have really changed. Even as they were raising us, they still taught us biblical principles and they tried to show us how a man and woman should love each other in a marriage but because they were not there for you when you needed them, they never really got pass that either. Maybe, you can help them to get passed their hurts as well. Maybe you can lead them in the passage to forgive themselves as you forgive them." Rosette said, "Perry, I know. Ronnie has also tried to talk to me about this same thing several years ago. I know you mentioned it five years ago when I came to support you in one of your final NFL games. Hopefully, with therapy and actually allowing the power of the Holy Spirit helping me to forgive, I finally will. I will be set free from this bondage that I have held on to for all of these years." Perry said, "Yes, Sister. I will be helping you pray for strength. We want to see some little Rosette running around here with our children. Hopefully, that will come before they become adults, Lol."

Rosette said, "Yes, maybe so, big brother. Hopefully. I now can see myself going toward that now. I have made strides to wanting that. At first, I could never see that in my life. I was burdened down in grief. I want to that you and Peter for being there for me along this terrible journey. You guys, have been my life source with the help of the Lord to get up in the morning and still thrive even though in my heart it was so.........hard. Yes, my friends helped me to. Thank God, I was able to still have some happiness and joy in my life in my basketball career and educational studies. All of you have definitely kept me sane through all of this. "Thank you, Lord." Rosette got up praising the Lord." Perry's wife and his three children ran into Perry's office where he went in for quite time, to see what was going on.

Perry said to them, "All is well family. Rosette is finally getting her breakthrough. It's been a long time coming, but I feel the Holy Spirit in this room." Stephanie said, "Yes, baby. I feel his presence as well. This Spirit is peaceful and full of Grace. Wow, this feeling is so full of completeness." Sister, I feel your healing coming on." Rosette, praised the Lord for a good five minutes. Perry and Stephanie 's children recognized when the Holy Spirit was present because they witnessed this occurring many times at different church services. Perry and Sabrina were raising their children in the Lord just as Peter and his wife are doing. They both made that choice to become faithful to the Lord in their college years and they sought out Christian believing women so that they could be equally yoked. They were blessed to find Stephanie and Penelope.

Rosette started to squat down on the floor and tears flowing from her eyes and she sat there still as a statue. Her nieces and nephew hugged their aunt to comfort her until she came to herself and looked around and saw them and her handsome brother and his beautiful wife coming near her and their children to squat down on the floor and started to pray God, loving power to come into Rosette's heart, mind, and spirit, to help her to move forward and not stay in the same grief and pain that she has now lived in for 14 years. They prayed that she will forgive all that did not assist her in raising her baby and for those that left her, Ray, in her mind, whom she had a hard time forgiving because he was the love of her life. Loving him with her whole heart has been a blessing and a cursing. A blessing that they created their son. A cursing because she had to give him up for adoption and it seemed that Ray left her when she needed him the most.

Perry's children gather around their aunt. Encircling her by joining hands with their parents. The spirit of the Lord came through Rosette, Jacqueline, Rochelle, Lavone, Stephanie, and Perry as their heart began to burn and tears of joy flowed from their eyes and all of their countenance of their face was lifted and they all were happy in their heart and smiled. Rosette felt free. She actually felt the heavy burden of grief and pain had lifted from her. For the first time since she was 16 y/o she finally felt like she could go on with the rest of her life. Love and be loved. She realized she was in darkness and depression all of those years and finally that weight was gone. Rosette got up from the floor with her brother Perry and her nephew Lavone helping her. Rosette said," Family, for the first time in years, I feel free from my grief and pain. I don't have to pretend anymore to be happy. I am happy. Thank God for his deliverance Than God for my family praying for me. It was at this very moment that God chose at this time to set me free. Thank God, Almighty. I am free." They all did a group hug with each other and Stephanie said, "Now, let's eat. I put the food in the oven to stay warm while you and Rosette were in your study talking.

They all set at the table and ate homemade Lasagna, Corn, salad, bread sticks, and Stephanie's famous peach and apple cobbler in one pie with ice cream for dessert. They all ate well, laughed, and talked. Perry asked Rosette to spend the night with them. They had an extra bedroom. Perry said, besides isn't this your home away from home. My goodness you have a dresser full of clothes that my wife had washed for you. We might as well say, "This is Rosette room, and have the other two bedrooms for guests." Stephanie and Rosette said at the same time, "I agree." Those two were peas in a pot. They got along instantly possible because they were so much alike and had all things in common. Stephanie and Rosette were like sisters from the same parents as close as they were. The two them would spend hours together just talking about life when Rosette would spend the night. The two of them were also close to Penelope, Peter's wife. They went out to dinner, shopping, movies, and spa events all the time. Yes, Rosette was blessed t0 have her brothers still very close to her especially since she had distanced herself from her parents. She did have her friends she made in college and that were on her college and WNBA basketball team. She could bond with women but she had problems bonding with love interests even though she was still greatly attracted to them. She just maintained her distance and therefore that inhibited her from forming a bond and a trust with them. Unfortunately, each relationship would fizzle out as quick as it came.

Perry and his family hugged Rosette as she said her goodbyes. Rosette headed home after stopping for some take out at her favorite restaurant. She ate her meals and took a long hot bubble bath and afterwards went to sleep in her cozy bedroom with the most amazing mattresses. She slept very well.

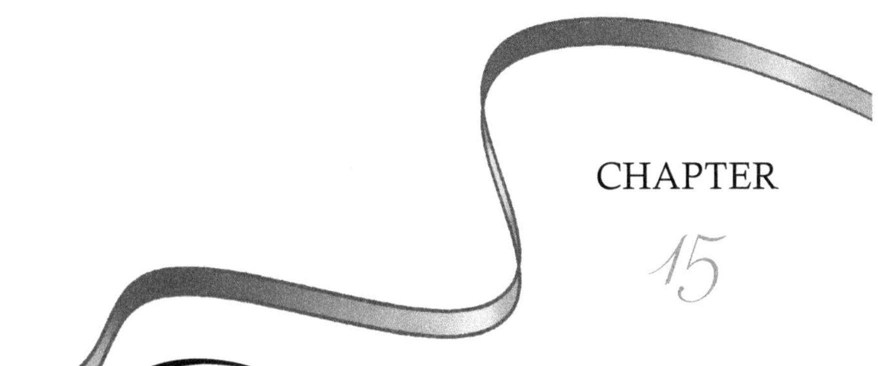

CHAPTER

15

Tom finished his work day and was travelling home when he noticed someone that looked like his ex-wife, Nancy going into a nearby restaurant by the home he shared with her when they were married. Of course, after their divorce he had moved out. It was one of his greatest creations for residential homes. It was his made especially for his wife during their marriage. Nancy had informed Tom, her dream home. Tom had designed it would a few more bells and whistles aiming to wow her. Tom was successful in doing so. He could not see himself taking away the home he had specifically designed for her away in a long-drawn-out court battle. Tom pulled over into the restaurant parking lot, parked, and went into the restaurant to see if he could locate her. He had wanted to talk to her weeks ago but had not built enough nerve to do so. This was his chance, he thought.

When Tom steeped into the building, he did not see anyone that looked like Nancy, but as he turned around to go out, he heard the sound of her voice. He followed the voice that sounded like Nancy. There she was, as beautiful as ever. His heart started to pound very fast. He was excited and nervous at the same time. She looked up and saw him. He almost ran the other direction, but before she had a chance, Nancy called his name out, "Tom, Tom is that you." Tom said, "Hello, Nancy, yes, it is me. How are you?" Nancy said, "I am doing well. What are you doing here?" Tom, was not short of words and he was always frank about everything. That was one of Tom's characteristics that she loved. "Well, to be honest, I saw some that looked like you going into this restaurant, and because I needed to discuss something with you, I took a chance, pulled over into the parking lot of the restaurant to see if it was indeed, you." Nancy said, "Yes, it is indeed me. I needed to also discuss somethings with you as well. I was also meaning to call you but I figured you were still at work in late evening like you were accustomed doing, so I did not call because I did not want to disturb you." Tom said, "Yes, I have been putting in a lot of late hours trying to complex residential projects and designing some corporate building that I was hired to do, but please, next time, do not hesitate to outreach me. I still have your special ring tone alerting me that it's you, I will be sure to answer or return your call as soon as I can.

Nancy said, "Thank you Tom. To be honest, I still have your special ring tone on my phone and please do me the same honors, call me anytime. I don't mind at all." Nancy looked at Tom. She acknowledged; he was the most rugged, tall, handsome man that she is still very attracted to. She started to think over their romantic past and got lost in the moment for a minute. Tom was an excellent very passionate Lover. He used to say all the time, A marital bed is undefiled. So let us enjoy ourselves to the fullest with ecstasy. Tom had a way of wooing her romantically. She did miss him very much.

69

Especially, romantically. Tom was her 2nd Lover, so she knew the difference between someone that was merely having sex then one who was truly making love to only her. She burned with passion every single time we interacted romantically, but to her dismay, the sexual encounters became more and more less frequent, as their relationship began to dwindle.

Tom was talking to her and started to call her name, "Nancy, Nancy can you hear me?" Nancy was startled a little at hearing her name, finally. I t brought her out of her trance of thinking about their lovemaking which was very fulfilling. Nancy answered Tom and said, "Oh, hello Tom. Yes, I am still with you. I apologize. I got swept in my thoughts." Tom said, "Oh ok. I hope your thoughts were pleasant." Nancy was so happy he did not inquire of what she was thinking about. She said, "Yes, Tom. They were very pleasing." Nancy said, "Come have a seat with me Tom. I am just ordering a meal for tonight. I thought I might treat myself because I too, have been working long hours. Please, sit with me, order anything, it is my treat." Tom said to himself, "Wow, this is different. She always allowed me to pay for everything." Nancy said, "I know what you are thinking Tom. I learned how to read your nonverbal body language very well." As he set near her at the table, he leaned over to kiss her on her forehead and said, "Oh yea, what was I thinking about?" Nancy said, "I know you were thinking about, wow, she is wanting to pay. When we were married, I let you pay for everything. Tom, it was not because I wanted to, but because you always wanted to make sure you paid for the finances in our family." Tom said, "Yes, you are right. I thought I was supposed to do such, but you know, I was wrong. I should have not taken your independence away like that. That is something I deeply regret, now that I think back at things. That is the main reason why I wanted to talk with you."

Nancy said, "Oh my goodness, Tom. Just your acknowledgement, is something great because, I did not receive any of this when we were marriage. I thought you just shrugged things off as me complaining and you probably felt, I should have been more appreciative. Tom, please know I always was very appreciative as the man you are. You take care of your responsibilities. I just wanted my husband to include me in everything but it seems as if you just did it and that was that."

Tom said, If I could go back in time and correct my flaws. I would do that in a heartbeat. He looked at Nancy with his big green eyes into her beautiful hazel brown eyes and said, "Nancy, I am so sorry, I ruined our marriage. You are the only woman that I have known besides my mother, that I have the deepest respect for. All I wanted to do was to make sure you did not want for anything, just like I did for my mom. I started being the man of the family when my father left us because my mom was so devastated, she had sunk into a deep depression. I started working in carpentry helping my grandfather, uncles, and men in my grandparent's neighborhood that we had to move into because my mom could not afford the upkeep of our home with my dad. I thought for a while my mom was going to be lost to her grief. She was so dysfunctional. She loved my dad so much. My grandparents helped my mom to raise me until she became stronger. They often tried to encourage her to look at your beautiful son. They referred to me as being beautiful because my face was always angelic until I got about 16 y/o and started to grow facial hair that hid my angelic face. I try to keep a small beard with a mustache because it makes me look more rugged and less beautiful as my grandparents would say all the time. I am 6'2 and very slender and muscular but model like. I even did some modeling when I was growing up just to bring in some extra money when my mom and I moved into our own place.

Thankfully, my mom having strong loving Christian parents, it helped my mom to grow stronger each and every day because they constantly encouraged her to make her focus about me, the son she loves more than herself and the man that left us. With the help of my grandparent's pastor counseling with my mom and some of the other ladies in the church befriending her taking her out on lunch and shopping adventures. By the help of the Lord and people loving us through all of this, it helped my mom join life again. I never wanted the woman that I decided to marry and be with for the rest of my life to ever experience such a tragedy over the love of a man that was lost. Nancy, I guess, I was over compensating with you because I experienced such things with my mom. I wish I could go back and fix those flaws that contributed to the end of our marriage, now that I realize what was occurring."

Nancy looked at her very handsome, ex-husband with tears in her eyes, "Tom, wow, I knew you and your mom went through some rough patches when your dad left and you started to work very early in your life to help your mom get back on her feet financially, but I did not know of the impact it had on you presently. I guess, the old saying is, whatever happens in your childhood affects your adulthood if you don't come to terms with it and correct any negativity that could alter your life of ultimate happiness in one or more areas of your life. Wow, Tom. All I can say, it was not only you. I had some part in our marriage ending. I no longer was that sweet but strong woman you fell in love with. I became bitter and argumentative because I felt like you were never listening to me although I tried multiple time to share with you what things were bothering me in the way you would not include me in any of our marital affairs rather it was emotionally, mentally, or financially. I believe the only thing that remained a constant was out physical love making. It was always intense and very pleasurable, but even that became less and less frequent because we just were not getting along."

Tom said, "Yes, you are right. I was not listening. I was just too task oriented and stuck in production mode. That is possibly why I am so success now, as an architect. Nancy, if it is okay with you, can I take you out on a date from time to time. I do not want to impose if you have someone else, but I wanted to show you, this is not something, I take lightly. I have truly changed and I want to show you that I am the man that I should have been when we were marriage. I am sure that if we would have been open to counseling and I was determined to look pass my own faults, we would not have ended up divorced."

Nancy, was truly crying now. She looked at Tom with intense passion and said, "Tom, bless your heart. I can see you have changed. I hear it in every word you speak. Tom, I do not have anyone in my life. I am still grieving over my marriage to you. Tom, I am not looking to start a new relationship without knowing what went wrong in ours. I do not want to carry the baggage that we have to someone else. I wish not to go through this nor do I wish you to. To answer your question, yes, I will. I will go out with you. I would rather us to keep talking and sorting things out than start a new relationship. I do have a one question before we start these discussions. "May, I ask the question?"

Tom said, "Yes, my sweet. You may ask me anything. What is your question?" Nancy said, "Tom, do you still love me and think things can work between the two of us? One more thing if I may? Tom nodded his head yes. Nancy continued, "Do you believe that we can continue to talk things through like we are doing now? I don't want to look backwards, but before, talking to you was like talking to a brick wall. You were so unyielding and task oriented that I never could get anything through to you, at least it seemed that way." Tom grabbed Nancy hand and kissed her on the forehead and looked at her so dearly and said, "My dear. I will be honest, it will take some time and work but if we both put in 100% and not walk away when times get hard, along with much prayer and guidance from the Lord. I believe we can make it happen." Tom pulled Nancy close to him and kissed her passionately as if he never wanted to let her go. Nancy returned his affection and before they got too carried away with passion that was clear they continued to burn deeply for each other. "They came to themselves, and looked at each other with longing in their eyes and said at the same time, we are drawing attention to ourselves." They both started to laugh. Tom said, "Can, I call you later this week?" Nancy said, "Of course, Tom. I will look forward to us talking again. I believe the more we talk the closer we will get. At least, I am hoping so." Tom said, "Yes, my dear. Me too." Tom walked Nancy to her car and they both drove home with ecstasy feelings toward one another as a result of what happened between the two of them. There was no change in how they were passionate toward one another, but the real change was how they were able to talk things through. That never occurred before when they were married. Nancy, wanted to see if it lasts and it is just because they were missing each other.

When Nancy made it home, she text Tom, "Good night. I made it home. I enjoyed talking and seeing you this evening." Tom text back and informed her, he was pulling up to his driveway and that he had also enjoyed talking and seeing her as well and could not wait to see and talk with her again." They both slept peacefully.

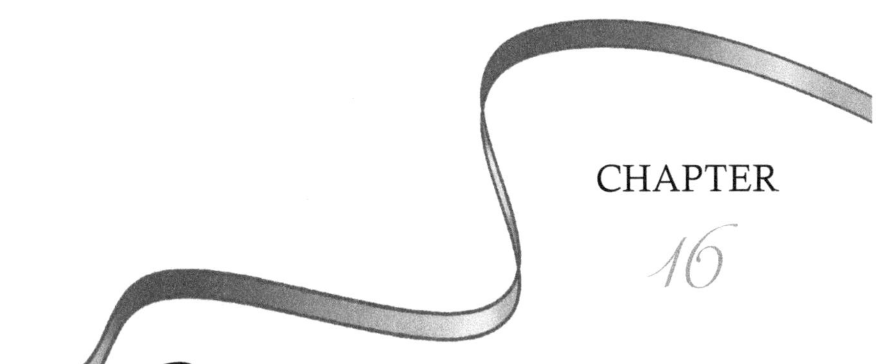

CHAPTER

16

onday morning came around too quickly. Jasmine and Romeo had kept up with each other by phone because Romeo was recuperating from his Rehab. He had finally made it home and was resting in his own home. He exhaled and said to himself, "It is so good to be home." He began to think about Jasmine. He wanted to call her but he knew she was at work and seeing patients. It was only 11:00 am. Romeo heard a knock at his door. He asked who is it from his chair. The female voice said, "It is Jasmine Romeo. I am checking on you to see if you need anything." Romeo got up from his recliner and as quickly as he could made it to his front door, to let her in. Romeo unlocked his front door and opened it. Jasmine was as beautiful as ever. She had her white lab jacket still on under small black chemise dress that came to her knees with black wide based pump for comfort when walking. She also had her glasses on. Romeo never seen her with glasses on in her lab jacked before. He thought to himself, "So this is her professional side."

Jasmine said, "Excuse me Romeo. I saw my last morning patient and wanted to come that you have everything conveniently by you so you want have to over exert yourself." Romeo said, "Thank you Jasmine. That is so thoughtful of you." Jasmine said, "No problem at all. I remember when we spoke last night over the phone you had informed me that you will be discharged home from Rehab in early morning today." Romeo said, "Yes. Thank you for remembering but I did not want to interfere with you seeing your patients." Jasmine said, "Oh no. It was not an issue. I was more concerned about not being able to see you make it hope then my busy schedule at work. Why didn't you call me. I would have picked you up." Romeo said, "Jasmine. I would have loved that but my father spent a night with me on my last day at the Rehab hospital so that he could take me home. I did not want to disturb your busy schedule."

Jasmine said, "Oh, okay. Just long as you made it home safely is what matter. Please know that it is never a bother. I just want you to know you can count on me." Romeo said, "Jasmine, thank you for saying that. I had a good feeling you was that person for me early on. Thank you for confirming it." Jasmine said, "All is well. Don't hesitate to call on me. Beforehand if possible. Even if it is the same day, please don't hesitate to call." Romeo said, "I understand. I will call upon you if needed without hesitation." Romeo felt as if he could not grow more in love with her but today, she proved to him that the love for her is endless and it will always have potential to grow. Romeo asked Jasmine to come sit by him. She did so. Romeo leaned toward her face and kissed her softy with great passion. Jasmine returned the passion with great tenderness. She knew she had already fallen in love with him but she also realized her passion was growing for him each time they talked or saw each other. She burned for him a likewise she felt that he did for her as well. Non visible fireworks went off in each of their bodies so much so they thought they would explode if that fire was no resolved. So, when Romeo start kissing her the way he was she was also able to let some of the steamy passion out that she was feeling as well.

Romeo kissed her passionately at the same time laid her body on his couch that they were sitting on and climbed on top of her. He put his hand underneath her dress and begin to caress her breast. Jasmine began to moan with ecstasy. Jasmine could feel him rising. She thought to herself my goodness, I did not expect him to be so endowed. She began to reach for him and fondle him as she felt him grow. Both of them burned intensely for each other. Romeo began to pull her lace panties down to her knees. She moved her leg so that he could smoothly finish taking them off. He lifted his body and began to pull his pants off, and then his shirt. He grabbed himself where he was growing between his legs and was just about to penetrate her when Jasmine cell phone began to ring.

That is when Romeo looked at her and realized that their passion had taken over. He did not want their first time to be rushed so he pulled his body away from her and pulled his pants back up his thighs at the same time Jasmine was saying, "No, Romeo. Don't stop. Don't stop." Romeo looked at her while she stayed in a lying position as she was trying to pull him back on top of her so that they could finish what they had begun. She had been hoping to finally be with him in that manner. Romeo stared at her naked body. She was absolutely stunning. She was slender but she had curves all in the right places. He was just about to lay back upon her when her cell phone rang again. This time, Romeo got up, and went to his closed and pulled out a plush light blanket and laid it upon her body.

Jasmine did not know why he stopped exactly but she answered the call. It was her mother. Her mother called to asked her was she coming back to the office because she had an emergency and she wanted her to see her afternoon appointments. Jasmine had informed her mom that she had taken the rest of the day off but informed her that she would come in to see her patients. She asked her mom to give her an hour than she will be there. Jasmine's mom thanked her and the call ended. Romeo came out of the bathroom with another set of Nike jogging pants and shirt on. The colors were dark green and black. It accented his gorgeous eyes and olive skin tone. He was as if he was a Greek God. He was very handsome; she could not stop staring at him. Romeo said, "Jasmine, dear are you alright.?" Jasmine barely heard him. Romeo said again, "Jasmine are you okay?" Jasmine came out of her trance and said, "Oh my goodness. I am sorry Romeo. I had my mind on other things." Yes, on him. She wanted to finish what they had begun. She was still in the heat of the moment, but she knew she had to prepare to go to see her mom's patients this afternoon. She had hoped to spend the evening with him to make sure all was well with him so he would not over exert himself.

Jasmine said, "Romeo you are looking good. I am sorry. I wanted us to keep going. Why did you stop?" Romeo said, "Jasmine, trust me. I wanted you so much but I wanted you to feel my entire love foe you as I make passionate love to you. I did not want to rush things between us. Like, I said I want our relationship to last and not rush things. As you can see. I am yet a man and I wanted to fulfill my fleshly desires for you but I know that only lasts for a moment but I want our love to be full of this kind of passion but also enduring love that surpasses all of the earthly desires. Don't get me wrong. As, I speak, I still want to lie you back down and enter you to feel your warm body next to mine and your inner warmth as well, but……"

Jasmine placed her index finger on his lips and said, "I know Romeo. I know. I feel the same way. You are not alone. Maybe it is fate. Although both us yearn and burn for each other, timing was just not right now. That was my mother. She wanted me to come back into the office. She has an emergency that came up, and she needed me to see her afternoon patients. I had taken off the rest of the day to make sure all was well with you since you were just discharged home from Rehab. By the way, I was going to ask how are you doing, but you answered that on how quickly we went from saying hello to almost making love in a matter of minutes. I guess the time away from each other in person had built up and we needed to release that passion that was inside of us."

Romeo said, "You are right my dear as usual then he leaned over and kissed her lips." Jasmine had managed to pull her clothes back up and asked Rome could she use his bathroom to freshen up? Romeo informed her yes, anytime. Jasmine went into the bathroom and washed her face. She re applied a light covering of her make up and lipstick and took her comb out of her purse and pulled her hair in a pony tail and placed her glasses and lab jacket back on. She finished refreshing herself and walked back out to Romeo. Romeo loved Jasmine so much and his love was ever growing. Jasmine felt the same way. They hugged each other tightly and kissed each other with loving longing within their bodies. Jasmine almost stayed and took her clothes off again but she pulled away and kissed him again, and asked him could she call him when she got off. Romeo said, "Of course. You never have to ask. You can call me anytime." Jasmine left and Romeo turned his TV on, and tried to concentrate on the movie he had turned to but he could not. He could not think of anything other than making love to Jasmine. He wanted her so intensely.

Jasmine was mesmerized by Romeo. She did not actually know how to picture him intimately, but now she had some indication that he was well endowed and from what she had gathered in that heat of the moment he was a very passionate lover. She thought to herself how ready she was to take their love to the next level but she was somewhat happy they are waiting. She made it to the office and inside the building at least 10 minutes giving her time to look at the patients charts she was to see and the last progress notes. She had three of her mom's patients to see this afternoon they were 30 minutes apart which gave her a little extra time to look at their charts again to learn each patient's physical and mental history so she would be properly prepared. Each patient was very delightful and had their own individual issues that her mom was doing a follow up on. Jasmine's mom was brilliant. Her dad was too. Thinking about it, she had no choice than following in their footsteps of studying Medicine because it was all in her genes.

Jasmine saw her mom's last patient and wrote their prescriptions and ongoing diagnostic testing and gave it to her mom's nurses to call the medication into the pharmacy and schedule the diagnostic testing for each patient and call them with the details of the scheduled testing. Sometimes, the nurses rotated between the doctors of the group but there was at least one head nurse to each physician. It just worked better that way. Jasmine finished her day in the office and was headed out of the building when her dad, called out to her. Jasmine turned around and saw her handsome father and asked her day, "Dad, hello, did you need anything from me before I left for the day?" Jasmine's father said, "No, I just wanted to say, hello, and see my beautiful daughter before she left home for today." Jasmine said, "Oh dad, you always know just what to say, Mr. Casanova." I can see why mom and your wife fell head over heels in love with you. You not only have the looks but you are a charmer as well."

Jasmine's dad said, "Oh well, daughter. You know me all too well, don't you?" as he chuckled. They hugged each other as she was stating her good byes. She told him that Romeo was discharged home this morning and she wanted to make sure he was okay before she went home. Jasmine's dad said, "It is great that he has made it home safely. I am sure you will take good care of him. I want to invite you two over for dinner or take you two out with us. Have a night on the town. We work too much. We need to have good life and work balance." Jasmine said, "That is true dad. Let us know and we will make it happen. "Jasmine dad said, I will do. I will also invite your mom and her husband as well. Thank God, we all get along." Jasmine said, "Yes Lord. Thank God." Jasmine got into her car and put her seat belt on and reached into her purse to get her cell phone out. She put it on the cup stand cell phone holder and allowed the car to pair with her cell phone so that she did not have to talk with the cell phone in her hand.

She called Romeo and checked on his progress and to see if he needed her to stop by with food. Romeo informed her that he had already eaten a sandwich and chips and he was all good. Jasmine informed him that she was a little exhausted and she was heading home. She will call and check on him tomorrow. Romeo thanked her for checking on him as he prepared his clothes to go into the office tomorrow by 12N. He had already discussed it with Frank. Frank was excited to have him back. He informed him that the Student Psychiatrist would also be present and he would like to do some counseling meeting with him tomorrow if he was up to it. Romeo said as long as the patients is fine with it, I have no issues with it. Frank informed him he had already received verbal and written consents from the two patients he wanted the student Psychiatrist to sit in the counseling sessions with Romeo. Romeo said, "Sounds like a plan."

Frank asked if it was okay to stop by this evening to check in on him. Romeo said, No problem. You are definitely welcome to stop by." Frank kidded with him by saying, "I did not want to interrupt any rondevues with you and Jasmine. I am just saying. I know you all have only talked on the phone lately since you have been in Rehab. You home now, it is no telling what hormones have run while with the two of you." Frank laughed out loud and Romeo laughed with him saying, "Man, you know what time it is. I am a man but I want us not to rush too fast into the sexual intensity but more so get to know each other mentally and spiritually if we have enough self-control to do so. Frank said, "I am not trying to interfere with the endless love portion of you all love affair but passion is passion. It will definitely find a way to exert itself." Romeo said, "Man, don't I know it."

Shortly, after Jasmine had called, Frank was knocking at the door. Romeo ended his call with Jasmine and answered the door and let Frank in. Frank said, "Man, I brought you some soup and crackers with your favorite Lipton tea so you did not have to cook while you are recuperating at home. I know you are coming in tomorrow but don't rush it. I got you covered. I just wanted to give you an update on the patients that I saw while you were out. All of them are progressing very well. All of them had some breakthroughs that will help them to get closer to their goals." Frank finished giving Romeo the reports and they looked at a basketball game of course with opposite teams and enjoyed the rest of the evening laughing, talking, and enjoying the game. Frank left late that evening for home, and Romeo took a shower and went to bed dreaming about making love to Jasmine."

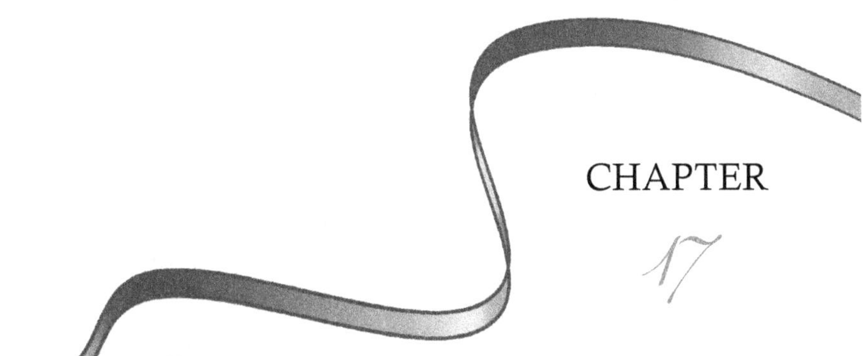

CHAPTER

17

Friday, Saturday, and Sunday were good fast days, Monday came in like a Mighty rushing wind. It was time for Romeo to get back to work. He was excited. He missed counseling others. Helping others to have breakthroughs to get to the next level in their life successfully. Romeo pulled up to the office parking lot in hi black Mercedes Benz. The year of the car was current. He had a white shirt with a designer tie and dressy black pants with Stacy Adams black silver toes limited edition shoes to match his outfit. Romeo dressed for success going into work daily. He was taught how to always look dabber and professional by his grandparents and his father. Yes, he could not have had a better childhood.

Sylvester was sitting in the lobby waiting until Romeo made it to the office. Romeo came into the office and seen one of the patients he was counseling 2-3 years ago. Very traumatic story. The woman was outstandingly beautiful and fit. Her name was Mary, he was trying to remember. She caught his eye and stood up with her right hand outstretched. She said, "Hello Romeo. How are you? It has been a while." Romeo said, "Yes. Yes, it has. What brings you hear and please remind me of what your name is?" The woman said, I am Mary. I say you about three years ago. I was a victim of sexual and physical assault and you helped me to get on with my life. I t was so hard, but I could not quit." Romeo said, "What brings you here?" Mary said, "I had just drooped my nephew off for his rotation with you and Frank. Rome shook Mary hand and went over to Sylvester and shook hand and as well. Romeo introduced himself and inquired of Sylvester, how may Frank and I be of service?

Sylvester stated, I am here to learn become like a human sponge. Romeo said, "You are in the right place. Sylvester said, "So you and my Aunt Mary know each other already. Mary said when I was in my mid 20'. s I was involved in a sexual and physical assault and Romeo helped me, by God's grace, to move forward in my life, successfully. Enjoying what all this world has to offer." Mary said, Romeo, I don't believe I would have made it if it was not the spiritual manner you guided our counseling session." Romeo said, "Yes, indeed. It was a challenge seeing your broken spirit. I had come to look forward to our session because with every session you little face begin to light up more and more each session we had." Sylvester said, "It was my Aunt Mary that informed me about your practice, and thought you would be the idea person to be my mentor. Romeo blushed and said, "I would not mind doing so one bit."

Frank set back and looked at Mary with great admiration. He remembered being with Rosette and her at one of the local restaurants. He felt so close to both of them. It was very easy to be yourself and still have fun and have a spiritual connection with others that you have not known very long. Rosette was definitely who he had this connection with but she felt as if I deserved someone that is whole so that the person he is with would meet every passion that he brought to the relationship. Rosette felt she was not in the frame of mind to be with anyone in that way but nevertheless, she could not stop the great friendship that was developing between the two of them. Frank believes the very reason, Rosette was drawn to him was the very reason why she felt that her friend, Mary, who was like her blood sister, was the woman that would truly make Frank very happy. Frank felt that she was just trying not to give in to love but as he saw Mary, talking with Romeo and how loving and caring she was to her nephew, Sylvester. He felt that Rosette was truly right.

Frank pondered, He felt ashamed because he did not recognize Mary was the young lady that Romeo counseled some 3-4 years ago. That Mary was shy, broken, and never met anyone at eye level. She was ashamed of what had happened to her. The Physical assault and rape had taken its toll on her. She actually was just living, not really enjoying life. That is why when he met Mary through Rosette, he had no idea that she was the Mary that he had described earlier. She was so different. She was beautiful then but her spirit was broken, but when he met her through Rosette, wow, what a transformation. She was not only beautiful but her spirit was bubbly, bright, and lovely that made her beauty even the more powerful. She was well spoken, smart, witty, and quite a fun person to be around. With that one meeting with her and Rosette was enough to tell him that she would make someone a great partner, a wonderful wife.

Frank knew that she was still playing professional basketball and she had at least 3 more years until she retired. Rosette was a fellow player of hers until she became injured and she was such a teacher, that they hired her as a coach. Frank found out through Rosette, that Mary was instrumental for Rosette coming to their clinic for Romeo to counsel her. She knew this because he counseled her with more than education and theory but with spiritual guidance from God. He never preached Jesus to her, but yet it was more of a lifestyle for him. Yes, indeed, he always made reference of Jesus, but to him Jesus was his friend, his brother, his guide, and it showed so vibrantly of his love for Jesus because he served all he met, counseled with, and sang to with the blessed gift that God had given him.

When Romeo was finish with their re acquaintance with Mary, he and Sylvester walked Romeo's first client into his office. Mary set down in the Lobby and pulled out her book. Frank and Mary had spoken to each other earlier before Romeo had arrived. They were happy to see each other. They hugged each other and things just felt so comfortable like he had been knowing her for a long time, even though, he knew that he had not. At least not as a friend. Frank checked in the next client. He was a little early, but he came because something was heavy on his mind. That was the thing about Frank the reason why he was so effective as a psychiatrist. He had a very keen discernment. He could tell what was on others mind. It was their spirit that he felt.

Frank looked at the man and asked him to please come to the counter where he often helped Romeo check in others for their counseling sessions with him. The man's name was Lester. Lester was very troubled today. Usually, he is very alert and peaceful but today he seemed very agitated and his head was hung down. Lester walked up to the counter and his head was held low, and he looked up at Frank and said, "Hello Frank. Did you need something?" Frank said, "No, not exactly. Lester, you know me, I care about the people that we serve here. I noticed your countenance was very bothersome and sad today. Very unlike the upbeat person you usually are. If you need to talk to someone now, I am available."

Lester said, "Would you mind? You are a great observer. I wanted to talk with Romeo, but I really need some relief of some of the things I have experienced over the last two weeks." Frank said to Mary,

"Excuse me Mary, can I get you to greet the other clients that come in the clinic and check them in. I show you, our process.?"

Mary said, "No problem. I will love to help." Mary walked to the counter. Frank showed her how to check in the clients in the appointment book and showed her the recreation area where people could just digress and relax. It was a room full of bright red, yellow, purple, white, blue, tropical flowers, and green plants and large plastic trees. This room was very botanical. It was truly a room that made you feel at ease. She remembered this room but they had added more tropical flowers and added meditation music and electric aroma pots that ministered to their five senses. He also showed her the beautiful play room for the parents that could not get a baby sitter, they could have the children go to the play room and have a good time. Listen to music, use the computers that were donated to the clinic, and also all kind of academic and knowledgeable books that would take them unto another world withing their minds. There were students and older ladies and men that would donate their time to watch the children while they were counseled. They believed in what Romeo and Frank were doing because they were used by God to help so many people to get well in their mind, body, and soul.

Frank walked Mary back to the counter in the front of the clinic. He asked Lester, to please follow him to his office. Frank asked Lester to please sit in the leather chair or lie on the leather coach. Whichever on that would put you in a relaxed mood. Lester chose to lie on the leather couch. Frank began to talk with Lester. "Lester, how have the two weeks that you were telling me about affected you? Please do not leave out anything." Lester said, "Well Frank, those voices are starting to come back. Those troubling voices that want me to do harm to others and myself. I thought I had got passed that. I have not heard them for years." Frank asked Lester, "Lester, I want you to be honest. Are you still taking your medication every day and the dosage that has been prescribed?" Lester said, "Yes, Frank. I have." Frank said, "Can I see the dosage that you are taking now, maybe it needs adjusted."

Lester reached down in his pocket and pulled out his prescription of Quetiapine (Seroquel) 25 mg 1 tablet by mouth twice daily and Temazepam (Restoril) 10 mg one tab by mouth once daily. Frank took out his prescription pad and wrote Lester a prescription for Quetiapine 50 mg 1 tab by mouth three times daily and Temazepam 30 mg 1 tab nightly before bed so that he can rest at night. Frank handed

Lester the prescription and asked him to get it filled today and stop taking the lower prescriptions strengths and start taking the increased dosages. Frank asked Lester has anything changed about his lifestyle and activities. Please share with me some of your day-to-day things you have been doing. Lester said, "I met a woman. She was very nice and beautiful. She has a family that I really do not care to be around. They practice witchcraft and Voodoo and I don't like being around that kind of stuff. The woman I am seeing does not take part of those practices but she loves her family so she overlooks what they do because to her, they are loving parents and her siblings are all very helpful to each other. I know that this type of thing is very unsettling to me but I really do like this woman and I want our relationship to blossom into something special."

Frank asked Lester, "How did he know that her family practices witchcraft and Voodoo?" Lester said, "I know they practice these things because I seen some of the artifacts and readings in one of the rooms they use in these sort of rituals as I was going to the bathroom one day, she and I was visiting them." Frank said, "How do you know about these artifacts and readings that are used in witchcraft ad Voodoo?" Lester said, because I was born in West Africa and am a Nigerian, I noticed these practices in our land as I was growing up. My parents or anyone in our family did not practice this religion because they were Christians, it was still prevalent, nonetheless. We still had the witchdoctors that some of the families still relied on to help their sick and troubled people. They did not want to wait on God, they wanted a right now fix as they often called it." Frank said, "Wow, Lester. I knew you had a slight accent but I did not know your heritage." Lester said, "Yes, I know. It is not very apparent because of my appearance. I appear to be a white man but I am not. I am a black Nigerian man. My mom and dad are black Nigerians but they come from parents, whose parent were enslaved by white masters that went unto our women and impregnated them and these children became people that dwelled in their masters' home. They were taken out of the fields and took care of their Master's and family in the comfort of their master's home. That is when the great divide of our people began to occur because the Master's children who they never claimed as their children were lighter in complexion then most of the field slaves. Often times when these children that grew into adults became older, they mixed with the slaves of the field which normally were darker in complexion. Every so often the genes of their slave master would show up in their children and they would appear as white men and women but in truth they were black. That gene is present within me."

Frank was speechless. He never thought, no, not once, that Lester was anything but a white man. Frank said, "Lester, I always assumed you were a white man because of the color of your skin. I Never would have dreamed that you were a black man or Nigerian because of you name." Lester said, "I know. I am not ashamed of who I am. I do not even hide it. I just don't bring the subject up unless it is relevant. Such as when I hear someone say a racist thing that is hurtful to others."

Frank said, "I have always been comfortable around black people. In England where I am from there are many prominent black people. Back in the day, King George fell in love with a black woman and married her. She was our Queen for a long time. My parents would share stories about their love that their parents and grandparents told them. Now, it is a little different, Authoritative people around the world mix and interact with others and people divide into their small cultures instead of being one people sort of like as it is spoken in the bible, "His people although they are many are one body in Christ." Lester said, "That is what I like about you and Romeo. You all do not preach Jesus and cram it down our throats, but you speak of him and the biblical teachings in such respect and gratitude. It is definitely not mere words that you all speak of, it is a lifestyle for you two, because it is ever present with your dealings with others."

Frank was touched by the words of Lester regarding he and Romeo. Frank never thought of it as such. He just felt commissioned to love and accept people as they are and try to reach them in some way to help them to start living a better life full of enjoyment and peace. Yes, he did admit they went beyond their educational practices and dealt with the spiritual part of man. He felt that God helped them somehow to reach the darkest part of their being to heal them and bring the light unto their world somehow. Frank said, "Thank you Lester. I appreciate your candor. Please share with me more regarding your new friend's family. Did you share with your friend your diagnosis of Bi Polar and Schizo affective disorder?" Lester said," Yes, I did. I also informed her that I take my medication as prescribed daily and I lead a very normal life."

Frank said, "Do you think she mentioned it to her family?" Lester said, "I really do not know. I am not ashamed of my diagnosis. I would not have become upset if she did. It is a lot of people in the world that we interact with that have some sort of mental illness rather they are taking medications like me or merely practicing other things to manage it." Frank said, "This is true but there are some that are not getting treatment at all and they could be a time bomb if aggravating circumstances were to occur."

Lester said, "Yes, that is true. I have seen it firsthand." Frank asked Lester, "If you do not mind me asking, where is your friends' family from? By the way, what is her name?" Lester said, "Her name is Abby for short. Her real name is Abigail. Her family is from New Orleans." Frank said, wow, New Orleans now there is a city with a lot of culture and spirit." Lester said, yes, that is true. Her family are French."

Frank said, "What type of people are they?" Lester said, "They appear to be very open, friendly, and accommodating. They like to feed people." Frank said, "Oh yea. How many times have you eaten with them? Lester said, "Numerous times. Almost every Sunday since I met Abby. Abby is a RN and she works a lot during the week so she never really gets to spend any time with her family much. She lives about two hours away from them and she tries to keep the family tradition of eating together on Sundays. The have a big spread of food and it is quite tasty."

Frank though within himself, "Could it be, that Abigail did tell her parents and family about Lester's diagnosis of schizo affective disorder and Bi Polar and they were somehow trying to cure him because they did not want this disorder to be passed to their grandchildren if their daughter was to marry him. Surely, they most likely see the affect Lester has on their daughter and how she has fallen head over hills in love with him. They see how loving and kind their relationship is. Could they really be doing this? Frank challenged Lester as they closed their counseling session, to please think about over the next two weeks to not go with Abigail to her family's Sunday dinners. To come up with a truthful reason not too and to take her out that Friday or Saturday night because you cannot join her in Sunday. Frank also instructed Lester to make sure he took the prescription to be filled to his local Pharmacy and start taking the increased dosages of his Psychiatric medication today. Lester said, "I will do it. No Problem."

Frank and Lester walked out to the lobby together. Just as they were walking into the Lobby, Sylvester and Romeo was walking their client back to the Lobby. Romeo looked over at Lester and said, "Hello Lester. You are a little early today. Is everything alright?" Lester said, "To be honest, things were very heavy. I have been having troubling things to occur over the last two weeks and it has me in a downward mood." Romeo said, "I am so sorry to hear that. Did you go ahead and speak with Frank about it?" Lester said, "Yes, I did. I hope you don't mind. Frank noticed me looking very different and called me up to the counter and inquired about what was bothering me. You know Frank. He has that sixed sense about things." Romeo said, "Yes, I do know. That is why he is such an effective Psychiatrist. He is truly blessed with a gift." Lester said, "Both of you are. This is an amazing partnership you two have. What a blessing it is to us. This service is greatly needed. You all put a spiritual component into your practice that really helps us to overcome our struggles." Romeo said, "We do our best. We definitely share that passion. I am glad you met with Frank. I am sure you were helped."

Lester said, yes indeed. I definitely was." Frank looked at Romeo and apologized but I see the heavy load on Lester and I wanted him to talk about it to release that heavy burden he was carrying." Romeo said, "No Problem, Frank. I am so glad you are here with me. Our clients really benefit from having a Psychiatrist and a Psychologist in the same practice." Frank said, "I will give you an update later." Romeo said, "Wonderful, that will be great." They both said goodbye to Lester, Sylvester, the other client Barry and Sue who were receiving marriage counseling, and Mary. Before Mary and Sylvester left, Frank thanked Mary for helping them and asked could he treat her to dinner sometimes this week? Mary gave Frank her number and informed him that he can call anytime he needed someone to talk too. Frank looked at her with amazement of her witty personality and said, "Look at you flipping the script. I like that about you, with your witty self. Will do. I certainly will call you." Sylvester and Romeo looked at each other and then looked at Mary and Frank and shook their heads, as they smiled at the mere thought of two deserving people getting to know each other better, would be a good thing.

Mary and Sylvester left and Frank and Romeo stayed over to talk for a little longer before leaving the office. Frank informed Romeo that there were some pertinent things that he needed to talk to him about one of his clients before she came in tomorrow. Frank asked Romeo to follow him into the digress room where the botanical and tropical flowers were. Romeo said, "Frank it must be really serious we have to go into this room." Frank said, "It is all how you interpret what I tell you. I am going to be vague for a purpose but in one of your meetings tomorrow, I want you to pray tonight that God bless you with discernment and also the power to see things that you normally would not, event to ask the right questions to get the answers you are seeking, even if they become too uncomfortable for you to continue." Romeo said, "Man, what are you talking about? Just come out and tell me. I do not know what this could be. You have already given me report of the sessions you had with the clients you counseled when I was in the hospital and Rehab. I do not know where you are going with this."

Frank said, "Yes. You are correct. I have and I did not leave anything out but I had a peculiar meeting with one of your clients that reminded me so much of people that you and I know." Romeo said, Who? Who was the person?" Frank said, "Your Father, Ray but the conversation was inconclusive. I did not have enough information to draw any other conclusions but the person she was describing made me think of a younger version of your dad." Romeo said, "So the client you are talking about is a female. Well that is in inconclusive because the population of my clients is 90% women." Frank looked at Romeo, "Man, I am serious and you giving me sarcasm."

Romeo laughed, "Man, I am not trying to be sarcastic. I am just trying to put everything together with the information you are telling me." Frank said, "I wish, I could go further, but I can't. I was only commissioned in my dreams to give you this information and tell you to pray and prepare yourself. I have not been able to sleep well in a week." Romeo said, "I want ask you anything else. I know this quite serious in all of this preparation. Besides, I know you and I trust you like the blood brother I never had. I was not blessed with any other person besides my younger sister. She is about 10 years younger than I am. My dad was dating her mom when he was in the NFL. She is about 18 years old now and is getting ready to go to nursing school. She wants to be a Certified Nurse Anesthetist. She informed her mother who is a doctor, our father, Ray and myself she has always been interested in that type of work. She voiced if she liked it, she would go on to be a Spinal Surgeon. She is very beautiful and tall. She will work as a model in the summer to pay off her tuition. She knows that her mom and dad can pay for her tuition but she insists she wants to pay for a great portion of her tuition or to be her own sole provider. She said God will show her how to make money legitimately to get her through school. She does not want people to think she is privileged and spoiled."

Frank said, "Wow, she sounds amazing and strong." Romeo said, "My sister is doing some modeling jobs in our town. Her and her mom are coming from San Antonio, Texas where they live and although our father and her mother never married, they managed to stay best friends. My sister's name is Leslie Walker and her mom's name is Ro Sarita. Ro Sarita recently got married her husband is a doctor as well and he will be accompanying them. They will meet up with my father and he will be taking them to put up their things. He insisted they not get a hotel but stay with him. He has plenty of room. My dad has a wonderful heart. I will introduce you to all of them tomorrow. They will be meeting me at the office and I will be taking them to meet my dad at his home before he takes Ro Sarita and her husband Michael out to dinner.

My sister asked me to take her out because she needed to talk to me about something. It sounded very serious. She is just like the women in my life. My grandmother, my aunts, my cousins, Jasmine, and her mom. All of them are so beautiful and have a great spirit to help others. I did not have another choice but love a strong woman like the ones that I have come to know. Jasmine is the woman that I picture asking to marry me. Have and raise children with me. I feel in my heart she is my soul mate. I have never felt closer to any other woman." Frank said, "I can see that. Yes, I definitely believe this to be true." They hugged each other at walk out together to their cars and they both went straight home, showered, and went straight to bed. They were exhausted. Frank lived in a condominium near the office and Romeo stated on the other side of town about 5 miles away.

The next morning, they both seemed refreshed and Romeo could not wait to see his sister, Ro Sarita and her new husband, Michael again. They were at their wedding. Ro Sarita had asked his father to give her away because her father and brother could not make it to the wedding in time. There plane had been delayed and they made it after the ceremony had started. Her parents and her sister and brother witnessed them making their vows and was able to attend the beautiful reception but missed the moment they had intended from the beginning to walk Ro Sarita down the aisle. She wanted the most important men in her life to give her away and that was her father and older brother who helped his parents raise her and her younger sister. He was 12 years older than she was and their little sister was five years younger than she was. Their parents had a little trouble having children and had to rely a fertility drug to help them conceive. No matter, they made beautiful loving parents. They even fostered other children to this day Ro Sarita and her siblings call them their brothers and sisters.

The phone began to ring it was 2:00 pm. Frank answered the phone. It was Rochelle. Rochelle informed that a team meeting and practice was called later own this evening and it conflicted with her 4:00 pm appointment with Romeo today. She asked Frank to please reschedule her and let him know. Frank rescheduled her for next Friday at 3:00 pm. Frank informed Romeo but admonished him to continue to pray about what he had told him yesterday evening. Romeo's sister, Leslie and her mom, Ro Sarita, and her husband, Michael showed up at the office at 4:30 pm. They were excited to see each other. Romeo introduced them to Frank. Frank was taken back by the beauty of Leslie and her mom, Ro Sarita. They both were tall and beautiful. They were beautiful, strong, black women. He immediately felt their essence. Michael was handsome but of course, Frank is a man he did not care about that.

Frank and Romeo gave them a tour of the office. They were amazed of how they made everything to stimulate and soothe the five senses in a relaxed state to create positive energy and spiritual enlighten. They felt and ease and calmness within themselves that left them feeling light. Romeo and the others said goodbye to Frank. Romeo led them to his father, Ray two story home off the lake. He had a beautiful; home on 5 acres of land they seemed more like an oasis. They had all the family events at this home and property. Of course, his home was accompanied with beautiful pool and pool house to relax after a nice swim. It had all the bows and whistles with beautiful fire place pit grill. With beautiful lounge furniture that could be comfortable while you are wet or dry. Romeo helped him to bring a botanical scenic appearance of beautiful colorful flowers and greenery. It was truly amazing. Ro Sarita and Michael were amazed. Ray came out and hugged all four of them and said, "Welcome, Me casa is your casa. Make yourself at home."

That was the second time Michael met Ray. He was accepted the fact that Ro Sarita and Ray was once a couple and share a passionate love affair that brought Leslie into the world. A child born out of sheer hot passion that grew into love but distance separated them and over time it destroyed their relationship but not their love and respect for each other. Ray was ending his NFL career and wanted to move back home to be by Romeo, his parents, and other family members. He was also secretly still in love with his first love Rosette. He never really got over her. Whenever he looked at his son Romeo, and noted his high intelligence, with, and those amazing green hazel eyes, he saw Rosette. That is also possible why he loved Romeo so much. It was more than he was his son. It was about him reminding him of Rosette the woman he could never cease loving. Ro Sarita was finishing up her Residency in the town Ray was playing professional football and she was offered a once in a life time, position as a staff doctor in one of the major hospitals in that city. That is where she met Michael. They were best friends first and they fell in love after five years. They were a match made in heaven. They complemented each other in every way. They had so much fun with each other and they bounced off of each others wit. Michael knew this but he was confident in himself and their love for each other, that Ray was Ro Sarita's past and he was her future.

Ray knew that when he met Michael that it was something between the two of them that was stronger than what they had but he was not worried because he knew he wanted to return home anyway but had also hoped that Ro Sarita would return with him especially when she had informed him that she was pregnant with their child. Ray did ask Ro Sarita to marry him and return home with him but Ro Sarita did not want to turn down that amazing doctor's position at one of the major research hospitals in that area. She felt terrible because she really loved Ray and wanted them to raise their baby together but they both agreed to shared custody. Ro Sarita had Leslie through the simmers and Ray actually raised Leslie the first five years of her life and her mom would come down and visit as often as she could. Ray was not living in the home he is now. He had everything built from scratch along with the landscaping. Romeo helped his dad raise his baby sister. That is why they were so very close.

This worked out well for Ro Sarita since she was starting her first job as a doctor and she would be working long hours. Ray's parents helped also raise Leslie and she was always around their extended family. Romeo and Leslie hugged her parents and Michael goodbye and they went out together. Leslie wanted to talk to Romeo alone about something very serious. They drove into town and Romeo took his sister to her favorite restaurant and they got a private table so they could talk and hear each other well.

Romeo turned and faced his sister after they ordered their dinner and said, "Sister, dinner is on me. I know how independent you are, but let me spoil my little sister. You are the only sibling that I have." Leslie said, "Big brother. Of course. You can buy me anything you want especially since you are going to become an uncle in about 5 months." Romeo looked at her with amazement. He knew his little sister said exactly was on her mind with little to know small talk. She always stayed focus and on point. Romeo said, "Little sister. I know I heard you correctly but I am going to repeat it again, are you expecting?" Leslie looked at him and said, "Brother, you heard me correctly. You know I don't do well with small talk and fillers. I am four months pregnant and my baby's daddy wants to marry me but I have not given him an answer yet. I wanted to first get through school and then get married. This pregnancy is unexpected. I was a virgin and he was my first. I had originally planned on staying a virgin until I got married and then after my career got off the ground, we would have children. I was only with him once but it was very memorable and I can't stop thinking about him and us making love. Am I wrong for that?"

Romeo said, "Leslie, I am at a loss of words. You are my little sister and I want the best for you. No, it is nothing wrong with falling in love and loving someone. You do love the guy, don't you?" Leslie said, "Yes, I do love him. I believe I got that first love and first-time syndrome going. I just did not want to get married and I have not accomplished my educational goals yet and started my career yet." Romeo said, "Well, what about the baby?" Leslie said, "What do you mean, what about the baby?" Romeo looked at Leslie bewildered and said, "Yes, Leslie, what about the baby?" Leslie said, "I am going to have and keep my baby regardless of what happens with my baby's father. You know me better than that. You know dad and our grandparents raised us to accept everything that life brings us. Besides, they taught is that no matter what, family is always there to help." Romeo said, "Yes, you are correct. Dad and our grandparents as well as the rest of our families have always told us that no matter what we are always here to step in when we need them. So, Leslie my beautiful little sister. What can I do to help? I thought you told your parents and your step dad you wanted to work and take care of your own tuition?"

Leslie said, "Yes, I did say those things but I did not know I was pregnant then. I still plan on going to school but that is why I asked to meet with you." Romeo said, "Yes, what else?" Leslie said, "Well, change of plans. I was going to go to Duke University, but now, I wanted to go to University of Texas of Houston. It is still a division 1A school and it has all the classes and the degree that I wanted to pursue." Romeo said, "So, you are going to be a doctor like your mom and step dad?" Leslie said, "No, there is another plan. I admit. I did want to originally become a research doctor to study genetics but now, I wanted to pursue, Psychiatry. "Romeo looked at Leslie and said, "Psychiatry, huh?" Leslie said, "Yes, big brother, Psychiatry." Romeo said, "Well, you know I am both a Psychologist and a Psychiatrist, but thank God, I also work with a brilliant Psychiatrist that use the same Theoretical and Spiritual approach to help our clients."

Leslie said, "Brother, why do you think I said Psychiatry. I could pick of his brilliance as he spoke to us. He was so warm and intelligent." Romeo said, "Yes, he is. What makes things a little more different, is that Frank will not allow me to pay him because he is very wealthy. He basically is there to help me with the business and see my more severe abusive related clients of all situations. He is torn between two opinions rather to stay in the states or go back home to England to be with his siblings and parents to join his father's practice and possibly take over it or stay here and open his own practice or become a full fledged partner with me. Right now, he is a silent partner picking up clients here and there to help me and act as my assistant. Of course, everyone soon finds out how brilliant he is when he begins to talk, he knows so much about the human mind and a mastermind at getting people to open up about their issues." Leslie said, "Yes, I gathered that." Romeo said, "I am happy you want to follow in your big brother's footstep, but do you even like the study of the mind and wanting to help people with psychological issues? Also, what else would you like for me to do?

Well, I want to earn extra money to help me go through school by being an intern when I actually go through my rotations and until then be your student psychologists for the children that parents come to see you and Frank." Romeo said, "Wow, that is a great idea. We get people here and there helping us with the children but no one consistent. That will be great. As far and I am concern, I have no problem with it. I have to talk it over with Frank. As I said, he is my silent partner. I am sure he will have known problems with it at all. Frank is not a flirty guy, but he loves being in the company of beautiful women." Leslie smiled and said, "It does not matter that he is tall and super handsome. His blonde hair, blue piercing eyes, chiseled body, brilliance, and accent is a recipe for hot, hot, hot....."

Romeo said, "Alright, little sister, slow down. You already are pregnant and what about the baby's father? Besides, all of that what is his name?"

Leslie said, his name is Christopher Cornelius James. All of his friends call him C.C. By the way, he is tall, dark, and handsome too. He is biracial. Mixed with black and white. His father is white and his mother is black. They have been married for 35 years since their youth. They were high school sweethearts that married right after high school and they both got a Master degree in education and switched times to get their doctorate in educations. They still teach at one of the largest colleges in our area. They are Professor Jennifer James and Professor Donnell James. They remind me of our grandparents. They are so in love. They were around 22 or 23 years old when Michael was born. Michael has an older sister that is one year older than he is and a younger brother that is actually 10 years younger than he is. He is getting ready to graduate high school. We have so many similarities. His parents, mom and dad are my inspirations that I can have my baby and raise him/her with their dad because I have great family support."

Romeo said as he leaned over to kiss his little sister on her right cheek. Yes, you do my dear. Yes, you do have the support of not just some but all of our big family." Romeo continued as their server continued to set the food, they ordered on the table so that they could eat. "Little sister, when are you going to tell your parents and your step dad. Not to mention grandpa and grandma?" Leslie said, "Well, big brother. I was hoping you would be there when I tell them. I will invite our grandparents over to dad's house while mom and Michael are here. Besides, there is no time but the present. Besides, I only have five more months left before my little one comes into this world. Romeo, I love kids. I always pretended that my Barbie and Ken was married and they had five children and a white ranch home on a lot of land with a beautiful landscape with a white picket fence."

Romeo, said, "Yes, little sister. You can definitely tell you was raised in Texas most of your life. Well, Leslie, where are you and the baby going to live?" Leslie said, "I was hoping I could stay with dad. He has that big house and only invites his friends and church member's family to stay with him when they come into town. I am sure he would not mind." Romeo said, "Leslie, you know dad can never say no to you. He is not going to like that you are pregnant now, but he will be all in to help you with the baby. You already know that our grandparents and the rest of the family will pitch in to help with your child while you finish school and start your career. How do you think your mom and Michael will take it?"

Leslie said, "Brother, I will be honest. Mom will be disappointed but if I know my mom, she is going to be happier of being a grandparent than me getting pregnant. Besides, she knows how determined I am. We made it through when she had me when she first started her Residency. Michael, he is my second father and has always been supportive so I know that he will be equally helpful but also a little disappointed as well because he only wants the best for me.

Romeo and Leslie finished talking and making a plan how Leslie would tell the rest of her family she was pregnant but she will be changing her major to Psychiatry instead of being a medical doctor. Leslie undoubtedly will inform her family that she will go to university as plan and it is a good thing that she had already completed an associate degree of her general classes while in high school that enabled her to start in the university as a Junior.

Romeo and his sister Leslie had also planned that she will be mentored by him as well as Frank as long as he was in the U.S. and even if he was to go back home to England to join his dad's Psychiatry practice, she could do interns there in the summer. They had called and discussed the plans with Frank and he had brought up the idea that if he does return to England and joins his father's practice, Leslie could come to England in the summers while she is in school to do interns there. Leslie was so happy her brother and Frank was so willing to assist her in her career goals and her brother helping her to raise her child with or without marrying the child's father.

Romeo did encourage her to marry him if she loved him and saw them as a lasting couple in the future. God will bless you both in Grace and Mercy as you guys grow in age. He encouraged them both to join a local church and be baptized and be servants in the church and society as God leads them. Leslie thought the world of her older brother. She knew that he was not carrying the Minister title and was not perfect but he truly lived the life as a Minister sharing the Joy of Jesus. Romeo and Leslie enjoyed themselves laughing and talking. They really got along very well. Romeo thought to himself how he was very attracted to strong women like Jessica. It dawned on him that he had not seen or spoke to her in about two weeks. They have never been apart or not said hello to each other since they decided to be a couple. Romeo and Leslie continued to enjoy each other's company. He pulled out his phone and was just about to call her when Ray, his dad called him.

Romeo answered his dad's call and said, "Hi dad. What's going on? Ray said, "Son, are you and Leslie still eating." Leslie said, "Is that dad?" Romeo said, "Yes, it is." Leslie asked, "Can I speak to him." Romeo informed Ray, "Dad, Leslie wanted to speak to you." Ray said, "Yes, hand her the phone." Leslie grabbed the phone and said, "Dad, I need to talk to you, mom, Michael, and our grandparents, can you call our grandparents to ask could they come over to your house around 7:00 pm tonight. I have to feel you all in of my futuristic plans." Ray said, "Sure, my sweet girl." I will as soon as I finish talking with Romeo. Romeo grabbed the phone back from his sister. "Dad, I'm here." Ray said, "Good. I was thinking that we might surprise Leslie with a Graduation party from us and our family. I know we flew to see her graduate and went to the graduation party that her mom and Michael did for her but I wanted us to do something special for her as well."

Romeo said, "That sounds like a great idea. Let's do it. When do you want to do it?" Ray said, "Tomorrow evening. I believe Saturday will be a good day for family to get together. Most of our family will be off of work and it will be such a blessing to have us all together again. We have not been together for a while now since Leslie's 12th birthday." Romeo asked Ray, as he was walking away from his sister, Leslie, "Is it a surprise or can I tell her?" Ray said, "Yes, let's surprise her. What do you think?" Romeo said, "Yes, let's surprise her." Romeo walked back to his sister and said, "Leslie are you ready go?" as he hung up from speaking to his dad. Leslie said, "Yes, brother let me finish this little bite left on my plate then I will be ready to go." Romeo and Leslie had made it home. Just as Leslie had requested all of them were waiting on her big announcement, as well as her grandparents. Leslie and Romeo entered the living room and everyone hugged them. Leslie was never one for a lot of words she simply goes right to the point. Leslie began to say, "Thank you all for gathering at the last minute at my request.

Thanks, dad for letting everyone know to be here. Romeo, you are the best as usual. Dad, Mom, Michael, grandmother, and granddad, I called you hear to let you know of the life changing events that I find myself in. I am four months pregnant and I did not want to let you all know until I was passed that iffy first trimester. Don't worry, I am still starting college in the fall. As you all are aware because I took my General Education courses when I was in high school, I will be starting out as a Junior." Everybody looked at her with surprise and a little disappointment. Leslie could tell by their facial expressions they were not taking the news that well. Leslie said, "Please don't be upset with me. It was one moment of weakness that occurred. It was my first time, and even though we both took precautions, I was one of those statistically rare people that regardless of the precautions you take not to get pregnant, there is always a slim case in which you will. The other thing I wanted to tell you all is that I have decided to change my career goals from being a medical doctor to becoming a psychiatrist, to study the human mind. Which has always intrigued and amazed me."

Ray and Ro Sarita almost begin to talk at the same time. Ray waited until Ro Sarita spoke. Ro Sarita said, "Wow, daughter. What a way to spring this on us. I know I am a medical doctor and so is Michael but you do not look pregnant at all, so excuse us if we are taken back a little. I know you are responsible and I personally am not concerned about you starting or finishing college, but I do want to tell you by experiencing it myself, it is not easy. Thank God for your dad, your big brother Romeo and Ray and My parents for helping us but you need to know the baby comes first and he/she should be your highest priority. Trust me, I know you can do this, but I will be less than a professional doctor and a loving mom if I did not tell the truth about such matters. Of course, I am sure we all will be here to help you. I know that we are in Washington but the summers, you can rest assured that Michael and I will help." Michael was nodding, yes, the whole time Ro Sarita was talking and she was looking at Leslie and Michael the entire time.

Ray said looking at his daughter, Leslie, and Romeo and his parents, "On the behalf of Romeo, my parents, and Romeo, we will also be there to help. You are still going to college here in Houston, Texas, aren't you? Leslie, I want say I am disappointed because I too have not only experienced this with Ro Sarita but also with my firstborn, Romeo. I thank God for my parents helping me to raise Romeo when I was so young. His mother, bless her heart. I loved her so much, and she wanted us to raise our son together, but her parents did not want that and they forced her to give the son she truly loved up for adoption. I want to tell you that destroyed the relationship that we had because she never got over giving up the baby she loved so desperately. She went into a deep depression and only the Grace of God brought her through. She went on to college. She too was like you, Leslie, she completed her Associates of Science while still in high school and started in the University as a Junior. I do not know if she ever forgave her parents. I hear from her brothers from time to time and they rave over her successes. She does not know that it was me and my parents that raised our son and that his name is Romeo. She heard that he was adopted by wonderful people but her parents talked us out of letting us tell her that we had our son. To this day, I know that my parents and I truly regret keeping this information from Romeo's mom and he was deprived from knowing such a beautiful and caring person who I know would have made an amazing and loving mom to our son. I hear she is very successful, now, but I can't help but wonder how it would have been if her parents would have also helped raise Romeo even if it was in separate homes. I still think Romeo would have benefited in knowing his mom as his mother as well. That was the key factor of us drifting apart because I could no longer allow her over to our home because we had Romeo here and she would have wondered who the little boy was, plus she would have known it was her son because she actually saw and held Romeo when he was first born, but her parents, had the nurses to come to get the baby so that she would not bond with him. I personally believe it was love at first sight. She did not want to let Romeo go and she cried hysterically, when they took him away from her. The doctor ordered sedation so she could rest, but she never was the same after that."

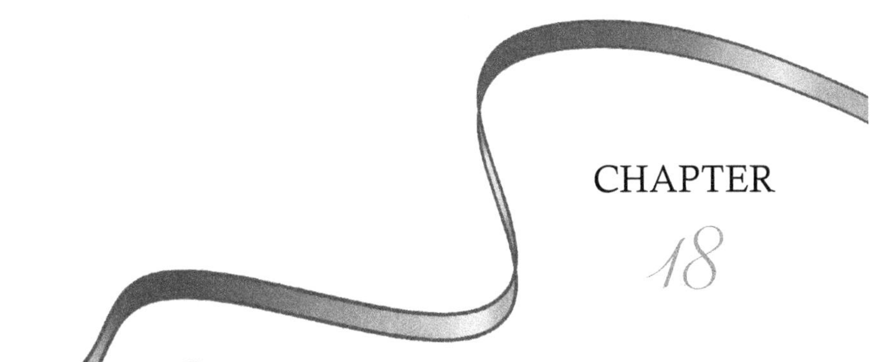

CHAPTER

18

Jasmine picked up her cell phone out of her top left drawer of her office desk and she looked at the pictures Romeo and her took at the Medical Conference in Hawaii a few months ago. They looked very happy and they were a very beautiful couple. She wondered to herself why she had not heard from him all week. She decided to give him a call. The call was unanswered and it went straight to voice mail. She called again a couple of hours afterwards before she left her office but it went to voice mail again. She thought to herself. Now, that is strange. Romeo usually answers my call on the 1st or 2nd ring due to sheer excitement to hear my voice so he had told her. Jasmine wondered what was going on that was so obviously different. She decided to stop at one of the local restaurants and she walked in to place her order. She wanted fish this evening, preferably fried catfish, French fries, and coleslaw.

Jasmine walked to the counter and looked around before she decided to eat in or get take out. Jasmine saw Romeo over in the corner table talking to a beautiful woman. She did not want to impose but she felt as if they were in deep conversation and it bothered her that he did not answer her calls. She decided to order out and waited at a nearby table closer to the register to receive her takeout. When the lady walked to her table bringing her the food. She quickly paid for it and left. She was upset but did not want to jump to any conclusion. It was Wednesday afternoon and she had not heard from him in a week. That was strange for him. She decided to go straight home without calling him for the rest of the evening and if he wanted to talk to her, she would wait before she outreached him, after all he had her number and he could easily recognize if she had called.

Just as Jasmine was walking into her living room, she heard her cell ring. It was Romeo. She answered it. "Hello." Romeo said, "How are you dear. It is so wonderful to hear your voice." Jasmine said, "Wow. I have not heard from you in two weeks and you tell me, "It is wonderful to hear your voice." Romeo said, "Sweetie, I missed that sense of humor." Jasmine said, "What sense of Humor?" Romeo ignored her sarcasm. He could tell she was upset with him. Romeo said, "I am sorry. I have not called you. I started back to work and we got so busy, and then my sister, her mom and step dad came down. We just finished eating. I took her out to eat at a restaurant near your home because she needed to talk with me."

Jasmine felt bad because she saw him at the restaurant and she did not say hello because she felt like the beautiful woman, he was with was his new girlfriend and he was cheating on her. She should have known better. She knew that he was an upright man. She felt ashamed. Jasmine paused for a little and said, "Romeo, I saw you at the restaurant with a beautiful young woman. I will be honest. I thought she was your new lady and you were cheating on me. I stopped by and got take out."

Romeo said, "Baby. I will never cheat on you. I love you." Jasmine had a sign of relief, "Of course not. I should have known better. I know the kind of man you are. A very good one. By the way, I love you too Romeo. I love you very much, my dear." Romeo's heart filled with joy. He started to talk with such delight. "Jasmine, as I said, my little sister Leslie, her mom and step dad are here and my dad called to asked me to help him to throw her a surprised graduation party. Her mom and stepdad gave her a graduation party when she graduated but my dad's side of the family could not make it besides our grandparents. They are at everything we do. I don't know what we would do without them. Sweetheart, my dad, Ray, said he wanted to do it tomorrow evening. Do you have any plans? I would sure love it if you would be my date. I can't wait for you to meet her. Besides you, my grandmother, and my aunts being very strong, beautiful, and intelligent women, I simply adore my little sister and her mother, Ro Sarita."

Jasmine said, "I would enjoy being with you tomorrow and your family. I can't wait to meet your sister. Did you say her name is Leslie?" Romeo said, "Yes, sweetheart. Her name is Leslie." Jasmine said, "For what I can see, she is very beautiful and tall. It looked like you both get along very well." Romeo said, "Yes, we do. I am 10 years older than she is, so it is like I helped my dad and her mom raise her. Her mom had her when she was going through her internship at one of the major hospitals in Washington. My dad asked her to marry him, but she could not turn down the new job and internship she landed straight out of graduating as a Physician. She still loves my dad but that love grew more into a sincere wonderful friendship. She fell in love with Michael as they were going through their rotations. They are a good match. He is very good to her and Leslie. Plus, my dad and Michael have also became very good friends. They respect each other very much. Ray appreciates the way Michael took up with Leslie and became her second dad. Yes, Leslie with her sweet self, has the blessing of having two dads. They both are very involved in her life. What a blessing but then again, Leslie has always been a blessed little lady. She is strong and independent. She reminds me a lot of you."

Jasmine felt good how enduring Romeo sounded as he talked about his little sister and compared his little sister to her. Leslie said, "Sweetheart. I really have missed you. I started to call you when I was at work. I had pulled the phone out of my desk drawer. I looked at your picture and longed to be in your presence but I did not call because I felt by it being your second week back at work, you were bound to be busy." Romeo said, "Please know that I am never too busy to talk with you or see you for that matter. Even if I am unable to answer the phone. Please know that I will call you back as soon as I possibly can." Jasmine said, "I know baby and I feel the same way. By the way, when should I come to the party tomorrow?" Romeo said, "If is okay. Can I come and pick you up. I have something special I wanted to talk to you about?" Jasmine said, "Yes. No problem. Thank you for suggesting it." With Romeo it was easy for her to follow his lead because he was a man of God, and he really knew how to show a woman just how much he loves her.

Tomorrow came, Ray, Romeo, Ro Sarita, Michael, and Ray's parents were busy preparing the big event for Leslie. One of Ray's cousin daughter, Michelle came to pick Leslie up to go get Nexagen nails and Pedicure. Leslie and her mom made this a mother and daughter event as long as she could remember. Leslie and Michelle are about the same age and grew up together when her dad, Ray was raising her in Houston, Texas. Leslie and Michelle made the whole morning about spoiling themselves. After they had their nails and feet down, they went to a nice restaurant to eat a light lunch. They always enjoyed each others company. Little did Leslie know that Michelle was in on the surprise for her. Of course, Michelle had told Leslie it is her treat so that made the event even more, sweeter. Leslie informed her cousin, Michelle, that she was four months pregnant but she was not going to allow the pregnancy to stop her from starting school in the fall since her dad, mom and her husband, Michael, Romeo, and their grandparents had committed to help her with the baby. Michelle informed Leslie that she too would help her with the baby when she needed to study. Leslie was grateful. Michelle was one of Leslie's confidents, people she did not worry about carrying the information they talked about to others, when it was life changing.

Michelle and Leslie completed their adventure and they had a nice day out on the town. Michelle of course took care of everything. Michelle and Leslie were on their way to Ray's house when Michelle got a call from Ray. Michelle answered and said, "Hello, this is Michelle. May, I help you." Ray said, "Hi Michelle, we are ready. Are you two on your way here?" Michelle said, "Yes, we are. We had a great time. I will be dropping her off in about 20 minutes." Ray said, "Great sweetheart and thank you so much." Michelle and Leslie talked about how Michelle is ready to start a family. She said her and her husband, Billy have been married now for three years. They have finished college and started their careers and now it is time to start a family. Leslie told Michelle that her baby's father wants to marry her. She said it is not just because the baby. She said, we have been dating ever since high school. He is two years older than me and he actually wanted to give me a promise ring after he graduated high school but he knew me, I probably would not have accepted it then. Michelle said, "Do you love him and think that you and him would have a lasting relationship?" Leslie said, "I do love him and I believe we are a wonderful match. I have seen him with his nieces and nephews and I know he will be great with our baby, and knowing the way his parents are so loving toward each other and their children. I don't believe it is just for show. They really care of each other. "Michelle said, "So, Leslie, what are you going to do if he asks you?" Leslie said, "I am leaning toward yes. He has accepted my goals and he know how driven I am. I don't think I would find anyone better than him. I definitely, believe he would be good for me and our baby." Leslie started to smile and think about Christopher Cornelius and their relationship over two years. They get along so well. Then she started thinking about how they are together intimately. She knows they should have waited but she got caught up with the glories of Prom night. She knows that great love making is not what holds a marriage together it is mutual respect, kindness, and dependence on God's guidance. The best thing is she knows that Christopher Cornelius is a believer. He actually walks the walk as he talks to talk. He does not fake and shake when it comes to the Lord." Michelle, remind me what is this man's name that has you smiling all the time and is always in a good mood? Girl, that is rare." Leslie said, "His name is Christopher Cornelius James, but I call him C.C." Michelle said, "Well, girl when are we going to meet Christopher Cornelius?" Well, Mom, Michael, Dad, Romeo, and my grandparents already know him. We have been dating for two years. They absolutely believe he is great match for me. I believe that is why they were not so angry with me when I told them we were expecting. Of course, they knew who the father was when I told them I was pregnant. C.C. and I are thick as thieves. We share everything."

Michelle said, "So, when are you going to see C.C. again? May I call him C.C.?" Leslie said, "Well, that is my pet name for him and he really does not like nicknames but because it is me, he loves it. I believe it is only because it's me. He loves everything about me, it seems." Michelle said, "My goodness. I thought my man was the best in the world. I believe Christopher Cornelius is a close 2nd." Leslie said, "I know that is like you thinking everybody comes 2nd behind you my favorite cousin. I am sure your

Donnell loves you very much and would love to start a family with you. You are the best." Michelle looked at her favorite cousin and said, "Little cousin, you know me all too well don't you but seriously, the way you talk about Christopher Cornelius he is great for you and I know he will make a wonderful husband and father. I just have a feeling."

Leslie said, "Sweetie, thank you for your support. I love you Miss All That." Michelle said, "And you know this." They both started to laugh. Michelle pulled up to Ray's house. Nothing was out of the ordinary. They walked up the beautiful deck porch and entered the front door. Michelle said, Leslie you go ahead. "Leslie said, "Are you ok, Miss All That? You always like to be first in everything. Ok, but I don't know what is going on with you." Leslie walked inside and Michelle followed. Everybody said, "Surprise!!!!!" Leslie looked at Michelle, her mom, dad, Michael, Romeo, her grandparents and the rest her family and friends and just started to cry.

Leslie said, "What is this? You guys are something else but seriously, what is the occasion?" Ray approached his daughter and said, "Daughter, I know that we celebrated with you at your graduation when your mom and Michael threw you a surprise graduation party but your family here in Texas wanted to share this moment with you. They could not make it, but too most of them you were there baby too because they help raise you with my parents, Romeo, and I. You are our little darlin, baby. We love you sweetheart. There is something in the kitchen that I left for you. Can you go get it for me? Ray kissed Leslie on her left cheek like he did every night when he read to her before he laid her down to sleep. Leslie walked into the kitchen you saw a large present with a red bow on it. She told called out, "Dad, I can't pick this up. It is too big."

Someone came through the back door when she was headed toward her dad. Leslie and Ray walked back into the kitchen and Ray was about to pick up the package when they heard a male voice saying, "I will do it." Leslie looked around to look at the face of the person who said those words to her amazement, she saw the love of her life. It was Christopher Cornelius. Her baby had come once again to help her celebrate. My goodness he is at everything that has to do with her and she absolutely adored him for that. She ran into his arms and kissed him passionately and said, "Baby, when did you decide to come and visit?" Your dad called me and wanted me to make it. He knew that it would be wonderful to have me here. He knows how much you love me." Leslie said, "It's true C.C. I do love you very much and I want to spend the rest of my life with you." Christopher Cornelius said, "Baby, I know you do and I feel the same way. I know it is not idea of us starting a family so soon but baby life is not planned it occurs one day at a time and whatever presents itself, I know that we can make it through it with the help of God and our love and respect for each other."

Leslie, Christopher Cornelius, and Ray walked back into to the living room where the other guests were. They loved Ray's home and especially the interior decoration and the land scaping around the property. It was plenty of beautiful botanical gardens, green plants, and tropical plants that his son, Romeo helped him to landscape because of the serenity it brought. Romeo called Leslie and Christopher Cornelius over to him and Jasmine. He wanted to introduce them to Jasmine. Romeo said, "Jasmine and Christopher Cornelius this is my girlfriend, Jasmine. She is a brilliant doctor practicing in the east quarters." Leslie and Christopher Cornelius hugged Jasmine saying, "Happy to meet you. Welcome to the family." Jasmine felt very welcomed because of their sincerity. Romeo said. "Christopher Cornelius, I know that she will be a great resource for you since you will be going into your Residency in a couple of years. Have you decided where?"

Christopher Cornelius said, "I have not decided yet. I was thinking about maybe doing it here in

Houston. There are a lot of large hospitals here. I wanted to be near Leslie and our baby." Romeo said, "Yes there is. I did my Residency at Methodist Hospital of Psychiatry." Jasmine said, "I did my Medical Residency at HCA Houston Healthcare Medical Center as my mom and dad did. If you like, I can talk to some of the board members to see if they have any opening if you are willing to transfer. They like for you to attend college in Houston for at least two years before accepting participants for Residency." Christopher Cornelius said, "Wow. Thank you. That will be something for me to definitely give some thought to. First, I would like to talk about it with Leslie and my parents, as well as pray for God's direction. I believe the word when God's says, "In all thy ways acknowledge him, and he will direct your path." That is the very reason why Leslie's family respected him so much and was not worried about her being pregnant unexpectedly because they knew that Christopher Cornelius would take care of his own. He was a strong man and beyond his years. He was only twenty years old but he was already about to complete his bachelor's degree in Medical Science. He was ready to go through the second half of his medical studies.

"For that last statement Christopher Cornelius said, Jasmine said, "Also if you want to do a Medical Practice Residency or get some extra cash. I am looking for an assistant." Leslie said, "See, I knew it was something about you. I sensed your generous heart even before you spoke one word. Plus, if my handsome big brother cares to have you as his girlfriend you would have had to possess the character of me, my mom, and his grandmother's and aunts strong, intelligent, self-sufficient, generous women else he wants give you the time of day." Jasmine said, "I believe that. He mentioned that to me."

Romeo kissed Jasmine on her soft lips and almost had a rising but he tamed it. Jasmine was so darn tempting to him. She made him excited every time he was around her. In truth, Romeo had the same effect on Jasmine. Their attraction went beyond the physical it was also a spiritual connection as well. Michelle and Donnell walked over to talk with them as well. Other family members came to be introduced to Michael Christopher and Jasmine as well. They were pleased with Romeo and Leslie selection of people they entertained as love prospects. Romeo walked out to his car and when he had come back, he and Christopher Cornelius said at the same time, "Hello all, please gather around. I have an announcement." Romeo looked at Christopher Cornelius and Christopher Cornelius looked at him in amazement. Neither of them expected the other to be speaking at the same time as the other. Christopher Cornelius asked Rome to go into the kitchen with him. Romeo followed him.

Christopher Cornelius began to say. "Romeo, I am sorry. I had already asked you dad, Ray, Rosarita, Michael, and your grandparents for their blessing in asking Leslie to marry me. I had also planned to ask you too but when I looked for you, you had already left the home, I guess to pick up Jasmine." Romeo said, "Yes, when dad had gone to get you from the Airport. I went over to Jasmine's home to pick her up for the party. I am so sorry, I missed you, but yes, you definitely have my blessing. You are a wonderful man who we all respect and know will be a great husband to Leslie and a wonderful father to your children." Christopher Cornelius, laughed and said, "Children. Do you know something I don't know. I know we are expecting but is it more than one child, are we having twins?" Romeo, laughed, and said, "Oh no. That is not what I meant. I just meant if you all decide to have more children. You will make a wonderful dad to all of them." Christopher Cornelius said, "Thank you, Man. I really appreciate that. One other thing, If you don't mind me asking, what were you wanting to ask the family?" Well, my sixth sense tells me that you were all set to ask my sister to marry you, wasn't you?" Christopher Cornelius said, "Yes, were you going to ask Jasmine the same?" Romeo said, 'Yes. I was. Well, I guess we can tell the family we both have an announcement or do you think the ladies want appreciate it?"

Christopher Cornelius said, "Well it seems as if both of our hearts were in it to do so, so we might as well do it before the thought passes." Romeo said, "I agree. Let us go do it." They both walked back into the living room and asked the family to gather around. They both had a big announcement to make.

Just as Romeo and Christopher Cornelius came in the living room, there was a knock on the door. Michelle opened the door. It was Christopher Cornelius's parents, his brother, and sister. Ray and his parents went to greet them and welcome them into Ray's home. The family greeted them. Christopher Cornelius met their eyes and nod his head, "Hello" to them with a wide smile as if to signal to them it is about to occur. You all made it just in time. He had talked to Ray about them flying down with him as well to celebrate with Leslie with her second graduation and he informed them all he wanted to ask her to marry him they all supported him in doing so and was very happy in his choice. They spent a night at hotel last night when they flew in. Ray had asked them to spend their time with him and they did not have to pay for a hotel but they did not want to give the surprise away and said they will spend the night starting the night of the party. Ray said he will prepare their rooms and make sure it was plenty of food in lots of variety so they don't have to worry about going anywhere to eat unless they just wanted too. It was decided that they may definitely go out the following day at an intimate wedding proposal celebration at one of the 5-star restaurants that one of Ray's football friends had started when he retired from his football career. They felt confident that Leslie would say, yes. They knew the great enduring love between the two of them even if they were very young. The fact that they were very mature beyond their years. Their family felt confident they would be just fine.

Ray's friend who owned the 5-star Italian restaraunt was an amazing cook and he had married one of the best chefs in town and they had four children, 2 boys and 2 girls and they were all between the ages of 18-28 years old and they worked in the restaurant when they were not in college and technical school. They loved working together in the restaurant.

Family we both wanted you all to know what a special occasion it is for us to all to be together today. With that being said, Romeo asked Jasmine to come to him and Christopher Cornelius asked Leslie to come to him. Christopher Cornelius grabbed Leslie's hand and said, "Leslie, sweetheart, you know that I love you. Over these last two years, I have learned to respect the brilliant, beautiful, strong will, independent woman that you are. I know you come from a long line of them. It would be my pleasure to have you in my life forever as the mother of my children, and my wife. Leslie, will you marry me?"

Everybody signed and smile and was about to clap when Romeo said, hold on family, I have something to say." He called Jasmine over to him and said, "Jasmine, I know I have known you for close to a year now, but from our first date, I was mesmerized with your intelligence, beauty, warmth, and spirituality. You are accomplished and kind, Jasmine it has been a pure delight being with you and quite frankly, I can't see myself living another day without you." A knock was at the door, Ray let them in. It was Jasmine's mom and dad and their spouses, and both sets of her grandparents. Romeo had invited them to his sister, Leslie graduation party and had asked for their blessing to marry Jasmine. He wanted them to witness it. Jasmine looked and smiled but wondered why they were there. She was about to pull away from Romeo's grasp when she saw them but Romeo would not let her go. He said, "Jasmine just like I would not let your hand go when you saw your family come in, I never want to let go of you. I want you to be the mother of my children and my lovely wife as long as we both shall live, Jasmine will you marry me?

Now the family clapped and said both to Leslie and Jasmine, "Well ladies what do you say? Answer these two men. They are awaiting your response of their magnificent marriage proposals. Leslie ran to

Christopher Cornelius and said C.C. I would be so happy to be your wife, yes, my love, I will marry you." Jasmine ran to Romeo and kissed him passionately and would not stop kissing him until the family said, Jasmine, wait until the married night. That is if you accept his marriage proposal." Jasmine said, "Yes, my darling, Yes, yes, yes, I will marry you." Then all the family raced in hurriedly to hug and kiss them. They were so happy to witness this special occasion. They all said, "We are invited, aren't we?"

Christopher Cornelius, Leslie, Romeo, Jasmine said, "Of course. You all are our family. We will not be who we are if it was not for all of you." It was amazing night. The family enjoyed each other and decided to celebrate further by going to celebrate at Ray's friend Nigel Satalino 5-Start Italian restaurant. Ray had called him to alert him of the number of people that was going to show up at 8:00 pm for the wedding proposal celebration. Nigel was excited, after all, He was both Romeo and Leslie's God father. His wife Adalyn Naomi Olivia Satalino was their God mother.

CHAPTER

19

The family members that were not yet retired went to work Monday Morning excited about what happened last night and could not wait until the wedding proposal celebration at Satalino 5-Star Italian restaurant. The locals knew that the food there was affordable and amazing. They had a few dishes that were expensive but that is when you want to go beyond the usual day to day Italian food and wanted something that was simply amazing that most people had not eaten before.

Romeo had a 2-hour session with Rosette today. He remembered what Frank had told him last night at Leslie's Graduation celebration. Frank reiterated that Romeo needed to pray that the Holy Spirit presence would fill the room when he and Rosette have their next counseling session. Frank informed Romeo that God told him to let him know he will have life changing information that was going to be brought to the fore front. Romeo assured him that he was going to pray very hard. Frank was also led to tell Ray that he needed to meet with him along the same time of Rosette meeting with Romeo. At the last hour of the 2-hour session that Romeo was going to have with Rosette. Ray did not know the reason why but he trusted Frank just like he trusted Romeo. When those two said they needed to meet with you, Romeo had learned along the years, it was mighty important because they were not just Psychiatrists but they were both spiritual counselors as well and he knew they both moved through the prompting of the Holy Spirit. They both was very sensitive to the anointing of God's Spirit.

2:00 pm arrived and Rosette entered Romeo and Frank's office. Frank and Rosette were great friends they talked at least three days a week. Rosette even gave Frank floor seats at her team's home games and even away if they were not too far. Frank thankfully went to their games near and far. He and Rosette was more like siblings than a love match because it was common knowledge that Frank had fell deeply in love with her friend, Patricia. They were a perfect match just as Rosette imagined. She knew that he would be a perfect match for her as well if she was well and was not carrying so much emotional distress that has prevented her from committing to a long-term relationship.

Frank walked over to her when she was passing her desk saying, "Come here girl. How is everything?" Rosette said, "I am getting better and better day by day, thank God for sending me here to get counseled by you and Romeo. Patricia told me that you all were not only Psychiatrists and Psychologists but also Spiritual Counselors. I receive all that you all have done for me and I know I am forever in your prayers. I feel the difference." Frank said, "You know us very well. We are 100% here for our patients and you are one of our dear hearts that we have got to know on a personal level as well. It was inevitable for us not to be. It was definitely a spiritual connection." Rosette said, "Definitely. I agree with my whole heart."

Romeo walked out when he heard them laughing and talking, and came out to greet Rosette to walk her to his office for her two-hour counseling sessions. Rosette agreed to it because she missed the last two sessions and wanted to get caught up. So, she agreed to meet Romeo today instead her usual day on Friday. Rosette did not have practice with her team until 7:00 pm tonight. The stadium was near to Romeo and Frank's office. Romeo shook Rosette's hand and said, "Are you ready?" Rosette said, "Yes, it is great to see you and be here." Romeo said, "Feel free to lay down on the leather couch or the leather chair. Both of them are very comfortable." Rosette said, "I will lay down on the couch this time. I have a feeling that this session is going to be ground breaking." Romeo said, "Alright. Well, let's get started."

Romeo begins to ask very revealing questions, "Rosette, how far do you believe you have come over these last nine months? Frank brought me up to speed in regard to the breakthrough that you had when he counseled you when I was out performing therapy from injury sustained via the auto accident my girlfriend and I had just around the corner from both of our homes. It was mind blowing that we were so close to home and we had one of the most horrific auto accidents we had ever been involved in. It was terrible." Rosette said, "Yes, Frank informed me of how tragic it was. I am so glad you all are alright now. Romeo said, "Yes, I am to. Thank God." Rosette said, "Well, I believe I am at the point I have forgiven my parents and the man that was the love of my life." Romeo said, "What have you forgiven them for, exactly, If I may ask?" Rosette said, "I mentioned this to you before. When I was going on 16 y/o I became pregnant. I was going into the 11th grade. It was not planned. The guy I was telling you that I was in love with we would always be together because he was friends with my twin brothers, he was always over to our house. He was brilliant. He was my age but he was already in the 12th grade with my brothers. He played football with one of the twins and when basketball season came around, he also played basketball with the other twin. My brother adored him because not only was he highly intelligent but he was also gifted in all sports: football, basketball, and baseball. He was very quick on his feet. He ran 7 minutes in 100-yard dash. He was fast as lightning." Romeo was a little unsettled because if he did not know better. It seemed as if she was describing his dad, Ray. He had heard these type stories regarding him all during his growing up years. Romeo, nodded with interest asking her to please continue.

Rosette said, "Yes, I had become pregnant by a young family friend around my same age but he was a gifted young man and his parents skipped him two grades ahead. He could have actually started college in the ninth grade but they decided to let him skip the 10th and 11th grade to go to the 12 grades because his maturity level was so high but they did not want him mingling with young adults too soon, plus he was their only son and they were not trying to rush him out of the house too soon." Romeo by now was twitching in his seat because the man she was describing was becoming all too familiar as if she was describing his dad, Ray to a tee.

Romeo said, "Please go on." Rosette said, "I had the baby, and my parents made me give the baby up for adoption. I pleaded with them to help me to raise him, because they thought me and the baby's father was too young to raise a child by ourselves, and back then my parents worked all the time in the lawyer practice. They were divorce attorneys and they were world renowned in that business. The only drawback is it came with a price. They worked all the time, but they made it too all of our sporting and school events. Our Nanny practically raised us otherwise. She was a beautiful older black woman who when our parent wasn't around, we called Moma Rose. Moma Rose had three children of her own that were our classmates at our schools. We all were great friends and since they were all adored by our parents to sweetened the deal for Moma Rose to accept the job as our Nanny, our parents informed her that she could also have her children over as much as they or Moma Rose wanted them.

That was never a problem because my brothers played sports with Moma Rose three boys. They too were academic scholars and adored by everyone that they met. Heck, I was falling for one of them. The middle child. He was amazingly charming, but the guy, I was telling you about, who was my baby's father, beat him too it. He was sort of awkward around me at first because he was shy. I would tease him all the time for it. I was always outgoing, so I pulled that shyness right out from him. He and I became very good friends first because he did not want to disrespect my brothers for wooing their little sister. Like I said, this young man, was very mature for his age. He was set apart from the other young men even in the romance department. He was amazing." Romeo said, "I see. It was like he was too hard for any woman to resist with that kind of charm."

Rosette said, "Exactly. Now, you see why I became pregnant. He was simply irresistible, but he was the type that entertained one woman at a time because he loved the wooing part of the romance." Romeo said, "I see how this is going. His charm was mesmerizing it seems." Rosette, "Yes. Very much so much so. It was almost hypnotizing." Romeo was curious now, she not only was describing his dad, Ray, but also the latter was characteristics he got from his dad, as well. Romeo said, "Please, go on?"

Rosette said, "Well, after I hysterically cried and my parents and the young man that was my son's father comforted me, they allowed me to hold my baby because I was screaming so much, "I love my baby. I want to raise my son. I don't want to give him up for adoption. Please God, don't let them make me give away my baby. I love him. I love him so incredibly. Please don't make me give him up for adoption!" Romeo was shedding tears at this time, because Rosette was screaming this out so loud and it was shattering his professionalism. It was as if he was back there at that time period experiencing with her, her incredible screams and pain. He could feel someone grasping him tightly. Not wanting to let him go. Screaming at the top of her lungs, "Please let me keep my baby. I love him. Don't make me give him up for adoption. Please don't make me!" Rosette said, "Next thing. She saw my baby's father's parents and my parents walk out the door together and they allowed me and my baby's father to bond with the baby. They knew that it was going to crush Rosette when she had to let her baby go and sign the adoption papers, but they felt so terrible in making her do so that they decided not to allow someone that did not know their families adopt the baby but have someone who was very familiar with both families adopt her son. Rosette said, "I was so devastated that I did not read the family that was going to adopt my son. I just could not deal with the trauma of giving him away. I noticed afterwards, my son's father and I drifted apart and he kept making excuses as to why I could not visit him at his home anymore. I not only loss my beautiful son but also the love of my life!" Romeo, was just about to ask Rosette, what was the name of her baby's father. He felt it was very important for her to identify him as a real person and not just the man she loved and the father of her son. From the beginning she never mentioned or called out his name.

Ray had made it to the clinic and was in the session with Frank, and when they heard Rosette screaming, "Please let me keep my baby. I love him. Don't make me give him up for adoption. Please don't make me!" Frank knocked on Romeo's office door and asked, "Romeo, is everything okay. I heard Rosette screaming. Is it alright for your dad and I to come in?" Romeo looked at Rosette and said, "You know how Frank loves you and he is just concerned. My dad is very professional. Do you mind them coming in. We are at the end of our session anyway. I believe you had amazing breakthrough. How do you feel.? Rosette said, "Frankly, I feel like a big heavy load has lifted from me. I can't explain how light I feel. It seems like that dark cloud that kept me in a deep functional depression has lifted. Wow, that feel so good. Yes, they can enter." Romeo said, "Come on in Frank and dad. My client said it was alright for you two to come in."

Frank entered the room first and then Ray came in. He was alarmed and very surprised that Rosette was Romeo's client. All the things they had been through in her given up the son she loved that he had told his son, Romeo all of his growing up years, was literally sitting in the room across from the son, she gave up for adoption that he and his parents raised without her knowledge. He felt so much guilt that he was moved to tears when he saw her and the passionately enduring love, he had for her then that he never was able to cease came running back to him like a mighty rushing wind." Rosette saw, Ray, and started to cry. Ray, what are you doing here? I have not seen you in twenty-eight years. What is going on here. Romeo why did you call Ray, your dad? You said you were around 28 y/o. Ray, I hate to say it but were you cheating on me because our son would have been 28 y/o?

Frank had Romeo to sit down to listen a bit and let Ray and Rosette get reacquainted and sort things out. God had already revealed in a vision how this moment would come about. Romeo said, "Wait. Do you two know each other and dad why have you not mentioned Rosette's name before?" Ray said, "Hold on son. Yes, I do know Rosette. I also have mentioned her multiple times during your childhood but I never called her name." Rosette said, "Ray, there you go again calling Romeo your son, and Romeo is calling you dad. Again, Ray, did you cheat on me? I thought you was a one man to one woman kind of guy. I mean, I knew you was extremely charming but I thought we were so much in love. We had a son together." Romeo said, "What? You two had a son. Where is this son, dad. Why didn't I know of this?

Ray said, "Hold on son. Wait just a minute. Please Rosette, sit down. Let me explain to both of you what is going on. Rosette, I wanted to contact you many, many times over the years but your parents thought it would not be a good idea because you had finally become better emotionally and physically enough to graduate high school early and go to college. From that point on by me talking with your brothers, you were drafted in the WNBA after playing basketball and you stayed on the road a lot. Your brothers informed me that you had become injured and retired your jersey but because you were so great at playing and teaching basketball, they asked you to become head coach of the Houston professional women basketball team, and again you stayed busy with that. I just did not have the courage to interrupt your routine and send you back into a major depression episode."

Romeo said, "Dad I hear what you are saying to Rosette but why did you make sure I was sitting down. What does all this have to do with me?" Ray said, "Rosette don't blame your parents. They thought they were doing what is best for their little girl. I know you wanted to raise our son by yourself or together, either way you wanted to keep him. That night you had our son, you cried so hysterically begging your parents to let you keep our son, stating," I love him. I love my son. Please don't make me give him up for adoption. I want to keep my baby. I love my son." I remember this as if it was yesterday. It still haunts me at night. From that point on, it has been difficult or me to get a decent 8 hours of sleep. I get 5 ½ to 6 hours nightly at the most.' Rosette said, "Ray, please get to the point. Why is Romeo calling you dad?" Ray said, "You remember us drifting apart after you had our son and how I kept making excuses for you to come over to the house. There was a very good reason." Rosette said, "Ok, what was the reason?" Ray said because you cried yourself into a frenzy, my parents walked out with your parents and I stayed with you to try to console you, an attempt to calm you down from the frenzy of pain you were in. Well, according to the arrangement that my parents and your parents made,

they no longer wanted the baby to go to an unknown family. They wanted them to have a family that was known by both families to raise our son."
Romeo said, "No dad. I know that you guys did not do that to Rosette. My God all this time."

Rosette said, "Romeo, what are you saying. I don't get it. What are you saying. Clearly you were in the dark just like me at the beginning of this conversation. What is really going on?" Romeo said, "My God. Dad, I believe I have figured it out but please keep enlightening this news flash to us." Rosette said, "Please, Ray, please let me know what is going on. You owe me that at least."

Ray said, 'Please forgive me Rosette. Please forgive us." Rosette said, "Forgive you or you all for what? Ray, don't you know I never got over our love and the giving up of our son. I have not had a long-lasting relationship as a result. So, if you want to let me know something, the time is now. If not, I am going to walk out of here and I never want to see you again. Ray, it hurts so bad. This is the reason why I am in therapy now. I want to move on. I want to get married and have more children. I just wished I could have found our son. They sealed his adoption and they would never reveal who adopted our son. I never stopped looking for him. I never stopped looking for our son."

Frank walked over to hug and console Rosette because she had begun to cry. He did not want her to cry, but he could not console her. The tears kept rolling down her face. Frank tried to get her to sit down and calm herself but she could not stop no matter how loving Frank was toward her. Ray pulled out a handkerchief and said, something told me to put this fresh and clean handkerchief in my pocket. He walked over to Rosette and said, "Can, I hold you?" Rat gave her the handkerchief and was able to lead her to the leather couch in Romeo's office. He set beside her and said, "Rosette. I know what you have been going through with relationships because I never got over our love either. Sure, I want lie. I have had other relationships but not like the love we shared. It broke my heart to make excuses why you could not come over to my house again and to break up our loving relationship. I also wanted us to raise our son together. I hated the idea you had to give our son up for adoption. I pleaded with my parents and your parents to help us raise our son. I asked your parents and my parent's permission to marry you but your parents thought we were too young to get married and did not want to ruin our futuristic goals. I assured them we would still graduate from high school and go to college and begged your parents to let us get married. I never asked you because they were adamant, they did not want that for you. They said our marriage would not last and when you get a divorce it was like a literal death and they did not want us to go through that. So, I begged my parents to help me to raise our son and they agreed. I wanted to tell you and was about to tell you before you signed the adoption paperwork but because you had cried so intensely, you did not even read the names on the adoption paperwork was my parents. You just signed the paperwork and went straight to sleep."

Romeo said, "What are you saying? "Rosette said, "So, you mean to tell me you have been having out son all this time and did not tell me? Ray, how could you?" Romeo said, "So my suspensions were correct. I did not want to say anything because I was too just trying to help you heal, but when you were describing the man, you were obviously still in love with, sounded a lot like my dad. It was very puzzling." Ray said, "Again Romeo and Rosette, I am deeply sorry. I have no excuse but I knew you were in a bad depressed state, Rosette, and I just did not know how the news of where our son was would set within you. I did not want it to take you to a place that it would be too hard for you to come back from."

Rosette said, "I understand where you are coming from, but please tell me where our son is?"

Ray said, "Rosette, Romeo is our son. Romeo, Rosette is your mom. I never was able to tell you her name exactly because I knew you would find her but her parents did not think it was a good idea, but I did tell you often that your mother loved you so much and she never wanted to give you up for adoption and she was talked into doing so against her will."

Rosette starting crying again, "All this time mu therapist is my son. The son, I have always loved and never wanting to give away. My God. I can't believe this. Why would my parents do this? Why would you and your parents keep this from me all of these years? What is this? I don't understand all of this."

Ray said, "Your parents thought they were doing what was best for you, and we, did not want it to be such a strain on you to know we had your child and your parents did not want you to be aware of it because they thought you helping you to raise our son would be too much on you and you would drop out of high school and never go to college. I tried to tell them they were wrong and they obviously did not know you. Heck, they worked all the time. How could they know you or your brothers. Even Moma, Rosa tried to tell them that you were very intelligent and as far as school, they did not have anything to worry about, in addition, she said she would be there to help you raise our son. Your parents thought that would be too much for Moma Rose and for you as well. They worked all the time so they were not going to be able to effectively help raise him but I can tell you this, your mom wanted to quit her job to do so, but your dad did not have any other lawyers at their practice and they were swamped with clients. Your brothers and Moma Rose even said they would help raise our son, but your parents knew they were getting prepared to go to college for the basketball and football full scholarships they had got. It was just too much for them to endure at that time, but I assure you Rosette, they all was trying to work it out so that you could keep our son. So, when all was said and done, my parents agreed with me and said they would help me to raise our son and when the time would come, for us to tell you, we all would, but we kind of lost touch with you. You were traveling so much and you rarely came home. You cut all communication off with your parents and you barely called your brothers because of your hectic schedule and theirs."

Rosette began to cry again, this time Romeo, Frank, and Ray went over to console her. Romeo said, "My goodness. I don't know what to say. I am so sorry you had to endure all of that. I know from counseling you; it has been very traumatic for you. Rosette, if you don't mind me calling you by your name, in spite of our recent revelations, I am so happy to finally meet my mother. To be honest, I have dreamed of this my whole life. I just never imagined I would meet my mom in this manner. All I can say is God has a way of bringing things full circle. It may not be on our timing nor the way that we imagine but it is according to his perfect will. I am so happy to meet you as my mom. I hope that we can keep talking rather professionally or personally because I want to get to know you. I hope you want to get to know me as well. Maybe, I can help you to forgive and move on just like our original plan was so that you can go on with your life. If I did not say it plainly enough, Rosette will you allow me a chance to get to know you as my mom even if you as my client ends?"

Rosette said, "Yes, Romeo I would like to get to know you as my son and you to get to know me as your mother. Ray, I understand the strain you must have been under keeping this from me all these years. I do know you and I know how persistent my parents are too. Thank you for sharing with me how everybody wanted to help me raise our son, but they had exhausted all resources or my parents just thought it would be too much for all of us to do at that time. This will help me to forgive and move forward and even repair broken relationships." Ray said, "I hope we can repair our relationship at least to become friends again?" Rosette said, "I am willing for us to start communicating again to try to bridge the gap." Ray felt so good he ran and hugged her tightly. Frank said teasingly, "Ok Ray, she said you guys can start talking again to bridge the gap. She did not say that she was there yet." All of them started laughing and gathered their things to get ready to leave the office. Ray said, "Rosette and Romeo, please forgive me. I did not want to keep this from you two. I really did not want to do this especially all of these years. "

Romeo said, "I can only imagine dad. I can only imagine. I love you and we will get passed this. The best thing is that the truth has come out and God has brought us back together again." Rosette, Ray, and Frank said, "That is so right. That is so true." Rosette gave Ray a card with her contact information and Ray gave Rosette his card with his business on it. Ray was a private health consultant. He used all of that genius intelligence to get a doctorate in health administration. They promised to get together and talk. Frank wrote Rosette's next appointment down with Romeo. This time they would work on bridging the gap and merging relationships through forgiveness. They all went home and slept well and woke up to their busy lives on Tuesday morning.

The next two days were a blur. Rosette and Ray talked over dinner to reacquaint each other and to informed her of how Romeo's upbringing was. Rosette laughed at the stories of what a serious young boy Romeo was and how they knew as he grew up, he was going to be either a professor or a psychiatrist. Ray told Rosette that sometimes it was hard on him because a lot of Romeo's mannerism and facial expressions reminded him of her. Ray told Rosette, "When Romeo looks a certain way when he is thinking about something, he looks just like you." Rosette, loved hearing that. Ray said, "Romeo was a great ball player as well in basketball and football, but he preferred football. He played up unto college. Although he did not need the basketball scholarship, because I had put away money for his college as I was playing in the NFL, he wanted to really do it on his own. I have a daughter that is 10 years younger than Romeo. Her name is Leslie. I met her mom when I was playing professional football. She was in her last few years in her Medical Residency and she became pregnant. She had just got a lead Resident position at one of the Research Hospitals in Washington and it would have been hard for her to turn that position down, so she turned down my marriage proposal but asked could we share custody with our child because most of the time she would have long hours at the hospital. I agreed but I actually raised he with help of my parents and other family in Texas for her first 8 years of life. Her mom came to visit as often as she could. When Leslie turned nine, she went to live with her mom. Her mom was more established as a medical doctor and went into Private Practice and she had more control over her schedule and could spend quality time with Leslie. Leslie came back to be with Romeo and I on the holidays and the summers. I would love for you meet her. She is 18 y/o, now and going on 19 y/o. She is just as independent as Romeo."

Rosette said "Wow, it seems as if you raised two wonderful children." Ray said, "Yes, they turned out very well. I still wished we did not keep you from Romeo all of these years. I know he would have benefited having you in his life as his mom. I just know it. I don't know how I can make this up to you. I don't want you to resent me for being a part of keeping Romeo from you." Rosette said, "I know you were pressured, Ray. I know that it was left up to you, you and I would have been raising Romeo together. I forgive you, Ray. I have even forgiven my parents. I looked at through their eyes and saw things differently. It was difficult but I did it with God's help. You know Romeo and his partner; Frank are brilliant Psychiatrist and Psychologists. They are great pair and they really incorporate Spiritual counseling in their counseling sessions. They both helped one of my friends when she went through a tragic circumstance in her life. She was able to get better and she gave me Romeo's card and said he incorporates spirituality in his counseling and I believe he can help you to become healed and go on with your life. I know he helped me and pointed me in the right direction. Rosette said, "Ray, Romeo our son and his partner Frank did an amazing job to help me with God's guidance. I really thank God that he instilled the right tools for them to help me. I feel confident of it." Ray said, "That is wonderful Rosette. Romeo is very impressed with you as a woman and looks forward to getting to know you as his mom. I know my son and he is delighted to have you in his life and guess work, I know Frank is. He is very protective over you. I picked that up very quickly, even your last appointment with Romeo, when you and I met in Romeo's office after all those years. I am surprised he did not ask you out yet, but due to is Professionalism, he managed not to; I am sure." Rosette laughed and said, "Yes, but it was so hard for him to maintain because he was very attracted to me. Plus, we got along very well from the start. I knew I was not ready for the long-term commitment and the type of woman Frank deserves and is looking for at this time in his life. I was harboring a lot of bitterness, shame, and hurt feelings that prevented me from ever having a long-term relationship with a man. I introduced him to one of my best friends, Mary. Mary is the reason why I start seeing Romeo. Romeo had helped her to overcome her life trials of being assaulted and raped by someone she knew. She is such a different person now. She is whole again both emotionally, physically, and spiritually. Needless to say, I was still in love with someone that I never could let go."

Ray said, "OkAY. I think I am offended." Rosette said, "Why would you be offended Ray." Ray said, "Because Rosette, I never stop loving you. My love for you is just as intense and enduring as it was when we were teenagers. After all, our love for each other produced a love child." Rosette said, "I was talking about you, Ray. I have never got over you. I love you very much. All of the bitterness I was harboring went away when I saw you in Romeo's office. Even the shock of knowing that you raise our son and did not tell me was not enough to keep my love for you, from resurfacing so greatly. It did so because my love for you never ceased." Ray and Rosette embraced each other for a long 5 minutes. They did not want to let each other go. It was as if they were re-imagining staying in each others lives and the twenty -eight years never kept them apart. At least that is how they held one another.

The two of them ate the rest of their meals, and Ray dropped Rosette home at her apartments. She used to be so independent and sure of herself. In her younger years if she never had that tragic experience of giving her baby up for adoption and losing the love of her life, she would have bought and paid for her dream home already. Money was no issue for her. She was one of the highest paid athletes of her time. Rosette wanted Ray to know where she lived. She wanted their relationship to grow. She missed him greatly, and she could tell he missed her in the same like manner.

CHAPTER

20

Wednesday morning came and the evening appointment list for Romeo had shortened. He had one more appointment scheduled and it was for Tom and Nancy. The both have been talking a lot since their last individual therapy and was working on building their relationship and was talking toward getting remarried. Tom had asked Nancy to re marry him and promised things would be different between them. His counseling sessions had helped him to see a lot of his character that was not allowing his wife to be herself. He learned he must involve her in all decisions of the marriage together. Nancy also stated much of the same. She learned from being in counseling with Romeo, that she was transferring her feelings of her step father over to her husband Tom because they shared a lot of qualities. She realized what she most endures about Tom was qualities that her mom disdained in her step father that led them to a divorce. She learned that instead of embracing Tom's strengths as a man she crushed them because of what she had been through with her mom in how she felt about her step down. Nancy had also vowed to not do that and love Tom for the strengths that made her fall in love with him in the first place.

They wanted to go to pre-martial counseling to help them to get a better start and to make sure they continue to stay on track of a long-lasting relationship and successful marriage. They both knew that Romeo and Frank used biblical principal to help their clients to overcome challenges that goes beyond their scope or abilities to resolve. Nancy had accepted Tom's proposal to marry him again. They had spent almost three weeks sorting to the difficulties of their marriages that led to their divorce. They were now able to see things through the other spouse's point of view. They were determined to keep God first and their spouse second, and stop looking through the scope of their own eyes and getting things twisted as a result of their past. Their strong love for one another was not strong enough to keep their marriage from ending. They needed a strong path to success and they knew it was through a higher power than themselves. Rather it was through God which was a true path to success accompanied with spiritual marriage counseling for the both of them together.

Tom and Nancy met both Romeo and Frank for their first counseling session to get both of them a fresh new start than between Romeo and Frank they will determine and pray the most advantageous way toward their path to success. They arrived 15 minutes early and was able to choose their scenery conducive to learning and peacefulness. They chose the area in which the children go to play while their parents were in counseling sessions. It kept them busy and they were having so much fun they did not realize they were actually learning. The counseling session started. For the first time in their

104

relationship, they felt peace and not strife and ugliness, but they felt love that ran from breast to breast and heart to heart between each other with no other people from their past and present involved.

They laughed and talked openly about what they wanted in this second married between the two of them. "Reunited because it feels so good, reunited because we understood." was something that kept running through their minds. They signed a pack that if they came into a hot spot or troubling spot in their marriage they would pray and listen to his Holy Spirit and seek spiritual counseling from Romeo and Frank to keep them on the right road to success in their marriage. Romeo and Frank had the pack developed with some of their other colleagues when they went to Psychiatry and Psychology retreats and seminars. They learned a lot in their retreats and seminars. Tom and Nancy felt this time around was the charm that they will truly make it this time. They even held off the heat and passion they had for one another during their marriage and so much since their reunion, they managed to not consummate their reunion until they actually got remarried.

They came very close to several times because their passion for one another was not the problem in their relationship, it was the fact that they were allowing their past into their marriage. Tom and Nancy were excited about their new life together and they asked Romeo if he knew if his pastor would marry them this weekend. They did not want to wait any longer. They figured that they should have sought spiritual counseling together from the beginning when their marriage begins to go astray. Pride is a terrible thing. It has always bought down mighty men and women. They know that now. Romeo said, "Hold on you two. Let me make a call to my pastor. I have him on speed dial. He knows if I call it is for a good reason." Romeo dialed his Pastor, "Pastor Gary, how are you?" Pastor Gary Lawson said, "Romeo. Hello, how are things? I am well. Just sitting here talking to my beautiful wife Kimberly. It is good to hear from you. How may I help you?" Romeo said, "I am well. I have a beautiful young lady, I met a year ago, and my sister and I are getting married, soon. I was wondering are you two available for counseling the two of us. Also, I met my birth mom. Yes, I will tell you all about it. I am so happy. The thing is I was her Counselor before knowing anything. I just found out this past Monday. It looks like my dad and her are still carrying a heavy torch for one another. You might have three weddings to counsel and perform. Are you up two it?"

Pastor Gary said, "Yes indeed. I will always make room for your family. I know Ray, Leslie, and You do not pick just anyone. They have to be the right fit for you to even entertain spending time with. I know that the counseling sessions will be short and to the point. You guys are already spiritual enough to know that being equally yoked in a Christian sense is a super important task in a successful marriage. In the end it is God that binds the heart of two people to make things work even through the struggles." Romeo, Frank, Nancy and Tom at the same time said, "Amen." Pastor Gary said, "It seems as if I have an audience. You did not tell me that."

Romeo said, "I was intending to, but we got caught up with catching up. Pastor, the reason why I called was the couple you heard, Tom and Nancy, wanted to know are you free this weekend, to marry them?" Pastor Gary asked if they have already gone to get their Marriage Licenses?" Romeo looked at Tom and Nancy and both of them nodded, "Yes." Romeo answered Pastor Gary and said, "They both said, yes." Pastor Gary asked, "Have they went through any counseling, yet?" Romeo said, "Yes. Pastor, they have been married before for 10 or more years and divorced for about a year and ever since their Divorce they have been going through counseling sessions with me and they found their way back to each other because they learned to see things out of the others eyes and not through people and their relationships which destroyed their marriage. Frank and I just finished their first counseling session together and they have signed a pack to continue in the good and the bad times. First and far most they decided to keep God as the head of their marriage and be led through the Holy Spirit and not go forward in their own thinking. "

Pastor Gary said, "Great. I am aware of how you and Frank run your counseling sessions and I have heard of the great success that have occurred with your clients. Your reputation proceeds itself." Romeo said, "Yes. They are ready for this reunion. I feel confident they will make it this time around." Pastor Gary asked will it be Saturday or Sunday evening?" Nancy and Tom said, Saturday, if you are available? It is going to be short and sweet. We have a few friends and Families coming to witness us re marriage. Of course, Romeo and Frank you and your lady friends and family are invited. Frank and I have already made to dinner plans and the reception plans. They left the window of engagement open because they want and also feel confident that the great love that is between us is rewarding, and they want to bless us." Frank and Tom said they will ask each others girlfriend and fiance but even if they can't make it, we will come support you guys." Pastor Gary said, "Sounds like a plan. Kim and I will be here. I trust Frank and Romeo did a good job in preparing you all for a long journey of marriage. We will see you all Saturday."

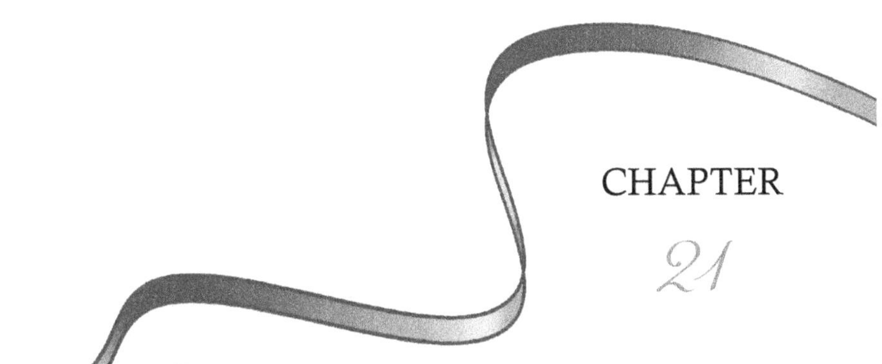

CHAPTER

21

ednesday, Thursday, and Friday were good days for Tom and Nancy. They finished their wedding arrangements and was now ready for their big day. They arrived at the church and their wedding party was there already waiting for their arrival. Nancy mom was on the front pew and her step dad and his new family ere there too. He had accepted Nancy proposal to walk her down the aisle and give her away. After all, he is truly the father that raised her since her biological father passed before her mom had a chance to inform her that she was pregnant. Besides, Nancy mom had asked Nancy step dad to forgive her because she would not allow him to fully be the man and the head of the household because she was putting too much pressure on him unknowingly to be her late husband, Nancy biological father, shoes. She admitted that what she was doing and because she had not dealt with the grief of losing the love of her life, she really subconsciously took it out on him. He forgave her and they began to talk again and became friends again. Nancy mom even made friends with his new wife and children. It was amazing how emotional healing and forgiveness can set things in the right order for futuristic blessings.

Tom's best man was his grandfather. He really looked up to him. He had best friends that were his high school buddies that he played sports with even in college but he asked them and their families to come but asked them to forgive him, but this time, he would be asking his grandfather to be his best man. He had also asked his father to stand up for him as well. His father was elated for him to ask him that. He hugged his son, greatly. He loved him so. Tom's mom and new step dad, his grandmother who he adored as his second mom, and the rest of Nancy and Tom's family were there to support them. Romeo, Jasmine, Frank, Mary, Ray, Rosette, Leslie, Christopher, Cornelius, Ray's grandparents, and other friends of Tom and Nancy were there. Wow, Nancy was so beautiful and Tom was as handsome as a make model. He was very angelic in his looks. He had shaved his beard for the wedding. Nancy step dad walked her in as she song her and Tom's favorite love song, "I will always Love You by Whitney Houston. Everybody turned around and said to themselves, "What! Who knew she could sing like that." The biggest surprise was when Nancy Step dad placed Nancy hand and his in hers, as a symbol that he is now, officially, giving his daughter away to Tom. Tom turned around and his dad gave him the mike and he started to sing, "When a man loves a woman, and everybody stood to their feet and applauded them both because absolutely none of their friends knew they could sing like that. Their family knew that they could sin, but not to that extent.

When the wedding vows were said, and they were very enduring, Romeo song, "Let's Stay Together, by Al Green in his natural tone and voice. It was magnificent. Fortunately for them, a song writer and music producer who was looking for a man and woman act approach them and Romeo after the wedding and asked could they meet with them Monday evening to talk about their ideas. They entertained the thought and said they would do so as an adventure. They wanted to maintain their day jobs. Everybody left the church to go to the reception at one of the town halls in town. It was beautifully arranged with white lace and crystal. The food was a mixture of gourmet and traditional comfort food to fit everybody's taste. It was absolutely beautiful. Everybody had lots of fun. Tom and Nancy had a beautiful life together. Nancy got pregnant within the first three months of their re-marriage. They had twins. A girl and a boy. Two years later they had another daughter, and then three years, later they had another son. God, truly blessed them for their faithfulness. They thought they were not able to conceive and had thought about adoption but God showed them both, "There is nothing too hard for God." Over the next 6 months Tom and Nancy alternated weeks with Romeo and Frank to get a comprehensive counseling session by two brilliant doctors that share equal spiritual gifts that each of them exercised in their counseling sessions. Tom and Nancy benefited from there counseling sessions and their marriage improved and became stronger in each session and as they had children, they taught their children how a man and woman should love each other and express their love openly within their marriage as they respect each other in love and patience.

Shortly after Tom and Nancy got re married, Leslie and Christopher Cornelius had their wonderful marriage. They went through spiritual marriage counseling with Pastor Gary and Pastor Gary encouraged Romeo and Jasmine to start their counseling sessions with him as well because they were going to get married with three months from Leslie and Christopher Cornelius marriage.

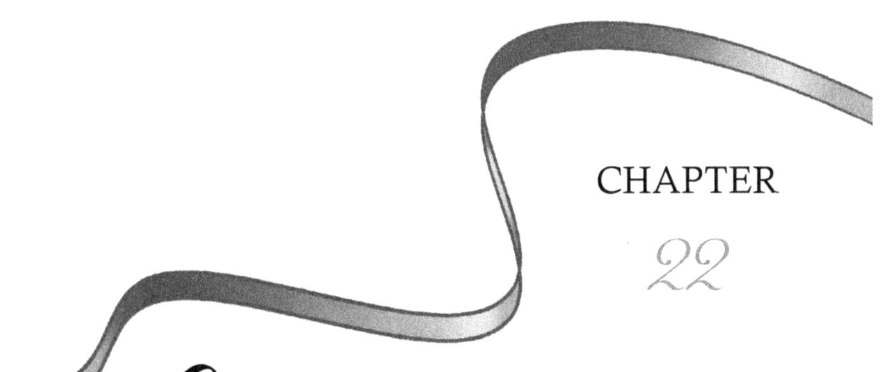

CHAPTER

22

Leslie and Christopher Cornelius had such a charming wedding. They too had their ceremony at Pastor Gary and Minister Kimberly's church. Ray walked his daughter down the aisle and Christopher Cornelius's dad, brother, and best friend stood up for him as his best men. Leslie's cousin and best friend, Michelle and Leslie's mom, Ro Sarita was her Maids of Honor and some of her younger cousins were here bride maids and flower girls. Romeo, Frank, Michael, Donnell, Michelle's husband, and two other friends of Christopher Cornelius that flew from Washington to Houston Texas to be a part of his grooms' men. The wedding was pink, yellow, violet, and white. It was so gorgeous. It was pink, yellow, violet, and white flowers everywhere. The greatest part was Leslie carried the baby more so in her hips and legs rather than her stomach so she just had two get two sizes up from her original size 6 wedding dress. She was absolutely model like. Leslie was so beautiful. Her wedding was spectacular. Leslie had a few of her of her high school friends fly down from Washington to Houston to sing songs in her wedding. Dennis song the song, "All of Me by John Legend." when she came down the aisle escorted by her father, Ray. Dennis song that song so amazingly that he had everybody crying before Leslie got to her husband to be. After Leslie and Christopher Cornelius said their vows, Leslie's other friend, Ronitha, song, "At Last by Etta Jones." Wow could she sing. Everybody applauded vigorously after she song as they stood on their feet as they watched the beautiful couple walk out of the church. The reception was fun and the menu was full of finger deli cases and sweets. It was very fun watching the older family members cut a rug with the younger people in various line dances. It was a lot of laughing, eating, and dancing at their reception. Everybody left happy, full, and exhausted.

Leslie and Christopher Cornelius, a weeks later had their first-born son. He was gorgeous. He had sandy hair and had his uncle Romeo and grandfather Rays eyes which were piercing blue mixed with her hazel eyes. His eyes were deep blue with specks of hazel within the blue encircled in hazel. His eyes were very alluring. Leslie, Christopher Cornelius, and their son George lived with Ray for four years gladly on the other side of his large home. It had its own pool section and it had two bedrooms and two bathrooms downstairs and two bedrooms with three bathrooms upstairs with a shared living area and a balcony. It was stunning. Not surprisingly, it had a very welcoming landscaping outdoors with a tropical feel to it even in the winter. They all loved living with Ray because he gave them their space but yet made his presence known because he loved playing with his grandson, George. Leslie finished her Psychiatry degree and Christopher Cornelius passed his medical degree and passed his Medical Board license to practice medicine. They both had very successful careers. Leslie had joined Romeo's

109

Psychologists/Psychiatry practice and was thriving. She learned so much from her brother, Romeo. She had the same like-minded in their approach to their field and utilized her spiritual gifts to better help her clientele.

Leslie and Christopher Cornelius had their second child in their fifth year of marriage. She had raven dark hair with light hazel eyes like her mom. She was stunning even as a baby and she grew up to be just as beautiful and model like as her mother and grandmother, Ro Sarita. Leslie and Christopher Cornelius careers were thriving but they always set aside time for family. They made it to all their children's events. By their 10th year of marriage, they had another little girl whose hair was reddish brown with light brown eyes. They named her Irish. She was a mirror to her grandmother Ro Sarita and when she made her facial expressions, she reminded them of Christopher Cornelius's mother. She was absolutely beautiful. In the 10th year they had fraternal twin boys that looked like Ray and the other one looked like Christopher Cornelius's father. They were named Ray Charles after Ray and Leonard James. They were so very handsome. Everybody spoiled them.

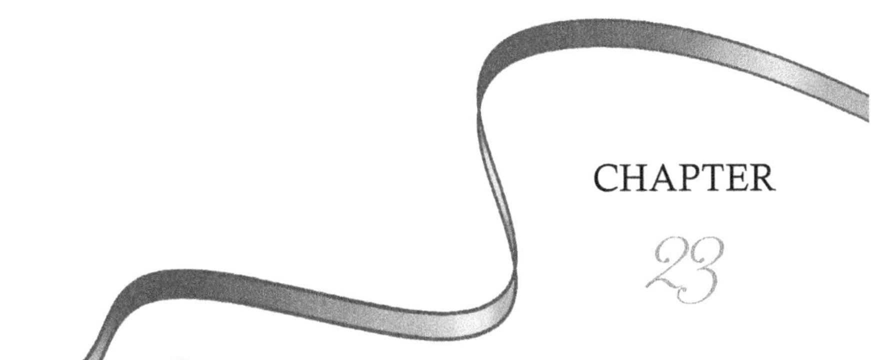

CHAPTER

23

rank had moved home to England the first-year of their marriage but he flew back to Houston to watch Mary play in Houston Comets games. He asked her to marry him and she accepted. She did propose for him to allow her to finish her last four years of playing professional basketball and then she would either get her citizenship in England and move their or stay in the U.S. and move wherever Franks wants to practice Psychiatry. They were hopelessly in love and they made a very attractive couple. They were equally yoked and complemented each other strength and weaknesses. They lived up to the expectations of them being a great couple. They even handled the long-distance love affair in great fashion. After the four years had passed and Mary retired her Professional Women Basketball career, she was offered a job at Houston University to be the head coach of their basketball league. She came highly recommended. She married Frank in England before she accepted the job to see what Frank thoughts were with the position.

Frank informed her that it was great and he supports her and that he wanted to moved back to Houston Texas and rejoin Romeo's Psychology/Psychiatric Practice anyway. Romeo and Frank continued to talk and be spiritual brothers during the time he was back home in England. Romeo had asked him what was his thoughts setting up practice in U.S. that is when Frank informed him, although he gained a lot of knowledge and experience being a part of his dad/s practice, he wanted to venture out on his own. Romeo offered him a full partnership with his practice and stated that Leslie is now an official Psychiatrist and is a part of his team. Romeo told Frank, "With you my friend our practice will be complete and we can grow our clientele. All of us are like minded and utilize our own spiritual gifts to best serve our clientele. That is what sets us apart from others. People need things other than the physical realm; their needs encompass the physical, they also have to have their emotional and spiritual needs met as well because this is the whole being of a person. That is why Romeo's practice has been so successful in helping others. They rely on a greater power than just their knowledge and their experiences. Frank accepted Romeo's offer and had already moved back to Houston Texas.

Romeo and Jasmine had flown to England to witness and support Frank and Mary's marriage. It was absolutely a dream wedding. It was very elegant and fancy. Frank paid for the airline tickets of Mary's parents, her brother and sister, and her best friend Rosette and her fiance, Ray. They had such a magnificent time. It was like nothing they have ever experienced in the U.S. Everything was so elegantly done. Even the reception was very class, but because Frank new all of the latest dances moves and line dances, he made sure it was very fun and entertaining for not only his bride but for his American

111

friends as wee. His cultured sophisticated family and friends joined in the fun and it was a memorable experience for all. Frank and Mary had two sons and one daughter and they were as gorgeous as their parents. They were beloved by their England and American family and friends. They were trained in very sophisticated England culture by their grandparents and family but played sports in America as their mom played and was very good. Their sport of choice was basketball and they exceed well in that as well as academically. Frank and Mary enjoyed their marriage. Sure, they had financial and physical challenges like most couples, but they persevered in hope and prayer, to God that he would direct their path. They were over comers and they taught others how to do the same through trust, belief, and prayer to God, that he will make a way out of No way, and in the end through their trials they will go through their fiery trials but come out as pure as gold.

Jasmine and Romeo continued to draw closer and closer as the years went by. They had a long engagement to get to know each other well. They prayed, laughed, talked, and ate together. They became strong as a couple before they walked down the aisle and officially became married. They were counseled by Pastor Gary and his wife, Minister Kimberly along with Romeo's birth parents, Ray and Rosette.

It is true, God had bought Ray and Rosette back together again, strong in their loves even more so than when they were younger. They were mature and in the right mindset now, for God to flourish their union. They were satisfied and retired from their busy sports careers. Although, Rosette continued to coach the Houston Comets, Ray would join her because he was set for life, financially. Rosette continued to see Romeo and receive counseling to get her stronger mentally and emotionally, and she forgave everyone that took part in the trauma she endured in given the son, she loved from conception and given birth to, up for adoption. Her relationship with Ray was not only restored but her relationship with her parents and Ray's parents were restored as well. Love and fellowship ran deeply between them. She now had her parents back in her life and Ray's family welcomed her with open arms begging for her forgiveness not letting her know all these years that they helped Ray raise their child. Although they wanted to tell her many times because of their convictions, they wanted to also not fall out of fellowship with her parents. They agreed they were more man pleasers rather than to do the right thing in which God had given them the heart to do multiple times throughout the years. They too confessed their wrong doing to God and asked in the future he will give them the strength to choose his path rather than anyone else. They were stronger as well from the cross they bared to keep this secret from her for all these years. It is something about the Grace of God. You can't buy it or earn it by your works. He freely gives it to the one he loves.

Actually, the most advantageous thing occurred, because of the significance of all that Rosette, Ray, and Romeo had gone through together both through the rough trials and the heart moving growth in compassion, love, and respect of their reunion, Jasmine discussed with them to have their weddings at the same time as a symbol of God restoring power of love. Romeo thought it was truly a terrific idea, and Rosette and Ray thought the same. They knew it was through God's guidance, patience, timing, and love that restored their reunion. Nobody but God to turn all of the hurt into a blessing.

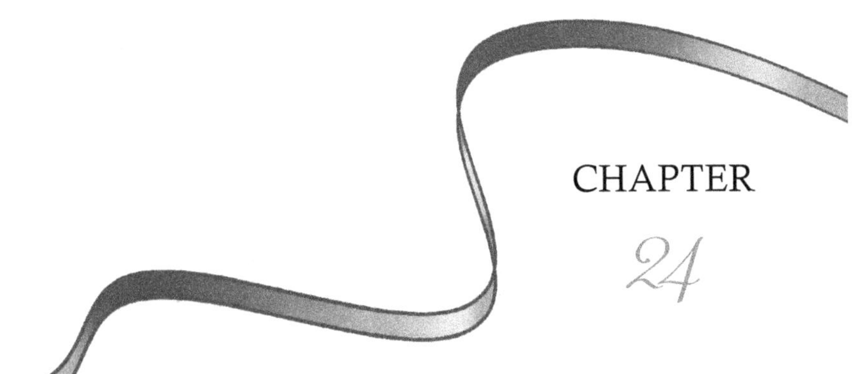

CHAPTER

24

The time had come. The spiritual counseling was complete, In the summer of July, Ray and Rosette, as well as their son, Romeo and his beautiful Fiance, Jasmine and both families combined with friends and colleagues flew to Hawaii to get married. Romeo and Jasmine paid Airline tickets for Pastor Gary and his wife, Minister Kimberly to perform their ceremonies together in Paradise. It was absolutely amazing.

They were surround by the serenity of the tropical flowers, green plants, water, and sun in the cool of the day. The wedding went without disruptions for the both couples and the ceremony was an occasion to remember. The song choice by their favorite singers played as both brides individually with their flower girls, bride's maids and the groom's men came down the aisles. Jasmine's father Ramon, walked her down the aisle and both he and her mom, Lorina gave her away. Lorina and Ramon's parents and a lot of their families came to support them in Hawaii as well. Rosette's father, Paul, walked her down the aisle, and he and her mom, Darlene, gave her away. Romeo's best man was Frank and Ray's best man was his father, Harland.

As Rosette and Ray's wedding party walked down the aisle, Tony Terry song one his favorite hits, "You."

As Rosette's father walked her down the aisle her favorite singer, Maria Carey song, "We belong together."

As Jasmine and Romeo's wedding party walked down the aisle, Tony Terry song, "Everlasting Love"

As Jasmine's father walked her down the aisle, her favorite singer, Yolonda Adams and Anita Baker song her signature ballot, "You Bring Me Joy."

After the vows were made by the couples, Yolonda Adams and Donnie McClurkin song, "We fall down but we get up in honor of Ray and Rosette reunion and their everlasting love for each other and Mariah Carey and Tony Terry song one of her signature songs, "Vision of Love."

Everybody was shocked of the famous singers that were there to support their love. This was a wedding present by Ro Sarita and Michael who knew Mariah and Tony Terry personally and from Ray's grandmother who was a gifted pianist and singer who have opened for Donnie McClurkin and Yolonda Adams from time to time when they really needed her to step in at concerts that were easy for her to get there. She would never accept any money because she felt like since it was a God given gift, she used it to minister rather than for financial gain. You would not accept Yolonda or Donnie's truths about the matter, "Your gift will make room for you in the since that God will provide through your spiritual gift if it is still used to bless others. Really, she was the type of person, that helped when she could, and at the end of the day that satisfied her more than monetary gain. Donnie and Yolonda still blessed her grandchildren, Romeo and Leslie and made donations to their church because they believed in blessing others in one form or another. In other words, they did a work around to still bless her for her services.

If you think the wedding was spectacular, the reception was serviced by the resort they were staying in the form of a Lua with the islander ceremony involved in it and the line dances back in the day and the most current ones. All of the jams of 70's-to current year was played to dance fast and for slow dances. They had a mixture of artists and songs because truly the couples and their families were all of different races, cultures, and socioeconomic status. What bonded them together was love and mutual respect for each other. Their multi culture and race that was represented with the merging of these two couples were a testimony of good old fashion, "Everybody is Somebody in the eyes of the Lord." Their merging was as beautiful of a blanket full of colors.

The reception carried on for three days in Hawaii each of them had a different theme. The themes were chronological as mentioned: Love and Happiness, Serenity and Peace, Forgiveness and Faithfulness which all had a tropical Hawaiian flare to it which made it very unique. Everyone loved the atmosphere and it stayed within their hearts for many years thereafter. When each of them that were present at the ceremony and 3-day reception themes, they would remember on the things that they witnessed and it encouraged them to keep on keeping on.

Rosette and Ray went on to have a beautiful enduring marriage. They were blessed with two more children. A boy and a girl one year a part. Their marriage UN shockingly lasted a lifetime until they were in their geriatric years. They both lived a fulfilled life of the ripe age of 98 for Rosette and 101 for Ray. They were blessed with their health, strength, memory, and the activity of their limbs. They never had to go to a nursing home or an Assisted Living Facility. They remained in good health until their hearts just stopped because God wanted them to rest from their journey. God truly blessed their latter lives rather than their initial lives together so much so they could not remember the 20+ years that they were apart. God gave them peace and a life full of joy as they received a second chance to raise the children that God blessed them with when they had lost the opportunity to raise the love of their life, Romeo together. Romeo was a great brother to his brother and sister even though he was old enough to be their father. He was a brother to them but also like a father figure. Romeo, Ray, and Rosette had a wonderful journey together with the new additions of their family, Ray Jr and Rosalyn.

Romeo and Jasmine continued to have successful careers. They enjoyed helping others. Romeo dealt with the mind and emotions and his wife, Jasmine dealt with the physical health and also treated her clientele holistically treating mind, body, and spirit. Romeo and Jasmine had five children. Twins: Jacqueline and Lena. Jacqueline and Lena were gifted in singing and playing piano. They both grew up being trained by Ray's mom and had successful and professional careers in their God given gifts. They were absolutely beautiful from babies, girls, to adults. Their attitude met their beauty. They both were meek but yet strong and milt temperaments. The two boys between were as handsome as their dad. Their names were Nigel and Tyler. They were so gifted in the following: Nigel in playing baseball and Tyler playing basketball. They both grew into their gift and mastered it and they had successful long careers in it. They also were taught financial good sense and learned and participated in knowing what stocks and bonds to grow their money into financial freedom to leave generational wealth to their families and their children.

Nigel and Tyler were two years apart. Leslie and Rosette's last child was a surprise, or should I say a blessing. Romeo was 50 y/o and Jasmine was 53 y/o and had not gone through menopause yet. They were blessed with a beautiful little girl that had her dad's blue eyes and her mom's beautiful curly locks. She was like her aunt, Leslie, tall and model like. She was absolutely stunning, but the way she carried herself was unselfishly. She was kind but yet a serious child like her dad was when he was growing up. She was as funny as her grandfather, Ray and as loving as his mom, Rosette. Their last little girl's name was Stella Louise. She grew up and wanted to pursue medicine like her mom. She met her husband in her last few years of Medical Residency. His name was William. William was part Indian, black, and white. He was a gorgeous young man. He was two years older than Stella Louise.

Stella Louise was also a gifted writer who wrote at least 10 best seller novels in her lifetime across the genres of Medical Good Sense and Family times. She and William moved from Houston and they planted roots in Hawaii. They loved the Serenity of the Island. It was a plus for their family because they had somewhere to come to relax from all the hustle and bustle of the city. It was a great change of pace for their visiting family. As Jasmine and Romeo became olde, Stella Louise and William asked both sets of parents to move to Hawaii to live with them. They had two living areas in their home and had a guest house on their land. It was convenient for them because their aging parents were close enough for them to assist them in all of their health and social needs if it was needed. In their parents of both sides did not necessarily need it because God had blessed them as previously described with Rosette and Ray but Williams' parents lived in good health in mind, strength, and health and the climate and peace of Hawaii helped them to live to their late 90's.

Williams' dad lived to 96 y/o and his mom lived to 99 y/o. They actually lived within Stella Louise and Williams' home and when Romeo and Jasmine were in their mid 80's their home in Houston, Texas and moved to Hawaii with Stella Louise and William and stayed in their guest three-bedroom ranch home with 2.5 bathrooms and a pool that made room enough for other family members to stay without having to get hotel rooms. Stella Louis and Williams home was surrounded by the tranquility of the Hawaiian ocean in their back yard. Their siblings and other living family member and friends loved to come to their home because it was always something exciting going on.

As other people they knew or came in contact with, witnessed how the blending of multiple races came together and produced love and harmony was a true testament of God's love for his people. Although our differences are what they are, in his eyes we are his large blanket of many colors that gives him so much joy when they put away the ugliness of racial wars and just love the humanity of a person than the world is a much better place to live and thrive in the blessings of the Lord.

Blanket of Many Colors

written by Rotonger Ronitha Burns-Walker